THE HOUSE NEXT DOOR

THRILLERS

JAMES PATTERSON

WITH SUSAN DiLALLO, MAX DiLALLO, AND TIM ARNOLD

GRAND CENTRAL
PUBLISHING

NEW YORK   BOSTON

Copyright © 2019 by James Patterson

Hachette Book Group supports the right to free expression and the value of copyright. The purpose of copyright is to encourage writers and artists to produce the creative works that enrich our culture.

The scanning, uploading, and distribution of this book without permission is a theft of the author's intellectual property. If you would like permission to use material from the book (other than for review purposes), please contact permissions@hbgusa.com. Thank you for your support of the author's rights.

Grand Central Publishing
Hachette Book Group
1290 Avenue of the Americas, New York, NY 10104
grandcentralpublishing.com
twitter.com/grandcentralpub

First Edition: January 2019

Grand Central Publishing is a division of Hachette Book Group, Inc. The Grand Central Publishing name and logo are trademarks of Hachette Book Group, Inc.

The publisher is not responsible for websites (or their content) that are not owned by the publisher.

The Hachette Speakers Bureau provides a wide range of authors for speaking events. To find out more, go to hachettespeakersbureau.com or call (866) 376-6591.

ISBN 978-1-5387-1389-1 / 978-1-5387-1407-2 (large print)
Library of Congress Control Number 2018945708

Printed in the United States of America

LSC-H

10 9 8 7 6 5 4 3 2 1

For the Karps—
your house isn't exactly next door, but it's
plenty close enough. We couldn't imagine
better neighbors or friends.

CONTENTS

THE HOUSE NEXT DOOR

JAMES PATTERSON

with SUSAN DiLALLO

PROLOGUE

"HURRY," I HEARD SOMEONE say. "He's losing a lot of blood."

Blood?

Stunned, I sat there for I don't know how long, listening to the whir of police sirens. Vaguely aware of flashing lights and a flurry of voices around me.

"Ma'am, can you hear me?" one of the voices asks. I squint and look up. It's a policeman, his face close to mine. He looks concerned. "Are you okay?"

I open my mouth to say something, but nothing comes out. I nod my head yes.

"Do you remember what happened?" the cop asks.

Do I? I'm not sure.

I remember being afraid. Very afraid. A scream. A crash. The screech of metal. And then—

Something is trickling down the front of my face. I taste blood. I lift my hand to brush it away, and a sharp pain rips across my elbow. I look down. A bump the size and color of a plum is throbbing there.

The cop calls out to an EMT guy. "She's conscious. But her arm looks kinda banged up."

Suddenly there is a commotion next to me. They have cracked open the door on the driver's side to get to the driver. More flashing lights. Another ambulance. More voices.

"Come look at this," someone says, and the cop crosses to the driver's side. They have lifted the driver out and put him on a gurney. Blood has seeped across his neck, down his shirt.

"He hit his head on the wheel?"

"That's what I thought, at first," says the EMT guy. "But look."

"Jesus," says the cop. "Is that . . . ?"

"Right," says the other man. "A bullet hole."

Suddenly, everything changes.

"Ma'am," the cop says, "I need you to step away from the car."

Cradling my arm, he helps me onto a gurney. As they wheel me over to an ambulance, I hear the crunch of broken glass. Then I see the second car, on its side, just to the left of mine. Half on, half off the road. The whole front side of it is smashed in. And slumped over the steering wheel . . .

I know that car. I know that driver! Slowly, bits and pieces of memories start to come back. A pop. A flash of light. And then it hits me: the horror of what I've done.

The two men I love—bruised, bleeding, dying— maybe dead?

And, dear God, *it's all my fault . . .*

CHAPTER 1

Six months earlier

YOU WANT TO KNOW the whole story? Let me start from the day when everything began to fall apart.

Just an ordinary school morning.

Joey is scrambling to finish his homework. Caroline is still asleep. Ben can't find his oboe. And my husband and I are arguing.

"This whole oboe thing is ridiculous," Ned says, gesturing with a piece of seven-grain toast. "The kid hates the oboe. He doesn't practice from one week to the next. And why he needs an oboe tutor..."

"So he can keep up with the other fourth-graders," I call out from the bottom of the hall closet, on my knees, searching.

"You're kidding, right?" Ned yells. But I know what he means. I've heard the school orchestra play. Even on a good day, it makes your teeth hurt.

Ben stands there, Pop-Tart in hand, watching as I push aside various snow boots.

"Would it kill you to help me look?" I say.

"Me? Why do I have to help?"

From the kitchen Ned shouts, "Because it's your damn oboe. You're the one who lost it."

"I left it right here on the hall table," Ben says. "Donna must've put it somewhere."

Donna is the cleaning lady who shows up on Mondays, cleans her little heart out, and for the next six days is systematically blamed for everything that's lost or broken. Poor Donna has had more things pinned on her than our local supermarket bulletin board.

I get up off my knees. Ned is standing next to me, still fuming. I know I have a choice: *Let It Go,* as Maggie, our couples therapist, has suggested, or *Push Back Gently*.

"Look. He's finally learning to play the scales properly," I say. Gently.

"And for that I pay seventy-five dollars a week?"

"Seventy-five dollars," I add, still in my gentlest voice, "is about *half* what you paid for the tie you're wearing. Which, incidentally, seems to have a small butter stain on it."

"What? Oh, for God's sake." Ned checks his reflection in our hall mirror. "I just got this tie. It's an Armani. Here," he says, carefully unknotting it from around his neck and draping it on the hall-closet doorknob. "Drop this at the dry cleaners, will you?"

He bolts up the stairs, two at a time, in search of another tie—then reappears and kisses me good-bye. His lips miss my cheek entirely. I wait to see if he notices that

I have chopped three inches off my hair since yesterday, and I've gone from Deep Chestnut to Honey Brown. He doesn't.

"Be home late again," he says, checking his reflection one last time in the hall mirror. "Asshole client meeting that doesn't start till six." Then he grabs his car keys and leaves.

We soon find the oboe, of course.

In the one place I'm never allowed to look.

CHAPTER 2

WELCOME TO BEN'S BEDROOM.

I am a Navy SEAL, cautiously making my way through enemy territory. I step carefully to avoid minefields.

No. Wait.

I am actually your basic forty-four-year-old suburban mom, cautiously making my way through piles of clothing scattered on the floor. It all needs washing, but I am under strict orders never to pick up anything I find lying there. This, as a result of accidentally laundering various dollar bills, student IDs, and cell phones left in pockets that I forgot to check.

A foot from Ben's trundle bed, I spot the corner of something leathery and brown peeking out from under an Imagine Dragons T-shirt. Sure enough, it's the oboe case. I lift it up, shake off some Cheez Doodle dust, and carry it downstairs.

Ben frowns and says, "Dad said I didn't have to go."

"He said no such thing. Now go get your backpack.

And where are your brother and sister? Joey! Caroline! It's eight twenty-five."

Caroline comes down the stairs, a vision of long blond hair and denim, holding her sixth-grade science project: a mock-up of the Mount St. Helens volcano, molded out of Play-Doh. She's only eleven. But with her blond curls and deep blue eyes, someday soon she's going to break some hearts.

Joey, age sixteen, appears on the top landing—high tops untied, hair gelled and standing straight up so that he resembles a hedgehog. He gallops down the stairs.

"Careful!" I say, as he zips past Caroline. "And would it kill you to carry that for your sister?"

"No! He'll tip it!" she says, hoisting the volcano high above her head.

"Fine. Whatever. Can we *just get going*?"

Then the usual mad scramble—lunch bags grabbed, jackets pulled from hooks, protein bars shoved into pockets, the three of them pushing through the front door and arguing over who gets the front seat. Another morning gotten through. I take out my keys and am about to lock up.

And that's when the phone rings.

CHAPTER 3

"MAYBE THEY'RE CALLING TO say it's a snow day," Ben says.

"In September?" I ask. But he has a point. When the phone rings that early in the morning, it's generally someone from the school phone chain with news of a weather day, an early closing, or—these days—a bomb threat.

I go back and answer it.

"Hello," says a male voice. "Is this Laura Sherman?" The voice is warm and friendly—two things I have no time for.

"Sorry. We're on the do-not-call list," I say.

I am about to hang up, when the voice gets more insistent.

"Laura, wait! Please. My name is Vince Kelso."

"Look, if you're running for office…"

"I'm your new neighbor. At thirty-seven Maple."

Thirty-seven Maple. The house next door. A total eyesore. The house had been vacant for quite a while. We were hoping someone would buy it and tear it down. But my friend Darcy, whose house is on the other side, said people moved in last week. She went over with brownies and rang the bell. No one answered. She left the brownies and a note asking them to call if they needed anything.

She never heard from them.

"My gosh. I owe you an apology," I say. "I've been meaning to stop by and bring over a plant or something and..."

"No problem," he says. "But I was wondering if I could ask a favor."

"Sure. I mean, I guess. Look, Mr. Kelso..."

"*Vince,*" he says. "Please. Call me Vince."

"*Vince.* I don't mean to be rude, but my kids are waiting in the car."

I look out the window to see if this is true. It is. Joey is in the front seat of our dusty Volvo wagon, practicing his best Justin Bieber pout in the rearview mirror. Ben and Caroline are in the back, arguing. As I watch, Ben hits Caroline over the head with his lunch bag. The bag breaks.

"I don't know a soul here. I was wondering if you could pick my son Vinny up after school today and take him to soccer practice."

"Today? Gee," I say, letting my eyes wander to our lawn. The grass needs cutting, and the garbagemen have left our big plastic garbage bins sprawled in the gutter. "Today's a little tough. See, Thursday's my busiest day. First there's my daughter's dance class. Then I have to get my son across town for his oboe lesson and..."

"I would never be asking," he continues "but my wife is suddenly quite ill. They had to take her away..."

"Oh. Gosh..."

"And you're my last hope."

"Me?"

I hear him take a deep breath. Then he says, quietly, "Honey, I'm all alone here...and I could really use a friend."

"Of course," I say.

"Swell," he says. Swell? Where is this guy from? The 1950s?

"I heard you were an angel," he says, sweetly. "I guess they were right."

Who's "they"? I want to ask. Certainly no one in my immediate family.

But he has already hung up.

CHAPTER 4

I LOCK THE FRONT door behind me and walk to my Volvo wagon. As I get closer to the car, I see Ben's peanut butter and jelly sandwich glued to the rear seat.

"Ben hit me with his lunch," Caroline says.

"It was her fault," Ben says. "She started it. She wouldn't move her stupid feet."

"Shut up," Caroline says.

"Hey! We don't use words like that," I say, pulling out of the driveway.

"Yes, we do," Joey says. "All the time."

"Well—we shouldn't," I say. So much for today's lesson in parenting. We drive past the post office, the Stop & Shop, the dry cleaners (*damn—I left Ned's tie hanging on the doorknob*). We drop Joey off at the high school. They are still arguing about whose foot belongs where.

But I'm lost in thought, wondering about the weird phone call.

"What do you guys know about Vinny Kelso?" I ask as we make a left onto the street that leads to the school.

"He's new," says Ben.

"Keep going. What's he like?"

"Nobody likes him."

"And why is that?" I ask. The crossing guard in a shiny yellow vest holds up a hand to let a bunch of students cross.

"He's a nerd. He reads all the time."

"Well, shame on him," I say. "How does he expect to make friends, with an attitude like that? No wonder everybody hates him. But I bet you've been kind to him. Right, Ben? Taken him under your wing. Shown him the ropes." I keep my eyes on the road, but I'm sure Ben is squirming in the back.

"Well...I heard his mother got sick," Ben says, desperate to change the subject.

"Really?"

"Yeah. Casey in my class said she heard two teachers talking."

"That must be pretty scary for Vinny. For all of them." Suddenly, my heart goes out to the Kelsos. New in town. Family emergency. No one to turn to.

"Why are you asking about him?" Ben asks.

"We're going to do his dad a favor today. We're driving Vinny to soccer."

"Oh, Ma. Please, no!" Ben says. A look of horror crosses his face. I get it: an unpopular, possibly uncool kid will be sitting next to him in our car. If anybody sees...Ben's a goner.

We are almost at the school parking lot. I swing the car

around and let them off in one mad rush of coats and science projects and lunch bags. The car gets very quiet all of a sudden. Then Ben, standing on the curb, taps on the window.

"Don't expect me to pay for your lunch," I say. "That's what you get for hitting your sister with a sandwich."

"No. I was just thinking: why did they ask us?"

"They didn't ask us. They asked *me*."

"Why didn't they ask Darcy? She lives next door to them, too."

"I dunno. Maybe they didn't like her brownies."

He shrugs and runs up the steps just as the bell rings. The heavy metal door slams behind him.

As I drive off, though, I realize the kid's got a point. Darcy left them a note, with her phone number on it.

So: why me?

CHAPTER 5

WHEN I GO BACK home to pick up Ned's tie, the dust balls meet me at the door. I know they've missed me, because they follow me from room to room. To kill time, I vacuum the whole house. Then I write a few checks. Then I empty the dishwasher.

I can put it off no longer. I've got to deal with Harry.

Harry, the *H* of H & M Cleaners, is standing behind the counter as I walk through the door. As always, he's frowning. He is a short, stubby man with deep lines in his face from intense scowling. Harry wears granny glasses that are always speckled with dirt.

"Hello," I say, pulling the butter-stained tie out of my bag.

"You'll have it Tuesday," he answers, curling the tie around his hand and dropping it on the counter. That's Harry's way of saying *Hello. Nice to see you again. How's the family?* Harry and my son Joey must be enrolled in the same charm school.

Harry punches a few numbers into his computer, prints a receipt, and peels it in half. I get the pink half.

"Can I have it tomorrow?"

"You want it tomorrow, you should have brought it in yesterday."

"But it only got stained *today*."

Harry shrugs. "So what do you want me to do?"

"I want you to have it tomorrow. Look," I say. Then I point to a huge faded sign that has been hanging there since 1967. "It says IN BY TEN, OUT BY THREE."

"Look yourself," he says. "It's ten fifteen."

"But today's only *Thursday*. What if I brought it in *tomorrow* before ten? Would I have it tomorrow by three?"

Harry shrugs. "I can't promise anything. Tomorrow is the weekend."

I get back in the car and slam the door. I'm annoyed at Harry, but just as annoyed at Ned, who insists I go to H & M Cleaners. I don't understand a lot of things Ned insists on. Mouthwashes that burn. Sitting in the first row of a movie theater. Then again, when we were dating and I accidentally got pregnant with Joey, another guy might've walked. But Ned insisted on marrying me. You've got to love a guy like that.

And I do. Most of the time.

Once Joey was born, Ned insisted we move to the suburbs. Overnight, I kissed my half-assed acting career good-bye. Okay. So my life isn't quite Shangri-la. But I can't complain (although I do, all the time, in couples therapy). I have a lot of laughs with the kids. Ned is a pretty good father. Life could be a lot worse.

And when I read all these stories about husbands who cheat and lie and put their family in harm's way—I know Ned would never do anything like that.

CHAPTER 6

"WELCOME TO BEST BUY, sir," the young salesman in the red T-shirt says, smiling as he greets the customer at the door. "Can I help you find something?"

"No thanks," Vince Kelso tells him, waving him off with his hand. He heads deeper into the store, toward the cell phone aisle.

Soon another salesman approaches—this one bald, with a bad case of acne.

"Just looking," Vince tells him. Vince wanders around until he sees exactly what he's looking for: a young salesgirl. She has long red hair and is standing by a cash register.

"I wonder if you could help me," he asks her.

"Sure, sir," she says. As he expected, she is sweet and perky—perhaps a trainee, determined to make a good impression.

"So many cell phones. What's an old guy like me to do?" he says. He shrugs helplessly and looks at the plastic name tag on the young girl's shirt. "Amber," he adds.

Amber looks him over. He doesn't seem that old—way younger than her father. She thinks he was probably cute as a teenager.

She gestures to the aisle behind them and begins the sales pitch they taught her in orientation. "Okay. So, a lot depends on how you're going to use it. So, like, if you surf the internet, or do a lot of texting..."

"Now, honey," he says, looking right into her eyes, leaning in so he's a lot closer to her. "Do I look like a guy who texts a lot?"

She blushes a little. It's sweet.

"No, sir—all I meant was..."

"Actually, I'm looking for one of those prepaid ones."

Her face lights up. "Oh. Like a disposable? Sure. Those are at the end, over there. They're pretty popular. The contract fees are much less, and you can..."

But he's already shaking his head.

"I'm a pretty simple guy, Amber. Don't even need a contract. I just want something I can use and then toss."

"Oh!" Amber says. "So, like, a burner. Here's the one most people go with." She reaches for a black phone in a blister pack, hanging on a hook.

"I'll tell you how good a saleswoman you are," he says. "I'm gonna take six of 'em." He pulls five more off the rack.

"Awesome," she says, all smiles. It's her biggest sale of the day. Maybe even her biggest sale ever. Vince turns one over, to see the price. He reaches into his pocket and pulls out a wallet. He peels off four fifty-dollar bills.

"I knew I could count on you, Amber," he says. "Why, I bet, if I come back here in ten years, you're gonna be running the place. Am I right?"

"Oh, I don't know about that," she says. She looks away shyly.

"One last thing," he says as he pockets the change. "I don't know this brand. Where do I find the phone number?"

"It's right inside," Amber says, cracking open one of the blister cases with the cash register key. "Let me show you." She pulls out an instruction manual. "Oh, look—you got a good one. 914-809-1414."

"914-809-1414. I like that," Vince says. "Easy to remember. Well, you take care now," he adds. "And remember what I said. Don't let me down."

"No, sir," she replies, smiling. "Have a nice day."

He winks, puts the phones and the instruction manual in his briefcase, and leaves without taking the receipt.

CHAPTER 7

THE TIME: 2:30 P.M., outside Copain Woods School. And it's starting. A snake pit of road rage as the SUVs line up, each driven by an impatient mom or dad, jockeying for position. I like to think of myself as an A-team player at this.

The minutes pass. Suddenly it's three o'clock. A bell rings. Doors open. Out spills a gaggle of students, grades one through eight. They scatter in all directions in search of a familiar car. Horns honk. Drivers shout names. Caroline spots me quickly and waves. Ben appears behind her. I pull closer to the curb and they both jump in.

"Where's Vinny?" I ask. My eyes search the crowd. Down at the end is a face I've never seen before. A boy leaning against the building. The kid wears a reddish-brown shirt the same color as the bricks.

"That's him," Ben says, pointing. Then he scoots down in his seat so none of the other middle school kids can see him. I pull closer to Vincent Kelso Junior and roll down the window.

"You must be Vinny," I say. "I'm Mrs. Sherman. Hop in."

Vinny walks slowly. Behind me, the honking grows louder.

"A little faster," I say sweetly. He has some trouble opening the door. *A nice kid,* I think. *But not too swift.*

"Perhaps you two can help?" I say. Ben, still crouched down out of sight, groans. He opens the door handle with his foot. Vinny slides in and fastens his seat belt.

I begin to pull out of the Circle of Doom. Once we're safely away from the school, Ben sits up straight.

"So how do you like Copain Woods?" I ask Vinny.

"It's okay, I guess," he says. I turn around and look at him. He's a little guy, a few inches smaller than Ben. He has thick brown hair and a nose the size of a small turnip. Cute kid.

"What's your favorite subject?" I ask.

"They're all okay." He shrugs and looks out the window.

"But I bet you really like soccer."

"I kind of did. In my old school."

"And where was that?" I ask. Suddenly, he looks frightened.

"I don't know. Pretty far from here."

"Oh," I say.

We pull up in front of the high school to pick up Joey. He's standing at the curb, checking something on his cell phone. He looks up and gives me his usual warm greeting.

"Did you bring my racquet?"

"It's in the back," I say.

"Where are my ballet shoes?" asks Caroline.

"On the floor in front with me. Next to the backup sneakers, water, snacks, and oboe. Am I missing anything?"

"Yeah," Ben says. "Mr. Wellman says I have to bring a pencil."

"Don't you have one? I bought you a few hundred before school started."

"All the erasers are chewed," he says with a shrug.

"He can have one of mine," says Caroline. She opens her backpack. Her pencils, like everything else about her, are perfect: impeccably sharpened and lined up like wooden soldiers in her Fancy Nancy pencil case.

"I don't want yours. Yours have cooties."

She gives him a dirty look. All three boys begin laughing as I gun the car around and head for the tennis court.

I pull into the Roger Raymond Recreation Center, a low, white cement building surrounded by willow trees. Joey jumps out and gets his racquet from the back.

"Next stop, soccer field."

Caroline makes a face. "But, Mom..."

"You can be a little late to ballet," I say. "Vinny needs to get there on time."

She stews quietly as I turn the car around and head back.

We drop Vinny at the playing field. The minute he's out of the car, Ben leans forward and grabs my seat.

"Why are you so nice to him?"

"His father is paying me a lot of money."

"Really?" he asks.

"No. *Jeez*. To think I gave up a promising career in theater for a chance to mold young minds, and this is how they turn out. Don't you remember the story of the Good Samaritan?"

"I thought that was just for muggings."

"You're hopeless. It's for anybody who's in trouble, who needs a helping hand. And that little boy..."

"He's in trouble?" Caroline asks.

"Well, I'm not sure. But...something's not right."

"Who cares," Ben says. He crosses his arms and sulks silently as I make my way through the afternoon to ballet and to oboe. After the drop-offs, I sit in my car and check my emails (*$350K in life insurance for as little as $153 a month!...Storm windows, 50% off!...5 Things You Should Watch Before They Expire From Netflix*). Then I head back to tennis, back to ballet, back to oboe, and back to soccer.

Vinny is waiting out in front, covered in mud from the knees down. He's got a big smile on his face.

"We won!" he yells. He jumps into the car and smears mud all over my upholstery. "Seven–zip."

And I shift into drive for the final leg of my Thursday journey.

We're going to Vinny's house.

CHAPTER 8

THIRTY-SEVEN MAPLE LANE. The house next door. A small gray house with a bay window.

Vinny jumps out with a quick wave and a polite "thank you." I park in my driveway and decide I'll walk over and introduce myself.

Two small ironstone flowerpots flank the front door. Each one holds a miniature pine tree that's turning brown. As I get close, I realize everything about the house is turning brown. Several gray clapboards are rotting on the corners. I am about to ring the bell when the door opens.

Vincent Kelso Senior is standing in front of me, smiling. He is wearing jeans, a light brown cashmere sweater the same color as his hair, and tasseled loafers.

He's in his mid- to late forties. Great smile. Great teeth.

"Laura," he says. He takes my hand and holds it briefly between both of his. His whole face relaxes. *Not a bad-looking face,* I think. And for a split second, I sense that he might be thinking the very same thing about me.

He keeps his sky-blue eyes locked on mine, except for one brief moment when they dart to the area where he thinks my breasts might be. But of course, they are so hidden under layers of sweatshirts and turtlenecks, he isn't even close.

"Thanks for doing this," he says. "I owe you, big-time."

"Glad I could help. You've got enough on your mind," I say. He looks confused.

"Your wife...?" I add.

"Oh, right," he says. "That sure made moving more complicated. Not knowing the town at all. Or where things are."

"I could put together a list for you," I say. "Local merchants. Plumbers. That sort of thing." *The sooner the better,* I think, as I let my eyes wander to the hallway behind him. Paint is peeling from the walls, and there is a huge brown water spot creeping across the ceiling.

"Oh, I couldn't ask you to go to that trouble."

"No trouble, really. It would give me something to do."

"Ah. A little bored out here, are we?"

"Is it that obvious?" I say.

"Let me guess," he says. "Like the comedian says: You feel like the whole world is a tuxedo. And you're a pair of brown shoes."

I laugh. "Exactly."

"Well, if you don't mind doing that list... I sure would appreciate it. Any local people I can trust. Or people to avoid."

"Harry at H & M Cleaners, for one," I say. "He's sort of

rude and abrasive. I just had a bit of a run-in with him myself."

"I'm sorry to hear that," he says, frowning. "A nice woman like you..."

"Yeah. Well. On the list of life's problems..."

I let the end of my sentence linger in the air.

"Vinny's a great kid," I say. "He really seemed to enjoy himself today."

"I'm glad," he says.

"And Coach Mike is always welcoming to new team members."

"I'll have to remember to thank him. What's his last name?"

"Janowicz," I say. "I'll add his contact info to the list."

"This is so kind of you," he says. "I sure got lucky to find an angel like you."

Angel. That's only the second time I've ever been called that. The first was him, this morning, on the phone.

He stares at me for a moment. He smiles.

"I've got to go," I say too quickly. "Gotta start dinner for the kids. I've got three. Ben's in the fourth grade. Joey's a junior in high school. And my daughter, Caroline. That's her out there now."

I point. Caroline is standing in front of our house, chatting with a neighbor who's walking her dog.

"She's lovely," Vince says. "I can see where she gets it from. What was the name of that dry cleaner again?"

"Harry. But don't tell him I sent you."

"Never," he says with great solemnity. He holds his

hand up as if he is about to swear on a Bible. I say good-bye. Then he closes the door and I stand there, not moving at all. It's after six, and getting dark, but everything seems a little brighter than when I first rang the doorbell.

CHAPTER 9

FRIDAY MORNING I WAKE up at six forty-five, stumble downstairs in my bathrobe, get out the mayo, and open two cans of tuna to fix sandwiches for the kids. Ned is already up and dressed and making impatient faces at the Nespresso machine. It's casual Friday, which means Ned has scrapped his usual Brioni suit for some J. Crew khakis and a J. Crew shirt. Tall, lanky, his thinning blond hair still swooping across his eyes, he looks the way he always does: handsome, but perpetually annoyed.

"Do you think Caroline looks like me?" I ask him.

"Don't be silly," he says. "She's blond. You're brunette."

I can see where she gets it from.

At seven fifteen, Ben walks into the kitchen.

"Have a good day, my man," Ned says to him. They pound knuckles as Ned leaves.

"Good morning, Sunshine," I say, cutting the crusts off Caroline's sandwich, putting tomato on Ben's, and smearing Joey's with salsa.

"What's today?" Ben asks as he takes a cereal box out of the kitchen cabinet.

"The fourteenth."

"Oh, no." He looks panicky.

"I thought you loved Fridays."

"Today's the day we're doing our Famous Artists presentation. I need to bring my van Gogh costume to school."

"What? Why did you wait till now to tell me?"

"I didn't. I brought home that paper for you to sign last week."

I check the refrigerator door—home to all notices, clippings, and other assorted reminders from my eternal to-do list. Sure enough, the Famous Artists Fact Sheet is there, right underneath a bill from the butcher. I freak a little bit.

"I don't even know what van Gogh looks like! Quick— let's google him."

Ben pulls out his cell phone. Before I can say "how-can-you-find-that-so-quickly-using-just-your-thumbs," he has pulled up a range of van Gogh self-portraits.

"Okay," I say, my eye on the clock. "He wore ascots a lot. Take your blazer to school. And we'll borrow a scarf from Dad."

I go to the hall closet. Ned's antique 1930s white silk scarf is hanging on a padded hanger.

I slide it out from the cellophane wrapper and hand it to Ben. "Make sure you bring it back. It's Dad's favorite."

"How do I tie it?"

"Like this." I drape it around his neck and make a simple loop.

"Now, what about the blood?"

"What blood?"

He rolls his eyes. "The blood from where he cut off his ear, remember?"

I find some gauze in our family first-aid kit. Then I dribble some red food coloring on it and wrap it around Ben's forehead.

"How do I look?" he asks.

"Like you've been in a train wreck," I say.

"Cool," he says with a smile, checking himself out on the selfie side of his cell phone. He puts the blazer, scarf, and gauze headpiece in a shopping bag.

As I finish making their sandwiches, my cell phone beeps. A text message.

I read it.

Thanks again for yesterday. If you need to reach me my number is 914-809-1414. Easy to remember.

CHAPTER 10

I DROP THE KIDS at school. But instead of heading home, I decide to visit my friend Darcy. First I stop at the Human Bean, our local Starbucks wannabe. I order a latte for me, a chai tea for her, a chocolate croissant, and an almond Danish.

On the way to Darcy's, I look in Vince's window. The house is dark. There's no car in front.

Of course. He must be at his wife's bedside.

Darcy is an artist—tall and red-haired, with a smattering of freckles across her face and wide green eyes. Darcy is quite beautiful. But she dresses like come-as-you-are day at Goodwill. So I am not surprised when she opens the door and I see her midsection is covered with hundreds of tiny blue dots.

"Let me guess," I say. "You're making wine from grapes. And you've been stomping them with your breasts."

"Not even close," she says. "I'm spatter-painting a deck chair. But I think I overdid it on the spatter. What's in the bag? Something rich and gooey, I hope."

We sit down at her oak kitchen table. She gets napkins, and I look around. The room is newly painted. It's an odd shade of pink. The color of tongue.

"You like it?" she asks. I lie and say I do.

"You certainly have a knack for this sort of thing," I say. "Maybe you can help our new neighbors get their place in shape."

"The Kelsos?" she asks. "I would...but I still haven't met them. Have you?"

"Just him," I say.

"I saw him once, at a distance," she says. "Saw the kid. Even saw the family cat, sitting on the windowsill—though it could have been a pillow. Never laid eyes on the wife, though."

I tell her about Vince's phone call, and about meeting him yesterday. She looks concerned.

"Hmmm. The whole thing's a little...creepy," she says.

"Creepy? How?"

"The place is a dump," she says. "What kind of family would move in there? Especially with a kid. I've seen the inside. It's like lead paint central."

"Maybe they're short on cash," I say. She frowns.

"So what's the father like?" she asks.

"Nice guy. Not bad to look at."

"How *not bad*?"

"Hmmm. All-American. Blue eyes. Interesting looking."

"Interesting like who?" she asks. "Channing Tatum... or Quasimodo?"

"Just sort of...preppy," I say.

"Preppy? In a house like *that*?"

I can see where she gets it from.

"Nice voice," I add.

"I bet," she says.

"What does that mean?"

"It means you're blushing."

"What? I am not," I say.

"Now don't go getting all huffy. This is *me* you're talking to. Tell the truth," she says, leaning forward, whispering as if we weren't alone. "Do you have feelings for this guy?"

"Darcy, I just met him yesterday! I've only seen him once."

"But obviously he's seen you," she says, licking chocolate off her fingertips.

"What do you mean?"

"I mean...it's just very odd that he asked you to pick up the kid. Why you? And where has his wife been hiding?"

I tell her what Ben heard his teachers discussing. A sudden illness. A middle-of-the-night ambulance.

"When was this?" she wants to know. "Monday? Tuesday? My bedroom faces the front. I would have heard something."

"I don't know. All he said was, they took her away."

"To United?"

United is our local hospital. It's where you go to have a sprained wrist bandaged, or a speck taken out of your eye. But for anything more serious, you go somewhere else. United's one claim to fame is that it's won the Hospital Gift Shop Award three years running.

"I don't know. He didn't say where she was."

"So, for all you know," she says, tossing the Human Bean bag into her recycling bin, "she could be lying in a ditch somewhere."

"Oh, come on…"

"No. *Listen.* You don't think it's strange—a new family in town, keeps to themselves, meets no one. Didn't even move in with any furniture, for God's sake."

"Is that true?"

"No moving van. No U-Haul."

"Well, now that you mention it…"

"One day the house is empty. Then boom, it's got tenants. No one meets the wife. Then suddenly, she's being spirited away in the middle of the night. I'm getting a weird vibe from the whole thing. Hey—can you hand me the Splenda?"

"What a wonderful imagination you have," I say.

"No, really. Think about it," she says, as she taps a few packets against her cup and tears them open. "And then, when they need a favor, do they ask the person who gave them her number and *asked* them to call? No!" she continues, pouring the Splenda into her tea. "This Vince guy goes out of his way to pick someone who didn't even know he was there."

Hell. I am soooo sorry I ever mentioned this to her.

"So, what do you think?" she asks.

"I think...you've been watching too many *X-Files*," I say. Darcy smiles her beautiful Irish smile.

"Maybe so," she says, waving half an almond Danish for emphasis. "But I don't think you've been watching enough of them."

CHAPTER 11

IT'S 6:00 P.M. BEN walks in the door as I'm making the salad dressing.

He has a big smile on his face.

"Hi, honey. How'd the presentation go?" I ask.

"Great. Everybody loved the bandage. They thought the blood looked cool."

"Good for you," I say. "Any mention of Mr. van Gogh's other achievements? His still lifes? His water lilies?"

"Oh. You mean his *paintings*. Yeah, I talked about them, too. But everybody liked the ear story best. Except— Mom, you're gonna kill me."

"Why?"

He rummages through his backpack and pulls out Ned's scarf. In the middle of it is a bright-red food-coloring stain, the size of an orange.

"Oh, no. Your father's going to kill *both* of us. I purposely gave you a plastic bag to put that in."

"I forgot," he says.

"Well, let's not tell Dad, okay?"

Just as I hear Ned's key in the door, the oven timer goes off.

"I'm home," Ned calls out. I grab some potholders and take the chicken out of the oven. A minute later, Ned walks into the kitchen.

"My car is due for an emissions inspection," he says, holding a letter from the state. "You can bring it in Monday, and I'll take yours to work."

"How will I pick up the kids without a car?"

"Wait there while it's being inspected," he says. He wanders over to the liquor cabinet and pours himself a bourbon. "What's new here? What's for dinner?"

"Chicken. Baked potatoes. String beans. And Caroline lost that ring we gave her for her birthday."

"Damnit, Laura," he says. "You let her wear it to school?"

I knew it was going to be my fault. I just didn't know how.

"I didn't 'let' her. She wanted to show it to her friends. Is that so terrible?"

"She lost it. So I'd have to say *yes*."

"And Joey got a sixty-two on his geometry midterm," I continue. I start to set the table.

"Not true," Joey says, suddenly appearing in the kitchen. "It was a sixty-three."

Ned looks at him and shakes his head.

"That's just great," Ned says. "Well, you can kiss any kind of tennis scholarship good-bye."

"It wasn't my fault! It's because the teacher hates me."

"That makes no difference in geometry," Ned says. "Your answers are either right or wrong."

"Should we get him a tutor?" I ask. Both of them stare at me. Wrong thing to say. I'm about to be blamed again.

"I got a better idea," Ned says. "Why limit ourselves to one. Let's hire a *bunch* of people. We'll build a little apartment over the garage. And they can all live here with us."

"He says the teacher picks on him," I say.

"And my boss picks on me. That's life. Get used to it," Ned says to him. "Y'know, if your mother didn't mollycoddle you so much…"

I put down the silverware.

This is starting to be a very unpleasant evening. And just when I think it can't get any worse…it does. Ned goes to pour himself another bourbon. That's when he sees the empty dry-cleaning bag hanging on the kitchen doorknob.

"Did Harry do that tie already?" he asks. Ben and I look at each other. I don't want to lie. But I know what will happen when I tell the truth.

"Not exactly," I say. "We had a little…accident."

That's when it all hits the fan.

"You used my *antique silk scarf*?"

(*Memo to self: Remember what your therapist said. You have control, as long as you stay calm…*)

"Well, it was last-minute, and…"

"Damnit, Laura," he says, slamming the bourbon bottle on the counter. "I ask *so little* of you! Of all of you!"

(*Stay cool, I tell myself. He's been under a lot of pressure at work this week. This month. This year…*)

"I bust my ass all day," he continues, yelling. "And when I come home, it's always chaos!"

"Well, I didn't think…"

"No, you didn't!" he says. "What else do you have to do all day, besides be on top of all this crap?"

What else? That's when I lose it.

"You mean, besides making lunches and dinners and dealing with teachers and waiting all day for the cable guy, like I did last week, who—by the way—never showed up?"

"Hah. You want to know what kind of week *I* had?" he says.

"No. I don't," I say. "Because whatever it was—it wasn't as annoying as wasting hours on hold with tech support, or picking out a birthday card for *your* mother—a woman you can't stand!"

"And that took you—what? All of five minutes?"

Okay. Now I'm *really* getting angry.

"Who do you think makes out the checks around here! And calls the insurance company! And does all the garbage that you're just too busy or important to do!"

I punctuate each of these by slamming a plate or a glass down on the table. The table shakes every time.

"Sure, I'll wait for your car on Monday. *You* pick up the kids. See how it feels to spend half your life in a crappy Volvo wagon that, by the way, is due for its eighty-thousand-mile checkup!"

At some point, Ben and Caroline have heard us arguing and wandered into the kitchen to see what's going on.

"See what you've done?" he asks, gesturing to the kids, who cower in a corner. "Are you finished?"

"I'm *never* finished!" I say. "It's called *keeping life together.*" I am yelling at this point. "Their life, and your life...and *mine...if you can call what I have here a life!*"

I pause. And then I do something I've never done before.

I scrape the chicken off the serving platter and dump it into the garbage.

All five of us stand there, stunned. Me included.

The kids go upstairs quietly. Ned wanders around with a hangdog look. Later, as I walk past him in the den, I see he's sprawled out on the sofa, watching a bunch of talking heads on TV and eating a bowl of Rice Krispies.

I head upstairs and read for a while. As I get ready for bed, I hear a *ping.* I check my cell phone. It's a text from Vince.

Linoleum buckling. Ants taking over the kitchen, he writes. He adds a frowning emoticon. Crappy night here. You?

Same, I write.

Need to run a few errands on Monday, he texts back. I could use some company. Interested? I smile. At least *one person* thinks I'm worth spending time with.

I do a couple of quick calculations in my head. I can drop the kids off, then bring Ned's car in and leave it there. Vince can pick me up at the Emissions Center. Two birds. One stone.

Sure, I write back.

I smile. Things have a way of working out.

CHAPTER 12

BY SATURDAY MORNING, I have cooled down. The kids are busy with friends, sports, TV, computer games, and their iPhones. Even Ned seems a bit contrite when I tell him I am going to take his scarf in. He offers to drive me to Harry's.

I say no. I'm still angry from last night.

I park across from Harry's. As usual, Harry is alone behind the cash register. When he sees me, he does something he's never done before: he comes out from behind the counter and opens the door for me.

"Hi, Harry. Listen. I was wondering if you could..."

"Mrs. Sherman! I have your tie ready. Crisp and clean. Like brand-new."

He reaches under the counter and pulls out Ned's tie, spot-free in a cellophane wrapper.

"You need it in a hurry, *I do it* in a hurry. Harry does his job!" he says. "You tell your friends."

"That's great. But I'm not here about the tie."

I pull the stained scarf out of Ben's shopping bag and hold it up for him.

He screams.

All the color drains out of his face. He puts his hands out in front of him, palms up, and slowly takes a step back.

"Blood?" he whispers.

"What? Oh, no," I reply with a laugh. "Food coloring."

"Don't worry. I'll get it out."

"You think you can? I've heard food coloring is a permanent stain."

"Is tomorrow okay?"

"Well, there's no rush, really. The weather's still warm, so I don't think he'll be needing it for a while. Besides," I add, "tomorrow is Sunday. You're closed Sunday."

"For you, I open."

"No, really. Monday is fine. Thanks. What do I owe you for the tie?"

"Nothing." He shakes his head.

"Nothing?"

"My way of saying sorry. Very sorry." For *what?* I want to ask. Being an asshole?

"Well, that's very nice of you. But really, it's not necessary."

"No, I insist. You leave it to me. I'll get this... this... *red*... out."

"Well, all right. Thank you again."

"And tell your friends," he says. "You make sure you tell them!"

I don't get it. Overnight, he's gone from a dybbuk to Miss Congeniality.

I pull out of my parking space and head home. As I pass Harry's window, I see him standing behind his counter, watching me.

CHAPTER 13

THE GUYS AT THE Emissions Center tell me I can have my car back in a couple of hours. As I get out and hand them the keys, I see Vince's car pull up in front.

He waves. I'm about to open the door and slide in, when he gets out of the car and opens it for me. He is wearing a gray sweater, chukka boots, and jeans. I laugh.

"What are you laughing about?"

"Nothing," I say.

A lie. I am thinking about what a friend of mine once said: If a man opens a car door for his wife, it's either a new car or a new wife.

"Thanks for coming along," he says. "We've got a dreary hour or two ahead of us. Think you can manage it?"

"I'll try," I say. But once we're on our way, the conversation comes easily.

"I thought you drove a Volvo," he says.

"I do. That was Ned's car. And he's..."

"...too busy to bring it in himself? Yeah. We men

are like that. My wife used to complain about the same thing."

I wonder if I should ask about his wife again. Well, of course I should. But I decide not to. Not yet.

"So what sort of errands are we running?" I ask.

"I need to see a few clients."

"What exactly do you do?" I ask. "I mean, for a living?"

"I sell medical supplies," he says.

"What kind?"

"Mostly ostomy products," he says "Colostomy bags, barrier strips, moldable rings. I'm a sales rep for a company that makes 'em."

I shrug. It sounds depressing. Then we talk about movies we've seen...rock groups we like...our kids... the high price of real estate (why they're renting instead of buying)...and where we grew up. (Me: Milburn, New Jersey. Him: Highwood, outside of Chicago.)

Our first stop is a pharmacy a few towns away. Then another one in the next town. I sit in the car and watch through the window. At both places, the scenario is the same: Vince goes in and talks to someone. There's a lot of hand shaking and head shaking. Then he gives them a card and leaves.

"Well, that's it," he says, getting back into the car.

That's it? I think. *Just those two stops?* That took all of twenty minutes.

"So...maybe we could grab a little lunch?" he asks. "That is...if you have the time."

Of course I have the time. He knows it. I know he

knows it. And he knows I know. Whatever little game he's playing...I decide I'm going to play, too.

"Well, there's some leftover tuna waiting for me in my refrigerator," I say.

"Do you think we could convince it to wait a little longer?"

I laugh. "Sure."

"I was thinking of La Lavande," he adds. Of course he was. La Lavande is the newest, chicest restaurant within fifty miles. I've been wanting to go there, but it's been totally booked. Some people wait months for a reservation.

I mention this to Vince.

"Yes," he says. "*Some* people."

CHAPTER 14

THE LA LAVANDE PARKING lot is filled with bumper-to-bumper BMWs and Mercedes and, every so often, a lone Porsche or Ferrari.

Inside, every table has a sprig of lavender in a small glass vase.

The maître d' seems to know Vince. They shake hands. He ushers us to a table in the back.

I excuse myself and go to the ladies' room.

I look in the mirror. *Not terrible,* I think. *Not terrible at all.* It took forever to get dressed this morning. I finally settled on my go-to outfit: a black cashmere sweater and black slacks. I like the look. It clings nicely to my backside, which sometimes seems too big, and it perfectly frames my breasts, which sometimes seem too small. But not today.

Did I mention a brand-new black push-up bra? *Victoria's Secret.* Mine, too.

I put on more lip gloss and comb my hair.

I smile at my reflection. Okay. So he really didn't need company for two short errands, and maybe this whole lunch thing was in the back of his mind all along. Is that so terrible? *I'm having a good time,* I think. I can't remember the last time I thought that. It isn't a date. But, damn, it sure feels like one. I'm nervous. I'm excited.

As I head back to my seat, Vince is studying a leather-bound wine list that's almost the size of the table. "I thought we could start with some wine. This is a nice little Médoc," he says, pointing out one of the wines. I take a look. All my eyes register is the name, "St. Julien," and the price, "$85."

"You up for it?" asks Vince.

"Sure," I say. This may be the first eighty-five-dollar bottle of wine I've ever had.

The waiter comes and takes our drink order. Soon he returns with a bottle and two wineglasses. He pours a taste for Vince. Vince takes a sip, swirls it around in his mouth, and nods. The waiter fills both our glasses.

"What shall we drink to?" I ask, lifting my glass. Vince shrugs and smiles sweetly, brushing a boyish lock of hair out of his eyes.

"To friendship. To autumn. And, of course, to you."

I feel my heart clutch. Then again, it could just be my stomach growling.

We clink glasses. I take a sip. Vince speaks.

"Actually, I wanted to talk to you about something."

I nod and nervously slide my wineglass on the table-cloth.

"Vinny had such a good time at soccer. I was wondering—do you think you could drive him there every week?"

Impossible, I think.

"Sure," I say. I can't say no. I don't *want* to say no.

"You're a peach," he says. We clink glasses again and I take another sip. The wine tastes warm and thick and gorgeous. I feel like I'm floating. I look around. The restaurant is fairly empty now; the lunch crowd has left. And the waiter is back with menus.

I order a quiche (*with apple-smoked Canadian bacon*) and a salad (*endive with toasted hazelnuts*).

"Very good, madam," the waiter says, with a small bow in my direction. "And for monsieur?"

"Hmmm," Vince says, studying the menu. "I was think-ing about elk."

Say, what?

I look at the menu again. *Seared New England Elk Tenderloin with Parsnip Mousseline.*

"I've never seen anybody order elk before," I say.

"Well, you've probably never been with anybody born in Montana."

"I thought you grew up in Illinois."

A beat. "I did. After we moved from Montana."

For dessert we share *Praline Chicory Coffee Soufflé, Coffee Anglaise, and Warm Beignets.* He pours me another glass of Médoc. Every time I look up, Vince is looking at me and smiling. I tell myself he is just being friendly. Neighborly. Another glass of Médoc and I have almost talked myself into it.

"So why were you so down in the dumps Friday night?" he asks.

"You go first," I say.

"Okay. Vinny doesn't seem very happy at school."

And, of course, he misses his mother, I want to add. But I don't.

"It's a pretty jock-oriented place," I say, remembering what Ben said: *He's a nerd.* "And it takes a while to find your level."

"Yes," he says. "I don't know what I would have done if I hadn't found you..."

If I hadn't found you? The phrase has a hundred layers of meaning.

Vince continues. "I can't even meet other *men*," he says with a smirk. "They all work normal hours. Okay. Now it's your turn."

I think back to Friday night. Caroline's ring. Joey's test. Ned's scarf.

"Well—a bunch of things went wrong. And Ned's been in a pretty crappy mood lately," I begin.

"It's that seasonal affective disorder thing he suffers from."

How does he know that?

"A lot of men do," he adds quickly. "They miss the whole summer macho thing. You know. Golfing. Barbecues..."

"That's what we should do!" I say. "Ned loves to barbecue. And you can meet a couple of the neighbors. What do you think?"

"Well...if it's not a problem..."

"Not at all," I say, wondering if that's really true.

The waiter comes by, bows, and drops off the check.

Vince reaches in his pocket. He pulls out a stack of cash, neatly folded with a sterling silver money clip around it. He peels off two hundred-dollar bills. I must look surprised.

"I don't use credit cards," he says, and shrugs. "Cards are for people who don't have cash."

The waiter takes the money. Vince says, "No change, please." And then what I really hoped might happen, but that I also hoped would *not* happen...happens.

He moves his hand to my hand. He touches my fingertips with his fingertips. Then he turns one of my hands right-side up and studies the lines on it. Slowly, he traces them with his index finger.

"This is your *life* line," he says, running his finger along a line on the fleshy part of my hand. "See how it curves around your thumb? Means you're a rock. People count on you. I can believe that," he says.

He moves his finger up a bit. It tickles. I try not to giggle.

"Now this one here?" he says. "That's the *head* line. Yours splits in half. That says you're sensitive to others. Willing to listen to both sides. Is that the case?"

"I guess," I say.

"Now *this* one...the *heart* line..."

I hold my breath as he traces it slowly, back and forth. "Yours starts high, ends low."

"And that means...?"

He catches my eye and smiles.

"Lot of feelings and emotions under the surface, waiting to break free."

I try to think of something—anything—clever to say. I can't.

"You are a lovely woman," he says. He lets go of my hands.

"But now I guess it's time to let you get back to your life."

CHAPTER 15

MAGGIE'S OFFICE IS IN a gray cement building. I take the elevator up to the fourth floor and enter. The brass nameplate on the door says it all:

MAGGIE TRELEVEN, MSW,
ADOLESCENT AND FAMILY THERAPY

I'm a few minutes early. And it looks as if Ned is going to be late. I sit there and look around at the artwork on Maggie's walls. It is all modern, vague, brightly colored—swoops and swirls that cry out for interpretation. *Kind of like therapy itself,* I think.

Maggie opens her office door and sees that it's just me. "Why don't we give Ned a few more minutes," she says. I am still angry at him for our big blowout last week, but she's probably right: we are here to make peace. I nod.

Six minutes later Ned enters, looking frazzled. "Lot of traffic," he says.

I nod again and we enter Maggie's inner office. Maggie is in her late thirties, slim, pretty, with dark hair pulled back into a professional-looking bun. As usual, she is dressed simply but elegantly: a white silk blouse tucked into a navy pleated skirt.

Ned and I take our usual seats on opposite ends of her aqua sofa.

"So. How are things?" she asks, as if she's a neighbor who just happened to bump into us at the supermarket.

I say nothing. Ned shrugs and says, "Fine." Typical.

"We had a terrible fight last week," I start.

"Tell me about it," she says. And I do.

And then I tell her what happened just last night, when I suggested we invite a few friends over for a barbecue. "He practically bit my head off. He loves barbecuing," I say. "I thought he'd enjoy a chance to do it one more time, while we still have the weather for grilling."

But even as I say it, I'm wondering if it's true. Was I really doing it for Ned's benefit? Or was I just trying to be nice to Vince? The one person who's been nice to me. I keep this thought to myself.

"It struck me as a dumb idea," he says. "A waste of a Sunday. I work hard all week. Can't I have at least *one* day to myself?"

"You can have *every* day to yourself, for all I care," I say, feeling my blood boil.

"Do you really mean that?" Maggie asks.

Yes. No.

"Sometimes," I say.

It goes on like that for quite a while. Neither one of us thinks we get enough respect…enough understanding… enough attention. Maggie just listens.

"The fight, the barbecue idea…" Maggie finally says, her eyes darting between the two of us. "I wonder if those are just symptoms of something else."

Ned and I look at each other. Neither of us says anything.

"What's bothering you the most, Laura?"

I take a deep breath. Where to begin? "Well, I don't know why he…"

"No," Maggie interrupts. "Don't tell *me*. Tell *him*."

I swivel on the couch to face him.

"Okay. I don't know why you even bother coming home anymore, Ned. You're always in a bad mood."

"That's because…"

"I don't care why!"

Maggie stops me. "Let him finish."

"…because my job is making me crazy," he says. "Managing other people's money. Even the smallest mistake can mean millions. And now the place is talking about making cuts."

Maggie nods slowly, sympathetically. "That's a lot of pressure. Laura, do you agree?"

I shrug. Maggie speaks.

"No. Don't just shrug. Tell him."

"Okay. I'm sorry your work is so stressful." I take a deep breath. "But I *hate* how you take it out on me and the kids."

Maggie taps her index finger on her desk, as she always

does when she is about to make an important point. "I think it's important you hear that, Ned. Did you hear it?"

"Yes," he says. And then he does the one thing guaranteed to make me melt: He makes his cute little-boy face—pouty lips, eyes downcast, like he's been caught with his hand in the cookie jar. A face that's hard to hate.

"You're right," he says, quietly. "I have been...a dick. And I'm sorry."

Case closed. Sort of.

"And another thing," I say. "You always..."

"No." She stops me. "No more blaming. We go forward from now on. Both of you need to listen to the other, and then disagree in *positive* terms. We have to stop now," she says, looking at the clock behind us. "But I want you to remember the things we talked about today."

I schedule an appointment for the following week. Ned looks annoyed. Did he think this session was going to cure everything that's wrong with us? But in the car going home, he seems more relaxed.

"I guess I have been a bit of a jerk," he says. A bit? "Want to grab a bite before we head home?"

"Well, I told the kids..."

"Call and tell them to fend for themselves," he says.

"It's better if I text them," I say. "When I call, they don't pick up."

"Ain't that the truth," he says. We both laugh.

So we stop for a burger and beer at Shenanigan's, our favorite local haunt, then sit and talk till ten. It's like the old days—sort of. When we get home, I rummage through my dresser drawer and pull out something Ned gave me years ago—a lacy red negligee—instead of the ripped cotton "Go Huskies" nightshirt I usually sleep in. To my surprise and delight, Ned remembers. "Wow! You still have that?" he asks.

When I come out of the bathroom wearing it, he's waiting in bed with his arms crossed. He smiles. He whistles appreciatively. I crawl in beside him, and we begin to make love—slowly, carefully.

Is this what the women's magazines call makeup sex? If so, I'm all for it. For a while, I can blot out all thoughts of kids, chores, errands—even Vince.

CHAPTER 16

I'M IN THE SHOWER. Washing my hair, shaving my legs. Kiehl's coriander body wash. I'm going to smell nice and natural.

Today is my first official day as Vinny's soccer mom. I haven't seen or spoken to Vince since our lunch.

I step out of the shower. Then the distinctive *ping* of a text message on my cell.

From Vince comes this: I'm bringing snacks 4 team. C U soon.

A few minutes later Vince is at the front door. He's holding three shopping bags. And I'm wearing nothing but a bathrobe, admittedly the most modest bathrobe I could grab—a navy-blue terry cloth that Ned wears, when he bothers to wear one at all. And nothing underneath.

"Is that what you wear to pick up the kids?" Vince says with a very wide smile on his face.

I ignore his comment, and hope I'm not blushing. Then I say, "Those bags are the snacks? Are you feeding the team...or the whole school?"

"It's my salesman background," he says. "Get the prospect to smile, and you can sell them anything."

"And what exactly are you selling?" I ask.

"Quite honestly? *My son.* I want the other kids to like Vinny. So if it means bribing the team with fancy snacks and drinks...I'm down with that. How's your week been?"

I think about the makeup sex with Ned and look away. Great. It's bad enough that I feel guilty about Vince when I'm with Ned. Now I'm feeling guilty about Ned when I'm with Vince. The bathrobe doesn't help.

"My week was...not terrible," I say.

Vince says, "I'm going to put these bags in the trunk of your car."

"And I'm going to go get dressed," I say.

"Don't have to do that for me," Vince says, the same smile lighting his face.

"I'll be down in a minute."

When I return I'm wearing fairly baggy jeans and a fairly baggy T-shirt.

"I liked your other look better," Vince says.

"Gotta go," I say, ignoring his comment. "I don't want to make Vinny late."

Vince holds out his hand to me, as if to shake. But when his hand touches mine, his hold is gentle and there is no shaking.

"Listen..." he begins, and then it feels like he's changed his mind about whatever he planned on saying. He lets go of my hand and says, "We're really looking forward to the barbecue on Sunday. Anything I can bring?"

"Nope. Just yourself and Vinny." I pause. "Well—see you Sunday."

Then Vince says, "I've missed you."

I don't remember driving over the speed limit, but I make it to the school in record time. All four kids are waiting for me.

"My dad bought me the shoes and everything else I need," Vinny says, jumping in and tossing a lumpy gym bag onto the seat.

"Great," I say. "And your dad dropped off snacks for the team."

"I know," Vinny says. Then he adds good-naturedly, "He's trying to get the other kids to like me."

I drive my kids to oboe, ballet, and tennis. Then I swing around to the rec center. Coach Mike sees me pull in, waves, and comes running over. Mike is a sweet-heart—craggy-faced, built like a fireplug. And he's a great coach. He's been doing it for twenty-five years. Tough and demanding, but patient.

"Your dad called and said he's packed us up a feast," Mike says to Vinny. Vinny beams as Mike takes the three bags from the trunk and carries them over to the side-lines.

It's a beautiful autumn day and I've got some time to kill. So I park the car and head to the bleachers. Vinny sits on a bench, puts on his shoes, cleats, kneesocks, and shin guards. He is high-fiving two other teammates. I can't wait to tell Vince that his son is fitting in perfectly.

I whip out my cell phone and check my email. Every so

often, I glance up to see how Vinny is doing. He's trying hard to do the warm-up exercises, but he's always a beat or two behind. My heart goes out to him. It's clear he's not a natural-born athlete. But it's also clear that he's having a good time.

A half hour into the exercise routine, I decide to leave. At the same time Coach Mike decides it's time for refreshments. He blows a whistle, and the team runs over and starts rummaging around two bags.

Two bags?

"Where's the third bag?" I ask Mike as I pass him on my way to the car.

"What third bag?"

"There were three. Three bags."

He cocks his head and smirks. He makes a joke. "Maybe it *felt* like three!"

"No. I never lifted them. But I'm sure I saw Vinny's father put three bags in my car."

"Nope," he insists. "It was just two."

Am I going crazy? Maybe I'm wrong. Maybe my mind is playing tricks. Maybe...?

I don't know what another "maybe" could be. Oh, well. I guess I made a mistake. And yet...

I don't get to finish my thought. My phone beeps. It's a text from Joey.

Ur late!!! Where r u??? What's going on???

Yeah. What's going on?

CHAPTER 17

WHEN I WAKE UP Sunday morning, the sun is shining. *The perfect day for a barbecue,* I think.

But then I start to panic.

My mind is suddenly filled with a million what-ifs: What if Vince says something about our outing or about our lunch, which I never told Ned about? What if I slip and do or say something, and Ned realizes how I feel about Vince?

How do I feel about him?

On and on I go. I'm making myself crazy. I feel like a teenager again, self-conscious and awkward around boys. And I hate the feeling.

At two fifteen, everything is cooked, cooling, coming to room temperature, or marinating. I go upstairs to get dressed. Then there's another text from Vince: Positive you don't need anything?

Other than a Xanax, no.

Darcy and her husband, Jake, are the first to arrive.

She shows up carrying a hand-stenciled basket filled with flowers from her garden.

"So where's the guest of honor?" she asks.

"He'll be here," I say.

Darcy smiles and says, "I'm sure he will."

Coach Mike arrives next, carrying a case of Coors. Mike has been divorced for years. Should I have asked him if he wanted to bring a plus-one? Well, too late now.

Mike shakes hands with Jake and Darcy. He hasn't seen them since their son, Alex, graduated a few years ago.

"He likes Stanford?" Mike asks.

"Loves it," says Darcy.

Then I hear the gate open again. I take a deep breath.

Vinny runs onto the deck first. "Where's Ben?" he asks. I direct him down to the basement, where Ben and his video games are.

Then Vince appears. He looks like he just got out of the shower. His hair is wet and slicked back. He's wearing the typical suburban dad uniform: a yellow J. Crew tee, jeans, and Docksides. He's carrying a shopping bag.

"Everybody—this is Vince," I say. "Vince, this is Darcy and Jake, your neighbors on the other side. Mike: meet the man behind all those great snacks. And that's Ned over there—the guy bent over the grill." Ned waves.

"You're the lady who left those delicious brownies," Vince says to Darcy. "So sorry. I meant to send you a thank-you note but..."

"No worries," she says, with a ladylike brush of her

hand. "I'm sure you've had enough to do. How are you liking it here in our neck of the woods?"

They begin a conversation about real estate, shopping, traffic, kids, sports, Vinny, and schools. Ned is busy at the grill, and everybody seems nice and civil to everybody else. I breathe a sigh of relief. I'm about to excuse myself to go into the kitchen when Vince pulls something out of the shopping bag he's holding.

"Almost forgot," he says. He hands me two bottles of Médoc. "I brought you some of that wine you like."

My eyes dart over to Ned, hunched over the grill. Has he heard this? For a moment I imagine him outraged, incensed, seething with jealousy.

But no. Ned is happily fanning the barbecue fire, stirring the charcoal, and not paying attention to any of us.

Okay, I dodged one bullet. I excuse myself and go into the kitchen again to check on the pies. I'm there just a moment when I sense someone behind me. I turn around. It's Vince.

"I need a corkscrew," he says, waving one of the bottles. I turn away, furious at myself for blushing at the word "screw." I point to the drawer where the silverware is kept. "Ned seems like a great guy," he says. Why does he say that? All Ned did was wave.

"Yes, he is," I say. I don't know what else to add. Having him here in my kitchen is making me nervous. Fortunately, he seems to sense this. He heads back out, corkscrew in hand.

As I go outside with a second platter of hors d'oeuvres—sliced salami wrapped around cream cheese and chives, toasted mushroom puffs, a wedge of brie—I see the conversation has gotten around to what people do for a living. Darcy is talking about her artwork, her stenciling, her oil painting. Ned shares the pressures of being responsible for other people's money. Vince nods politely to all of them. Then Jake mentions that he's a cardiologist.

Suddenly, Vince leans forward in his chair, intrigued.

"I've never been to a cardiologist," he says. "And I suppose I should. My dad died of a heart attack when he was barely sixty."

"How long ago was that?" Jake asks.

"Oh—thirty years, give or take."

"Was that his first heart attack?" Jake asks.

"No. He suffered from angina. What I remember most is how he carried those little nitroglycerin tablets around with him and put one under his tongue any time he felt a tingle."

"They don't use them much anymore," Jake says.

"Do you think I should be—what? Checked? Tested?"

"That's always wise, with your family history. Give my office a call, first thing tomorrow. Tell my secretary I said to fit you in."

"Thanks. I'll do that," Vince says. His hair has dried in the sun at this point, and he looks...cute. That curl has fallen into his face as it usually does, and he keeps brushing it back with his fingers.

Like a nervous hummingbird, I dart back into the kitchen. As I'm putting some bowls in the sink, Darcy appears.

"So?" I ask. "What do you think?"

"Delicious," she says. I turn around and see she has taken a fork and dipped it into the potato salad.

"I meant, what do you think of *Vince*."

"I know you did," she says. Suddenly, she turns serious.

"Okay. He's charming. I'll give you that," she says. "But I still don't like it."

"Because...?"

"Because if I was lying in a hospital somewhere, I'd like to know my husband was missing me, or thinking of me, or feeling guilty that he's at a party without me."

Darcy frowns.

"And *not* charming the pants off his new neighbor."

I desperately need to change the subject.

"Jake seems quiet," I say. "Is everything okay with you guys?"

"With us—sure," she says. "But he's preoccupied. He's in the middle of a big malpractice suit."

"Oh, my God," I say.

"Some patient is suing. Claims Jake made a mistake in surgery, and now he can't work. Jake says it's all bullshit. But until it's resolved, it's hanging over his head and he's a nervous wreck. Anyway, it's all kind of hush-hush. Frankly, I kind of wish he *would* tell someone about it, just to get it off his chest. He said he was gonna ask the guys' advice today."

I look out the kitchen window. Jake is talking. Vince and Mike listen, deep in thought.

"Looks like he's doing that now," I say.

Just then we hear Ned yell, "Dinner is served."

CHAPTER 18

WE'RE READY TO EAT. We all take our seats around the gray wood picnic table.

"To the end of summer," Ned says, holding up his glass. There's a lot of clinking, and I am beginning to relax inside. No cause for alarm after all.

As we finish eating, Joey appears on the deck. He says hi to Darcy, Jake, and Mike. I introduce him to Vince.

"Nice to meet you, son," Vince says, shaking his hand. "You're what now: a junior? How old are you?"

"Seventeen next week," Joey says.

"And he'll be going for his driver's license," Ned adds.

"Ah. The classic rite of passage," Vince says. "I remember when I first got mine. I was fifteen. Of course, the rules in Iowa were very different then."

Iowa?

He sees the surprised look on my face. "My grandparents owned a farm there," he says. "In those days, you could get a junior license at fifteen if you lived more than a mile from school."

"Hard to believe you're getting your license," Darcy says to Joey. "First time I met you, your mom was carrying you around in a Snugli."

"I bet you're pretty good with computers," Vince says. "Unlike us old folks."

"You bet," I say. "We think of him as our live-in IT guy."

"Y'know, Joey, if you've got the time, I could use some help setting up a new piece of software I just got. You familiar with Excel? Spreadsheets?"

"Sure," Joey says, circling around the table and filling his plate.

Why does this please me? Why does it make me nervous?

"That would be great. The company wants me to switch over from my old bookkeeping method, and I don't think I can master it on my own. I'd pay you, of course," he adds. "So you can start saving up for your own car."

"Cool," Joey says. He takes his plate and heads back inside.

"Perfect steaks, Ned," Mike says, sitting back in his chair.

"And great day for a barbecue," Jake adds.

"It *was*," Mike says. "But it looks like it's about to rain." Mike is right. The sky has turned a dark gray.

"Maybe we should head inside for dessert?" I say.

Just then, there's a crack of thunder and a few drops of rain. Then, suddenly, it's pouring. Hard silver drops slash against the deck. Ned runs around grabbing the cushions. Darcy, Jake, and Mike gather up the remaining plates and platters and bottles. I hold open the screen door as everyone rushes in and out. I get drenched in the process.

"I've got to close the windows upstairs," I say.

"I'll go with you," Vince says. Before I can protest, he's following me up the stairs, to the second floor.

By the time we get there, rain has already soaked a small part of the carpet. Vince moves quickly, slamming the windows shut in the hall bathroom, the boys' rooms, and Caroline's room.

Last stop: my bedroom.

We walk inside. He stands there for a moment, taking it all in: the lace curtains, the cream-colored duvet on the bed, the antique French mirror over the dressing table.

"Nice," he says. Nice? Does he mean the room? The afternoon? Being there with me? All of the above?

He looks around and sees my red lace nightgown hanging on the closet door. Then he looks at me and laughs.

"Well now," he says. "I guess I'll have to adjust my fantasies."

A small shiver passes through me.

Slowly, quietly, as if he has all the time in the world, he walks across the carpet and closes the window on my side of the bed. Then the one on Ned's side.

"A California king-size bed," he says. "You and Ned like that?"

"Yeah, most of the time," I say. "Sometimes it feels...I dunno...too big. A little..."

"Lonely?"

I say nothing. But Vince speaks.

"You don't know what lonely means until...you know...with my wife gone..."

There is a crackle of thunder behind him. Then a bolt of lightning that lights up the room. For a split second, he is backlit, a lone figure standing in the rain on the Yorkshire moors. He is Heathcliff.

And I am his Catherine.

He takes a step toward me. With a finger, he lifts my chin.

"Don't be afraid," he says, his eyes locked on mine. "You never have to be afraid of *me*."

He runs his hand through my hair. Then down my ear. And across my neck. He is tender. Oh, so very tender.

I freeze. Time stops. The moment seems to go on forever.

But then, with the back of his hand, he leans in and gently wipes a few raindrops off my cheek. I am relieved. Or heartbroken. Maybe a little of both.

Then we both head downstairs, as if nothing has happened.

CHAPTER 19

THE SHOP WAS CALLED Gussied Up. That was the first thing that annoyed Marlene.

Gussied Up sounded cute and fun. But the gowns they sold there were elegant and expensive—ridiculously expensive. Way more than what Marlene and her husband paid in rent.

The women who came in and tried them on and admired themselves in the store mirror rarely looked at the price tags. That annoyed Marlene, too. But she was in no position to say anything.

She needed a job. They needed the money.

When a man came into the store, Marlene and the other salesgirls were instructed to fawn over him. Offer a glass of champagne. Direct him to a chair where he could sit and watch his wife—girlfriend? mistress?—try on gowns and twirl for his amusement. Women with men always spent more, she was told.

And men alone spent the most.

So when Marlene sees the man walk in, she rushes to his side, picturing a big, juicy commission. He is nice-looking. Early forties, she guesses. Nice smile. He eyes a rack of fancy cocktail dresses.

"May I help you find something?" she asks.

"I'm looking for a gift for a lovely lady," he says. "I want her to know just how lovely . . . by getting her something special."

He is such a gentleman. Marlene sparks to him immediately.

"Were you thinking of a gown?" she asks.

"Probably not the best idea. I don't know her size."

"We have some lovely handbags and scarves," Marlene says, gesturing to a display against the wall. "Does she have a favorite designer?"

But the man is shaking his head. "I don't know. I don't know her that well."

He thinks for a moment.

"I have an idea," he says. "Why don't you show me the thing you like most in the store."

Marlene smiles. She knows exactly what she should show him.

She uses her key to open a glass counter, and pulls out a gold metal belt, studded with green and blue emerald-cut rhinestones, and decorated with sterling and gold filigree. "It's a one-of-a-kind Art Deco piece," she says.

She stretches it out on the counter. "It was custom-made for a very wealthy woman," she says, holding it up so he can get a closer look at the French pavé settings.

"Is it gold?" he asks.

"Pinchbeck," she says. "A kind of gold alloy invented in the eighteenth century. But the buckle part is eighteen karat. Magnificent, isn't it."

"Yes," the man says. He looks at the price tag. Marlene assumes he will flinch or decline graciously. He does neither.

"This is perfect," he says.

"Very good, sir."

"Please," he says. "Call me Vince."

"All right then...Vince," Marlene says. She clips the price tag off, then gently rolls the belt into a circle and wraps it in silver tissue paper.

To her shock, he reaches into his pocket and pays with cash. She has never seen that much cash before.

"Have you been working here long?" he asks, as she puts the belt in a large gold box.

She cuts off a long piece of gold and silver ribbon and begins to make a bow.

"No. Just a few months."

"I get it. Looking for something to do with your downtime."

She laughs. "Not quite. I needed..." She stops midsentence. She doesn't know how much to tell this man, but he seems so kind. "My husband has been ill for a while."

"Nothing serious, I hope." He frowns.

"Well—he's on disability. But..." She stops herself again. If the shop owner knew she was talking to a customer about herself, she wouldn't like it.

"Does he intend to go back to work?"

"Yes. Eventually," she says.

"But not until the lawsuit is settled."

Marlene snaps her head around. Suddenly, she feels very afraid.

"What...?!"

"I mean—that's what it's all about, isn't it, Marlene?" Vince continues.

How does he know her name?

"Your husband is a deadbeat. Always was. Even before the surgery. Missing days. Calling in sick a lot. One of those guys who's always looking for a free ride. Am I right?"

A chill goes through her. Who is this man? What does he want from her?

"You know," the man continues, *"insurance companies are onto people like you. Filing false claims. Making false accusations. It really isn't right, how you can ruin a good doctor's life with just one little lie."*

"No!" Marlene says, her voice starting to crack. *"It's not like that! That surgeon made a mistake! My lawyer says..."*

"Marlene. Please!" Vince holds up his hand. *"Do not insult my intelligence by referring to that ambulance-chasing brother-in-law of yours as an attorney, when both of us know the truth."*

She has finished wrapping the belt. She hands it to him. She is close to tears.

"What do you want?" she asks. She can barely get the words out.

"I want you to tell your husband to withdraw his case," he says.

"I don't think I..."

He leans in and grabs her wrist. She winces.

"Go home. Tell him a man came into the store and gave you a deal. A simple trade. He drops the case, and he gets to keep . . . the thing he loves most."

He is still holding on to her wrist. "That seems fair, doesn't it? I think you understand what I'm saying."

Marlene can hardly speak. She is shaking so much. She nods. He lets go of her wrist and turns to go.

"By the way," he says, turning back. "You can keep this, too." He hands her the wrapped package. "Consider it your very generous settlement."

He laughs. Then he walks out the door.

CHAPTER 20

IT'S BEEN OVER A week since the barbecue. Vince has written me several texts and emails.

> Laura, I miss u.
> Where r u?
> Come on, girl. We have to talk.

Do we?

Not until I figure out what I want to say.

Yet I can't help checking my messages twenty times a day, to see how desperate he's getting. How much he misses me. How much he wants to see me again. I'm like a lovesick schoolgirl with her first crush. And it feels...well, exciting. Before Vince, most of my messages said things like "Teacher needs to see you."

Or "Working late 2nite. Asshole client."

Suddenly, I hear honking outside my door. It starts out slowly, then gets more insistent. Someone is leaning on a horn, full blast. What the hell...?

I go to the door, determined to yell at whoever is creating such a racket. I should have known. I see Vince's car. The honking stops.

Vince rolls down the window and waves. Shit.

I walk to his car, unsure of how to play this.

"Hey," I say. "What's up?"

He is not smiling. "You know," he says quietly, "I don't like to be ignored."

Something doesn't feel right. But then he laughs, and he's the old Vince again. The angry voice is just a tease.

"You're a tough lady to reach," he says, turning on the charm. "Didn't you get my messages?"

"Yes, but…"

"Look. I was a little out of line on Sunday, scurrying up the stairs like that. So if I said or did anything to upset you…"

"No, really. It's fine. I've just been so busy," I say.

Both of us know this is a lie. Busy with what? Broiling lamb chops and folding boxer shorts?

"I want to make it up to you," he says. "Get in."

"What? *Now*?" I am leaning on his car. I take a step back.

"I said get in." That tough-guy voice again.

"Really, you don't have to…"

"I've got a big surprise planned," he says.

"I can't now," I say. "I've got to pick up…" But he cuts me off.

"Taken care of," he says. "I called Darcy. She's gonna bring the kids home. So come on. No more excuses."

I just stand there.

"Scout's honor," he says holding up three fingers. "You're gonna love it. Trust me. Get in."

So I get in. Is this a good idea? I don't know. A second later I'm buckling my seat belt.

Vince turns and we drive through town.

"We need to talk," he says.

"About...?"

"About my wife," he says. He looks over at me as we pass a row of fancy Victorian gingerbread houses opposite a small park. My favorite part of town.

"Okay," I say. He parks the car and I follow him out. We sit on a park bench. He is staring off into space for quite a while. Then he turns toward me.

"The truth is, my wife left me. Walked out on Vinny and me, over a year ago. Decided she just didn't want to...be with us anymore."

He turns away and I see him wipe his eyes with the back of his hand.

I am stunned. I don't know what to say.

"She's living—I don't know. Somewhere in Florida, I think. We haven't heard from her since. It's been terrible for me and Vinny. I still have a hard time even talking about it."

"So she's not...?"

"Sick? In a rest home, somewhere? No," he says sadly. "That's what I tell people. But I wanted *you* to know the truth."

My heart is breaking for him. He's lonelier than I could ever imagine. A minute ago I thought I was being kidnapped. Now I just want to throw my arms around him and tell him it's all gonna be okay.

So I do.

We sit like that for a while, hugging each other, cheek to cheek. I smell his aftershave—something spicy. Patchouli, maybe. Or musk. He runs his hand across my back. Then up along the back of my neck. He whispers my name over and over again. "Oh, Laura…"

I want this moment to last forever. Is that all I want? I'm ashamed of what I am thinking. But he seems so very unhappy.

Then he pulls away.

"Well now," he says, taking a deep breath. "Now that that's out of the way—do you want to know where we're going?"

"You mean there's more to this car ride?"

"You think I spirited you away just to tell you that? We're going into the city," he says. We go back to the car and he makes a left turn onto the highway.

"New York City?" I ask.

"Unless you'd rather go to Cleveland." We both laugh.

"What's in New York?" I ask.

"Look in the glove compartment."

I pop it open. Next to the registration and manual is an envelope. I open it.

It's two center orchestra seats to *Hamilton*. Today's matinee. Starting at two.

"I know how you love acting, music, all that stuff," he says. "So I thought maybe this was something you might want to see."

Might? The show of the century? Is he kidding? Last month I asked Ned about getting tickets. His response? "At five hundred dollars a pop? I'd rather watch Netflix."

The show is thrilling and gorgeous and full of wonderful moments. And Vince seems to really enjoy it. He applauds loudly.

And at one point, during a touching moment, he reaches over and takes my hand. We look at each other and smile. Has any moment in my life ever felt this joyful, this peaceful?

I don't think so.

We chat about the show all the way home. He pulls into my driveway. I can see the kids through the living room window, sitting on the couch. Caroline is reading a book. Joey and Ben are watching *Game of Thrones*. Nobody seems to be missing me.

"This was a lovely afternoon," I say. "Thanks. And Vince..."

"Yes?"

"Thanks for leveling with me about your wife."

"Thanks for listening," he says. He leans over to my side and gives me a quick and gentle kiss on the cheek.

One of the mysteries of Vince: how can a kiss this chaste and friendly feel so...well...so incredibly hot?

I stand there for a moment as he drives off. Now it's back to the lamb chops and the boxer shorts.

I miss him already.

CHAPTER 21

NED AND I ARE supposed to meet at Maggie's. But at the last minute, he texts:

Meeting running late. Can't get away. Go w/o me.

Ordinarily, I would be pissed. But today I am glad for a private session.

I need to talk to her about Vince.

Maggie knows something's up. She sees it in my face, as I sit down. I want to tell her everything. But I don't know where to begin.

"See, there's this guy..." I say.

Damn. Bad enough I feel like a teenager. Now I'm starting to *sound* like one, too.

"This *man*. He's new in the neighborhood. I drive his son places. He's charming and funny and nice to me. And his wife walked out on him, a year ago..."

"Go on," she says.

"Do I have to spell it out? Ned has been a dick and I spend time with a nice man who seems genuinely fond of me. He says I'm his only friend."

Her eyebrows go up a bit on that line. But then they settle down again.

"And I think I'm falling in love with him."

"Tell me about it," she says.

Then the floodgates open. Every fear and feeling and fantasy of the last few weeks comes tumbling out.

As I ramble on, I know what Maggie's thinking: how could I possibly hope marriage counseling would work, when all along my heart was elsewhere?

But if Ned hadn't been acting so awful these past few months...

"So this is Ned's fault?" she asks.

"Well—sort of," I say. "What I like about Vince is it's all so *easy*. He really cares about me. We don't get bogged down in the awful stuff."

"Awful stuff, like...?"

"Oh, you know. Dentist appointments. Mortgage payments. Blaming each other for things the kids did."

"The stuff of life," she says.

"Well, yes..." I say. "But it's more than that. I mean— what do I do here, Maggie? Nothing's happened between us—yet. But would it be so terrible? I mean, yes, for the kids, if they ever found out. They would be devastated. And Ned—it would be awful for him. Maybe. I don't know anymore."

She doesn't say anything.

"Oh God, Maggie. Don't just sit there nodding. Tell me what to do here! I'm a wreck!"

"You want me to give you permission to have an affair," she says.

I say nothing.

"You know I can't do that," she says quietly, smoothing down the pleats of her skirt. "Only you can decide. But if we keep talking about it…"

"No!" I say. It comes out louder than I thought it would. "I am *so damn tired* of talking, and thinking about this, and slinking around behind Ned's back, and feeling guilty about what I want to happen, and being angry at Ned for… for…"

"For not being more like Vince?"

"For not *being* Vince. A nice simple guy who loves me and has a good time with me."

"Once a week."

Oh. Low blow.

"Okay," I say. "Once or twice a week. What are you saying? That Vince would turn into Ned if we were married? That that's how all marriages get, over time?"

"Laura, I didn't say that. I just asked…"

"Help me, Maggie. *Please!* I feel like my whole life has turned upside down, ever since I answered that phone call."

And then, all of a sudden, my cell phone rings.

I look at it, prepared to let it go. But it's not Ned or Vince or any of my friends.

It's Ben and Caroline's school.

"I have to take this," I say to Maggie. Damn. What has Ben done now? I bet he mouthed off to one of his teachers. Or maybe he failed something.

I press Talk.

"Mrs. Sherman?" I hear a voice say.

"Yes," I say. I'm prepared to hear the worst about my son.

"This is Principal Wallace's office. We need you to come to school. There seems to be a serious problem...with Caroline."

CHAPTER 22

WE ARE SITTING IN Principal Wallace's office. Evelyn Wallace is a heavyset woman with short curly hair. She wears navy suits a lot. Even on a good day, she could pass for a prison warden.

Principal Wallace is usually cheerful—just what you want in a person who spends her life around small children.

But today she is not smiling.

And neither are we.

"This is outrageous," I say. Ned nods.

"There's no way our daughter could be involved in something like this," he says.

Mrs. Wallace is holding a small plastic bag. In it are a bunch of pills.

"I understand your concern," she says. "But these were found in her backpack."

How dare Wallace suggest such a thing!

"That's impossible," I say. If I sound huffy or pissed, it's because I am.

She shakes the bag. The pills dance around.

"I don't know how they got there!" Caroline says. She is crying. She'd been sitting on the bench outside Wallace's office crying even before we arrived. Her face is bright red.

I lean in closer and study the bag in Wallace's hand.

"Hah! That's not even the kind of *bag* we use," I say. "I never buy the ones with zippers." Case closed. Or so I think.

"We have two witnesses," Principal Wallace says. "Your daughter accidentally dropped her backpack when she was getting up from her desk, and this bag fell out."

"It isn't mine!" Caroline says, still sobbing.

"A boy sitting next to her picked it up and handed it to the teacher," Mrs. Wallace says. "The teacher brought it to me."

Ned has been seething. Suddenly, he explodes.

"I want the name of that boy!" Ned yells. "And I want to talk to that teacher!"

Good. I want him to make a scene. I want him to yell and scream and show this woman how wrong she is. My little girl? My baby? The whole thing is preposterous.

"What kind of pills are they?" I ask.

"Ritalin," the principal says. "Twenty milligrams. I showed them to the school nurse."

"Then I'll speak to her as well!" Ned yells.

"Mr. Sherman," the principal says, in the kindly voice we're more used to. "I know children these days are under a lot of pressure to do well. And your Caroline has always been ... a perfectionist. So it's easy to understand ..."

"Let's get one thing straight," Ned says. "My daughter does not take drugs."

It's clear our protests are falling on deaf ears. Or, even worse, the ears of a person who has already made up her mind.

"There are many children in the school who require medication," she says. "But the protocol is for a parent to give the prescription bottle to the *nurse,* who then doles it out."

"I don't think you heard me, Mrs. Wallace," Ned says. His face is almost as red as Caroline's. "I said my daughter *does not take drugs!*"

There is a pause.

"Not that you're aware of," she says quietly.

That's when Ned loses it.

"What are you saying?" he says, jumping up suddenly. "That my daughter is a drug addict? That's she's selling these? Giving them away?"

I'm torn between wanting him to reach across the desk and slug her...and afraid he just might.

"Please, Mr. Sherman. I'm just saying..."

But there's no stopping him.

"If I get my lawyer on the phone, I can have you removed just like that!" He pounds his fist on her desk. "How *dare* you suggest that my daughter, a *goddamn eleven-year-old*..."

"Mr. Sherman! There are children around!" Mrs. Wallace says. She stands up. Now they are eye to eye. "I'm not suggesting anything! I'm only saying...we have a drug-free school! If Caroline needs Ritalin to focus..."

"They're not mine!" Caroline wails. "I don't know how they got there."

"Let's get out of here," I say. Ned takes Caroline's arm and leads her to the door. He turns toward Principal Wallace one last time.

"You will be hearing from my lawyer about this. I can promise you that!"

I follow him out the door. Caroline is still crying.

"Dad, I swear..."

"I know you didn't," he says. "This is all a terrible mistake. And if she dares put this on your permanent record..."

He walks us to my car without finishing his sentence. "I'll meet you at home," he says. "I've got to...take care of a couple things."

"You're not heading back to the office, are you?" I ask. "It's after four."

"Yes," he says. But then a moment later: "No." He turns and heads to his car.

I get in my car and Caroline gets in next to me. "Mom, those aren't mine. Honest." She's still sniffling.

"I know. Honey, I believe you." And I do believe her. Really.

But then whose are they?

CHAPTER 23

NO DOUBT ABOUT IT. Tonight will be a "Freezer Night."

After our meeting with the principal, I'm too wiped out to cook. So I open the freezer and throw together a meal made up of anything I can microwave.

It's a haphazard menu, even for us. Frozen pizza. Frozen Brown 'N Serve sausages. (Can you put breakfast sausages on a pizza? Well, I'll find out soon enough.) Fish sticks. Two dozen pigs in a blanket. And chunks of frozen cookie dough for dessert.

The kids don't care. And Ned doesn't, either. Neither one of us has the energy to make conversation at dinner. As the boys chat away, Caroline is quiet. Her face is still puffy from crying. I look over at Ned. He looks like I feel: totally spent. Worse than spent. *Squandered*.

Later on, when I go upstairs, Ned is already in bed reading. It's the first time we've been alone together since our meeting at the school. I can't stop thinking of how the principal looked at us. The expression on her face as she shook that bag.

"What are we gonna do?" I ask him.

"I don't know," he says. "I don't want to talk about it now."

I feel the fury rise up in me.

"Oh. And you think *I do*?"

He shrugs and goes back to his book.

"Damnit, Ned. This is important! What do you think is going on?"

He doesn't answer.

"I mean, do you think...there's any chance that she...?"

"No!" He says. He slams the book shut and turns to face me. "Jesus, Laura! She's practically a baby! *No way* she would have those pills in her backpack. Hell, the kid can barely swallow a Tylenol. No way she's taking drugs behind our back!"

"Well, then how come...?"

"Forget about it," he says. He goes back to his reading. Book open. Case closed.

Forget about it? Does he really think I can do that?

"Okay, then. What *do* you want to talk about?" I ask. "The weather? The situation in Iraq? *Game of Thrones*?"

If my life were a movie, a little animated red-devil character would jump onto my shoulder at this point and whisper in my ear: "Go ahead! Tell him about *Hamilton*! Tell him about *Vince*! Tell him...*everything*!"

But of course, I don't.

"I do have one piece of good news," he says. "That guy Vince came by my office this week."

Wait. Did I say my life was a movie? Wrong. Minute by minute, it's turning into an episode of *The Twilight Zone*.

"What did he want?" I ask. I can barely get the words out.

What I really want to ask is: Did he mention me? Did he tell you how we hugged? Did he tell you we held hands in the theater, or how he kissed me good-bye?

"He asked if I'd be willing to take him on as a client. You know. Handle some of his money."

"And you said . . . ?"

"Sure. Why not. A commission's a commission. So we're going to get together again next week and talk strategy. I need to find out his level of risk tolerance."

"When was this?" I ask.

"Wednesday."

"This *past* Wednesday?" The day Vince poured his heart out to me? The day the two of us went into the city?

"Yes," he says.

Fear, anxiety, and adrenaline are racing through my body. There's just one thing I can do to distract myself: start my Lamaze breathing.

Of course, it doesn't help me any more now than it did during childbirth.

Ned may be lying about this, I think. Or is he? Did Vince stop by before he picked me up? I can't ask Ned too many questions. He'll wonder why I'm asking.

Maybe Ned is wrong about the day. But if he isn't, why

didn't Vince tell me what he had done? He sends me ten, twelve texts a day. Why didn't he mention this in any of them?

One of them is lying to me. Maybe both of them are.

(Memo to self: It's too bad you didn't pursue your acting career. Look how you're able to maintain a straight face when, inside, your entire life is falling apart.)

Ned goes back to his book and reads a few more pages. He yawns. Soon he turns out his light. He's asleep in a matter of minutes.

Me? I know I'm going to be tossing and turning for hours.

CHAPTER 24

WHY ON EARTH DID I agree to this?

I know why. I thought it might clear my head to get away for a day.

Besides, it sounded lovely on paper. A bus ride into the city. An afternoon on the water. A picnic lunch at the Statue of Liberty.

Of course, I forgot about the downside: I would be chaperoning ten noisy, rambunctious second-graders on a class trip, a group that doesn't even include my own kids. A bunch of kids who delight in being annoying and obnoxious, from the time we board the bus at school all the way down to Battery Park.

I brought a *Vogue* and a *Vanity Fair* to read on the bus. That's a laugh. I spend the entire ride breaking up fights. Making sure Dylan doesn't pick his nose—or, if he does, not to wipe it on Sophie. Getting vomit bags ready for Lacey, who gets carsick.

If I think a ride on the ferry will quiet them down, I am wrong. The water is rough. On the ride over, both Lacey *and* Tyler need vomit bags. Like an overtaxed mother hen, I get dizzy trying to keep an eye on my ten charges. They scatter between the benches and the rails. It's my job to make sure no one falls overboard.

And then I see the guy in the black suit.

He is sitting a few rows in front of me. A young man, mid-thirties, dressed like an undertaker. Black shoes, white shirt, black tie. He is wearing dark sunglasses and reading a newspaper.

The only person on the entire ferry who's completely alone.

Every so often, out of the corner of my eye, I see him move the paper to the side and look at me. The one time our eyes meet, he quickly turns away.

Call me crazy, but I could swear the guy is watching us. Watching *me.*

An admirer? A stalker? A pervert? This is New York. He could be all three. He is good-looking, if a bit bland. Certainly ten years younger than I am. So it's flattering. But odd.

Once the ferry docks at Liberty Island, he disappears in the crowd.

I help my group of kids off the boat and stand guard as they make bathroom visits. Mrs. Bolton, the teacher, announces that tickets to the top of the torch have been sold out for months. So we're only climbing as high as the pedestal.

This meets with a lot of groans, but I'm delighted. I'm carrying all their lunches. Two shopping bags filled with sandwiches, juice boxes, chips, and fruit, to lug up all the stairs.

When the photo taking is finished—a few New York harbor shots, and several hundred selfies—we head back down for lunch. Mrs. Bolton and I sit at a picnic table to eat. The kids prefer eating on the grass.

Then they line up for the final leg of our historical journey: a visit to the gift shop.

But as the kids make a beeline to all the Statue of Liberty green foam crowns, the rubber souvenir bracelets, and the *I ♥ Lady Liberty* T-shirts, I see him again: my Man in Black. Just standing there.

It's as if he's been waiting for me to show up.

Who is he? What does he want? Nothing to be afraid of, I tell myself. There are hundreds of people milling around. This is a public place.

Unless he's a sniper. Or a hit man. Or a terrorist.

Come on, Laura. Get a grip.

We board the ferry back. I look around and breathe a sigh of relief. My stalker is nowhere in sight. It's rush hour, so the bus ride back takes forever. Some of the kids start to doze off. The rest are tired, hot, and cranky. By the time we pull into the school parking lot, I'm feeling that way, too.

And then I see him again. In the school parking lot.

Same man. Same suit. Same sunglasses. Only this time, he's sitting in a parked Subaru in front of the school.

Okay. Now I'm really scared. Who is he? What's he doing in front of an elementary school at 6:00 p.m.?

And what do I do if he follows me home?

I don't give him a chance. Once the last kid is off the bus, I run into the school. I'm looking for someone who'll come with me, so I don't have to walk out alone.

I'm in luck. Mr. O'Brien, the gym teacher, is still there. He's over six feet tall, and a weight lifter. If anyone can protect me, he's the one.

But when we get outside, the man is gone.

Mr. O'Brien smiles and walks back inside. I jump in my car and lock the doors. Have I ever made it home in less time? I don't think so. Just to be sure I haven't been followed, I drive around the block a few times before pulling into my garage.

Who was he? I have no idea.

But something tells me he knows who I am.

CHAPTER 25

SAFETY VALVE. SAFETY NET. Safety first.

Every time Archie Monahan hears the word safety, *he has to smile. A "safety" was what they called a condom back in the 1940s, when his father first opened Monahan Drugs.*

Archie remembers all the young men who came in, asking to speak to his father. How they looked around nervously as his dad opened a drawer in the back. Then paid and left quickly, hoping they wouldn't bump into anyone they knew. How shocked his dad would be, Archie thinks, if he could see how things have changed. An entire shelf of condoms with names like Skyn, Rough Rider, and Pleasure Plus. Textured, ribbed, and studded. Some even glow in the dark.

And right next to them: Lubricants. Ovulation kits. Home sperm tests. Contraceptives. Vibrators.

Archie hears the front bell ring. That means a customer. He's prepared to give his usual welcome . . . when he sees who it is. He frowns.

"Hello again, Archie," says the man.

"Hello, Vince," Archie says.

The man extends his hand to shake. Archie ignores it.

"I was wondering if you've had a chance to think about the offer I made the last time we talked," Vince says. Archie makes a face.

"I thought about it. The answer is still no."

"Hmmm. Perhaps I didn't explain it well," says Vince. "What I'm promising is…"

"I know what you're promising," Archie says. "And I don't want any part of it."

Vince shrugs and wanders around the store. Archie stands and watches him. Vince picks up a tube of toothpaste and a bottle of avocado-scented shampoo. Then he circles back to the pharmacy counter to pay.

"You see, the thing is… I would understand your reluctance, under ordinary circumstances," Vince says to him. "Except, as of last month, your circumstances are anything but ordinary. Am I right?"

Stunned, Archie looks at him for a moment. Then he turns away.

"Sorry to hear about your boy," Vince says solemnly. "Damn shame, after all those commendation medals. A real hero he was, too. Where'd it happen? Afghanistan?"

"Iraq," Archie says. He practically spits out the word.

"Your son, God rest his soul, isn't around anymore to take over the store. And those two lovely grandchildren of yours — Luke and Justy? They're gonna need you, Archie. Now more than ever."

Archie says nothing. He just stands and stares. His eyes and his mind are somewhere far away.

"Stella can't handle them alone. Certainly not financially. And let's face it—business isn't what it used to be. Those big chain stores are killin' guys like you."

Archie has heard all this before. Slowly, he walks over to the phone.

"Forgive me, but you're not a young man anymore, Archie," Vince adds. "What's going to happen to all of them when you're gone?"

"I want you out of here," Archie says quietly. "I'm gonna count to three. If you're not out, I'm calling the police."

"And tell them what?" Vince laughs. "That a man came in and offered you a deal that'll put you on Easy Street? So you and Millie can travel, buy things for the grandkids, save for their college? Go ahead, Archie. Call them. And put the phone on speaker, so I can hear them laugh!"

Vince takes a step toward him. Is he going to hit me? Archie wonders. No, he thinks. People like Vince don't do that. They kill you with words, not fists.

Vince leans in closer, so they're almost eye to eye. "Let me ask you something," Vince says. "What would your dad have done, with an offer like this?"

"Don't you dare bring my father into this!" Archie is yelling now. "I'll have you know, my father was the most decent...honorable..."

"Easy, old man." Vince backs off a little. "All I meant was: Did he ever take a vacation? Buy a car that wasn't second-hand?"

"You know what my dad would do? He would toss you out on your ass!"

Vince shakes his head in disbelief.

"You're throwing away a golden opportunity," he says. He takes a few dollars out of his wallet and pays for the toothpaste and the shampoo. "Nobody has to know about it. It'll be our little secret. You'd be the silent partner here. I'm the one taking all the risks."

"Get out!" Archie says. He points to the door. His voice cracks.

Vince shakes his head in disbelief. He shrugs.

"I thought we could do this the easy way," Vince says. He heads to the door. "But if you're determined to make it hard for me..."

He leaves before he finishes the sentence.

CHAPTER 26

BY TUESDAY NIGHT, WE'RE already arguing about it.

"Nobody your age needs his own car," I say. "They won't even let you have one at school till you're a senior. So what's the big rush?"

"What will I drive when I go out with my friends?" he asks. "Not your crappy Volvo."

I resist the urge to tell him that he and his siblings are the ones who made it crappy. Sticky car seats. Potato chip crumbs. Muddy shoes.

"And Dad won't let me drive his new BMW," he says.

I am in the middle of sweeping. I stop. I put the broom down. I lean against a wall.

His new *what*?

"Uh, what makes you think Dad is getting a new BMW?" I ask.

"He told me," Joey says. "I asked if I could drive his car, and he said no, he's trading it in."

This can't be right. Ned is getting a new car? We just paid for an emissions checkup on the old one.

"So if I can't drive *your* cars," Joey says, smearing peanut butter on three slices of bread for his pre-dinner snack, "I guess I'll just have to use Vince's."

He sees the shock on my face. He misreads it as confusion.

"You know. *Vince.* The guy next door? He said when I got a license, I could use his car anytime I want."

"Uh, I don't think that's a good idea," I say. He stares at me, waiting for a reason. I say the first thing that comes into my mind. "I doubt his insurance would cover a second driver."

But Joey is already shaking his head.

"Chill, Mom. It does. I've been driving his car for a couple of weeks now," he says. "Helping him make deliveries."

(Note to self: that fluttering sound you hear is your whole life, spinning out of control...)

"I thought...you were helping him...with his computer," I say. It's getting hard to put together a cohesive sentence.

"Yeah. That took, like, an hour. But then he hired me to help with his business."

I'm still leaning against the kitchen wall, trying to process all this. Ned told me nothing about his new car. Vince told me nothing about Joey. And Joey—who usually tells me nothing, *ever*—spilled the beans about both of them.

I look at the clock. It's almost seven. Where the hell is Ned, when I desperately need to talk to him? How many asshole client meetings can one mid-level executive have?

When he walks in, he's in an unusually chipper mood.

"Hi," he says, all smiles. "Smells good. How was your day?"

I know I should wait. I know he likes to check the mail and pour himself a drink before he listens to my daily Family News Wrap-Up. But the anger is bubbling up inside me. I can't control myself. If I don't say something now, I'm going to explode.

"When do you get to pick up your new car?"

He freezes mid-pour. "How do you know about that?"

"Joey told me."

"I was going to surprise you," he says. He takes a sip of the bourbon. Then another.

"You were going to surprise *me*...with a new car for *you*?"

The irony of this seems to escape him.

"Wait'll you see it!" he says. He's like a kid in a candy store. "It's the five-twenty-eight-i sedan. Black sapphire. Mocha leather seats..."

I haven't seen him this happy in a long time. He goes on and on about enhanced Bluetooth, key memory, even a moon roof. And all I can think of is the years I've wasted clipping coupons.

"It's a beauty," he says. He is all smiles.

"And what does this little beauty cost?" I ask.

"Zero percent down," he says. Even *he* knows that this is not an answer.

"Ned—is this something we can afford?"

"I told you—I've got a new client. His portfolio is huge."

"Are you talking about...Vince?"

That's when it turns ugly.

"What do you care where the money comes from?" he yells. "Goddamnit, Laura. I make it all! I should be allowed to spend it the way I want!"

Bourbon in hand, he goes upstairs and slams the bedroom door.

Years ago, as a joke (sort of), I started making a list of all the things we fight about. Careless things (being out of stamps). Annoying things (his habit of leaving used dental floss on the bathroom sink). His mother. My brother. His drinking. My eating. On and on and on.

I thought we'd pretty much covered the gamut of things to argue about. But tonight, eighteen years into our marriage, there's a new one: a fifty-thousand-dollar car that I knew nothing about.

I am trying to sort this all out when the phone rings. It's Darcy. "Boy, I'm glad you called," I say. "I need to talk to you."

"Me first," she says. And then she shares a startling piece of news.

Coach Mike, our friend, our mainstay, our hero...has just been arrested for dealing drugs.

CHAPTER 27

THE NEXT MORNING, I text Vince.

Very upset. Must talk. Call when you can.

Seven minutes later, he rings my bell. He's holding flowers.

"You haven't been answering my texts again," he says. There is the beginning of a frown. "But see how quickly I answered yours?" Back to a smile. "May I come in?"

I take a quick look up and down the street to see if any of my neighbors are watching. There's no one around. Just me and the man I'm crazy about, standing on my doorstep.

And I'm crazy enough to let him in.

He hands me the bouquet. "Where did you get these?" I ask.

"Darcy's garden. I didn't think she'd mind."

He sits down on the couch. Do I sit there, too? He sees me hesitate. He pats the spot next to him and smiles.

I decide to sit on a chair. He shrugs. "Suit yourself," he says. "What's going on?"

I cut to the chase. "Exactly *when* did you go to see Ned?"

This startles him. "Why do you ask?"

"Was it this past Wednesday?"

He looks confused.

"Wednesday I was with *you*." He gives me his sweetest heart-melting smile. "Don't tell me you've forgotten *already*..."

But I'm in no mood for charm.

"Why didn't you tell me you were going to see him? And what's with you and Joey? Why are you driving my kid around, sneaking behind my back?"

"Whoa," he says, holding his hands up in front of him. "One thing at a time. About Joey: he wants to buy his own car. And I know you're not crazy about that idea. So yeah, he's working for me. But we decided not to mention anything about it for a while."

That makes sense. But I still don't like it.

"The Ned thing? Look: I know it hasn't been great between you two lately."

"You heard us arguing last night?"

"Honey—the truth? I hear you arguing a lot," he says. "I thought I could maybe do something to help. And I didn't tell you because...I wanted to surprise you."

Why the hell does everyone want to surprise me?

"Besides," he says, "I thought it was Ned's place to say something, not mine."

Good answer. Smooth answer. The guy should run for office. He's totally unflappable.

"I just thought, if I threw a little money his way, things might get easier for the two of you."

Okay. Now I'm angry. I get up quickly, holding the flowers.

"Laura—wait..."

"I need to put these in water," I say. I hurry to the kitchen to get a vase. Is that what this is all about? I'm some sort of...charity case?

"Get back here!" he calls out to me. And when I don't, he comes into the kitchen. I reach up to a shelf for a vase. He grabs my shoulders and turns me around to face him.

"Listen," he says.

"No. *You* listen!" I say. "You hijacked my family! I don't understand what's going on. Joey is even more distant. Ned has begun lying to me, for the first time ever. I can't deal with any of this." I start to pull away. "I want..." I hesitate.

"What?" he asks. "Tell me. Anything."

"I want my life to go back to the way it was! Before I met you!"

Suddenly I see fear in his eyes.

"You don't mean that," he says. "Please, don't say that. Don't do this to me."

And then he does something he's never done before. He pulls me toward him and kisses me on the lips. Slowly.

I whimper quietly. Or is that him? I'm not sure. I open my eyes. His eyes are still closed.

"Laura," he says, gently. "I've waited forever to do that." Great. Now, on the list of Vince's Positive Attributes, I can add one more: *Mind Reader*.

He takes my hand and leads me back to the living room. My heart is beating so fast, I'm having trouble breathing. I'm scared, because I don't know if I can trust him.

No. That's just part of it.

I'm scared because I've never been kissed like that by anybody, ever.

Not. In. My. Whole. Life.

A million thoughts are colliding in my brain, each more thrilling and terrifying than the next. And all of them are variations on the same theme: *Now what? Alone in My House, with Nowhere to Be Till Two Thirty,* I think. It sounds like the title of a country song.

And as he pulls me down to the couch, I think of another one: *I Want Him Out of My Life, But I Can't Stop Kissing Him.*

His fingers cup my face, stroke my neck. Then he gets more adventurous. His hand wanders down and fondles my breasts, and I let him. I think I am going to die of desire. We sit there for a while, making out (do they still use that expression?) like teenagers.

"Please don't go away," he whispers. He's practically pleading. "You're the best thing that ever happened to me."

"You should get out more," I say, trying to make him laugh. It doesn't work.

"Since I met you, I've felt more alive than I have in years," he says. "But if I'm hurting your marriage or causing you pain . . ."

"No," I say. Who am I kidding? He's the kindest, gentlest, loneliest man I ever met. I could never give him up. Not now.

His hand moves to my thigh, but I swat it away. Yes, I'm firing on all cylinders. And if my heart and my hormones had their way, I would give myself to him in an instant. Except—I can't. Not yet. Not until—

Until what? I don't know. Something is stopping me.

There are so many things I want to ask him—Why did his wife leave? Why, with all his money, is he renting such an old run-down place?—but I don't. I tell myself it's because I don't want to ruin the moment.

But maybe it's just that I don't want to know the truth.

CHAPTER 28

ANOTHER MONDAY. ALMOST HALLOWEEN, and today's to-do list reads like a scavenger hunt. A black cape, a blindfold, and a pair of nunchucks for Ben, who wants to go as a ninja. White face paint for Joey, who'll dress up as a ghoul. A silver headpiece, blue cape, and red tube dress and wristbands for Caroline. (She wanted to go as a cheerleader. I argued for Madame Curie. We finally compromised on Wonder Woman.)

As I'm pulling out of my garage, Darcy comes running over, waving her hands.

"Wait up!" she yells. "Great news!" I roll down my window. She's all smiles.

"They dropped the case!" she says. "I just spoke to Jake. That malpractice suit? Done, done, and done!"

"That's wonderful," I say. "What happened?"

She shrugs. "Nobody seems to know. Jake's lawyer got a call from the other lawyer. The guy just changed his mind."

"Just like *that*? I wonder why?"

"Who cares! Where you headed?" she asks.

"To the party store to buy Halloween costumes. Want to come?"

"Thanks, but no. I've got a celebratory dinner to plan."

"Well, congratulations," I say. This really is good news for them. The trial had been hanging over both their heads.

The party store is jammed, of course. A veritable wonderland of glitter, polyester, and hideous rubber masks. I am debating between two pairs of nunchucks (would Ben want plastic or polystyrene foam?) when my cell phone rings. A man identifies himself as Karl Wallace, an assistant pharmacist at Walgreens.

"I'm calling to let you know we've taken over all the prescriptions from Monahan's Drugs, now that it closed."

Monahan's is closed?

Monahan's has been a fixture in the community since . . . well, since forever. It still has the same dark wood paneling, the same old-fashioned wooden ladder that slides across the floor on little wheels. Even the same soda fountain and green leather stools since it first opened. When the kids were little, we used to take them to Monahan's every Sunday for ice cream cones. And now it's closed. The end of an era.

"Is Mr. Monahan retiring?" I ask.

"I don't know what his plans are," the new druggist says. "But we have all your family's prescriptions on file here, when you need them."

"Thanks for calling," I say.

Monahan's is located right on the main street in town. It's what's realtors would call Prime Retail Property. Once I finish at Party House, I decide to drive by and see if there's any indication of what the store is going to become. I hope it's not another bank. We could use a good restaurant in this town. A hip shoe store. Maybe even a Trader Joe's.

As I drive past Monahan's in search of a parking space, I see a sign on the door.

TO ALL MY VALUED CUSTOMERS it says, in big black letters. I am surprised to see that Archie has decorated the shop for Halloween. There's a huge spider web in the window, the entire height of the store. How odd that he would bother doing that if he was planning to close.

But as I get out of the car and get closer, I see it's not a decoration at all. The entire front window is completely cracked—shattered in the shape of a spider web, radiating out from the middle.

My eyes wander down. A chill goes through me.

Right in the very center is what looks like a bullet hole.

CHAPTER 29

REINHART, WILSON, AND SLADE *has its offices in one of those angular steel and glass buildings that looks like it might topple over at any moment.*

But inside, the financial services firm is as sturdy as a rock.

The company has two thousand employees worldwide and manages twenty-seven billion dollars in private money. Its offices are sleek, elegant... and very, very quiet. The thick beige wall-to-wall carpeting makes every noise as silent as a hand-shake.

Alice, the seventh-floor receptionist, makes it a point to re-member every name and every face she comes in contact with.

But today, there's a new one.

"Welcome to RWS. How may I help you?" she asks.

"My name is Parker Paulsen," the man says. "I'm here to see Ned Sherman."

"Do you have an appointment?" Alice asks.

"No," he says. "But I don't want to impose on your good graces. If you could just point me in the direction of his office..."

"I'm afraid I can't do that, sir," she says. "We have strict rules about unescorted visitors."

"See, the thing is, I'm an old fraternity buddy. Ned and I haven't seen each other in, gosh, must be twenty years. I'm just in town for the day and wanted to surprise him."

Alice frowns. Cold-calling is against company policy. But this man looks—well, like a potential client. Nicely dressed. Oxford button-down shirt. Brooks Brothers tie and jacket. She's waffling.

"Take a look at this," he says. He pulls out an old photo of himself in his college days. The photo is dog-eared and worn. "That's me on the left—and there's Neddy," he says. He points to another young man in the picture.

Is that Ned, with hair down to his shoulders? He's wearing a baseball cap that says "Chicago Cubs." And she knows Ned went to Northwestern.

"Well…all right. Whom shall I tell him is calling?"

"Just say it's an old fraternity brother from Phi Ep."

She rings Ned, who picks up on the second ring.

"Mr. Sherman—one of your old fraternity buddies is here. He says he wants to surprise you."

Ned is intrigued. He knows a lot of his frat brothers have done very well over the years—better than he's done. Could it be Corky Ballentine? Nico Ross? Or that Parker guy—what was his last name again? All Ned remembers about him is that he was independently wealthy.

"I'll be right out," he says. You just never know where a new client might come from these days.

As Ned gets to reception, he sees the man has his back to the door.

As he gets closer, the man turns and comes rushing at him. He swallows Ned up in a bear hug.

"Ned Sherman!" he says. "You old son of a gun. Why, you haven't aged a day!"

Ned freezes. He turns pale. The man sees the shock registering on Ned's face. He looks at Alice.

"You see? I told you he'd be surprised! Well, c'mon man," he says to Ned. "Let's not just stand here. Take me to your office. We've got a lot of catching up to do!"

Ned looks around. The security guard is nowhere in sight. But even if he was…

They walk down the hall to Ned's office. Ned is sweating. What is Vince doing here? What does he want? Up till now he's been able to keep his dealings with Vince separate from his professional life. But now…

Ned walks into his office. Vince follows and shuts the door behind them.

"Listen," Ned says in a loud whisper. "You can't just waltz in here like this."

"Oh, no?" Vince asks. "I already did!"

He lunges at Ned and grabs him by the throat, spinning him around till he has him in a powerful choke hold. Ned begins gasping for air. He can't breathe. And he can't scream—but even if he could, should he? That would bring people in, asking questions. And that's the last thing he needs.

"I got your message," Vince tells him, tightening his grip on Ned's neck. "But I gotta tell you: It's too late. Nobody walks away from me. You got that?"

Ned tries to answer him. He can't. His head is wedged tight between Vince's arm and his body.

"You're in too deep, my friend. And there's no going back. Understand?"

Ned starts to nod yes... but Vince is closing off his windpipe. Ned feels himself start to faint.

Then just as quickly, Vince lets go. Ned begins to sputter. Is he going to throw up? God, he hopes not. He knows his face is red.

Vince takes out a pocket comb and begins combing Ned's hair back in place.

"So don't go getting any fancy ideas. Y'hear? I need to know I can count on you. You're like my right ball. And Ned..."

"What?"

"Whatever crap you're using on your hair," Vince says, looking at his comb in disgust, "get rid of it. It's way too greasy."

CHAPTER 30

I AM TRYING TO make sense of all the changes in my little suburban world. But the more I try to sort it out, the harder it gets.

A beloved coach, arrested. A bullet hole in Monahan's window. Ned's secret slush fund. A bunch of random things, happening all at once, totally unconnected.

Or are they?

So I start doing what I usually do when I need to keep my body as busy as my mind: I clean. With a vengeance.

Armed with a spray can of Pledge, Windex, a few dust rags, and a half gallon of Mr. Clean, I slowly make my way around the house. As all the how-to-clean manuals advise, I start at the top (mirrors, picture frames) and work my way down (tabletops, kitchen counter) till I get to the bottom (rugs, floors).

Next, the kids' rooms upstairs. Now I really have my work cut out for me. All three of them are slobs. I tackle Joey's room first. It's a jungle of clothes, electronic gear, sports equipment, and leftover food, surrounded by posters of various rock groups—all of whom look like serial killers. I strip the bed and use lemon-scented polish on his dresser. At least part of the room will smell good.

On a whim, I start to organize his closet. Starting at the top, I pull down a shelf's worth of T-shirts and fold them, then straighten out the clothes on hangers. The bottom of his closet is filled with sneakers, tossed in a heap. Like a good mother, I pull them out to sort them into pairs. That's when I see the bag tucked way in the back.

Like a not-so-good mother, I open it and look inside.

The bag is filled with pills. There must be thirty bottles in all. All of them have labels hand-written in pencil. Some names I recognize: Percocet. Oxycodone. Some are just initials: R2. G. C. Big O.

My first thought: *These are all candy pills.* The kind that used to come in Fisher-Price medical kits, when the kids were young.

My second thought: *Who am I kidding?* These pills are real, all right.

But what are they doing in Joey's closet?

There's got to be a logical explanation. Joey's a good kid. Maybe he doesn't even know they're there. It's possible, right?

Oh, please, God, tell me it's possible . . .

I collapse on his desk chair, pushing aside all the clothes on it . . . and all thoughts of what this could mean.

Suddenly, Joey walks in the room. He sees me holding the bag.

"Where did you get these?" I ask.

"What are you doing in my room?"

"These are dangerous drugs, Joey. Who gave them to you?"

"Who gave you permission to go through my things?"

"Did Coach Mike give you these?"

He snickers. He throws his backpack on the bed, turns to me, throws his head back, and starts to laugh.

"Don't be ridiculous," he says. "*I gave them to him.*"

I am suddenly terrified of the tall, lanky teenager standing in front of me. My firstborn. My baby. When he was an infant I tied a red ribbon to his stroller—an old superstition to ward off evil spirits. I guess it worked for seventeen years.

But now...

There's so much I want to say. So much I need to ask. But all I can manage to blurt out is the dumb threat I used when they were little. "Just wait till your father gets home!"

And then I hear it again. That mean, awful, evil laugh.

"Yeah. *Ask Dad*," Joey says. "He'll tell you aaall about it."

Does Ned know about this? Is he somehow involved? Oh God. The money for the new car! Suddenly, it all begins to make sense.

I've got to call Ned. Now. No. I can't. I have to wait till he gets home so we can deal with this in person.

But I've got to talk to someone...

Of course. *Vince*. He'll know what to do. How to make sense of all of this.

I text him. He doesn't answer. I text him again a few minutes later. Still no response. So I dial his number. He doesn't pick up.

I'm about to leave a message when I get a better idea: Go to him. Sit on his doorstep until he gets home.

This time, I don't care how many neighbors might be watching.

CHAPTER 31

I RUN TO VINCE'S house and ring the bell. Nobody answers. Maybe he's in the back, I think. Or in his garden. Not gardening, of course. Pulling up weeds? Well, it's possible.

I go to the back. He's not there, either. And I can't tell if his car is in his garage.

I peer in his windows to see if I can spot him. No luck. I even yell his name. Nothing.

I'm desperate. I've got to talk to someone. So I cut across Vince's backyard to Darcy's.

Just as I am about to ring her bell, I see a caravan of police cars heading my way.

Oh God—they're coming to arrest Joey!

But as I run back home, I see the cars have stopped in front of Darcy's house. *Good*, I think. *They got the address wrong.* This will buy Joey and me a little time to figure out what to do next.

And what *should* we do?

Do I help him escape? Does he turn himself in?

Inside the house, I call Joey's name. No answer. Did he see the caravan? Is he gone already? I go to my living room window and look out. A dozen policemen are standing on Darcy's front lawn, as well as two men in business suits. One of them holds a bullhorn and talks into it. I can't hear what he's saying, but I see Darcy's door open. Several cops rush in. A few minutes later, they come out again. But they're not alone.

They've got Darcy's husband, Jake, in handcuffs!

As they push him into one of the squad cars, Darcy runs out of her house, yelling. She jumps into her car to follow them. Then one by one, all the cars drive away.

All except one.

The door to that car opens, and a man gets out. I feel myself break out in a cold sweat. I know that walk, that suit. It's my Man in Black. The Statue of Liberty stalker.

Who is he? What is he doing here? He's not a cop. Is he a plainclothesman? A reporter?

As I hide behind the curtain, I watch him. He pulls a small piece of paper out of his pocket and checks something on it. He looks around slowly.

Then he walks to my front door and rings the bell.

CHAPTER 32

I DON'T ANSWER. I won't answer. I can't answer.

Not until I figure out what he wants. And what I need to say.

So I stand behind my curtain and watch the Man in Black ring my bell. He rings several times and waits. Did he see me duck into my house? I'm not sure. Whoever he is, he's the soul of patience. He stands there for quite a while. Finally, he turns and gets back into his car and drives off.

It's almost six o'clock. Still no Vince. No Ned. No Joey. I go into the kitchen. On an ordinary day I would be getting dinner ready right about now.

But today has been anything but ordinary.

As I pass the refrigerator door, I see something scrawled on the calendar. I get closer. It says *PTA Meeting 6:30*. I have to smile. Months ago, when life was normal, I signed up to chair the annual Kiddie Carnival at the kids' school. And tonight is the kickoff meeting. Great. A couple of hours to argue the merits of face painting versus dunk tanks.

And try not to think about your whole family in jail.

I pull into the school parking lot. But just as I am about to walk up the steps to school, I hear a voice say, "Mrs. Sherman?"

I turn. It's the Man in Black.

CHAPTER 33

THIS TIME THERE'S NO escaping him.

"Yes?" I say. I'm too frightened to be afraid.

"I'm Special Agent John Witten. With the FBI," he says. He pauses a minute to let that sink in.

"We're trying to nail a drug dealer who's been working the area. His name is..."

I hold my breath. Oh, please, God, don't let him say Joey Sherman. Or Ned Sherman.

"...Nick Milligan."

I laugh. Did he see how terrified I was? Did he read anything in my eyes?

"Sorry," I say. "Can't help you. I don't know anybody by that name."

I knew this whole thing was a mistake. My husband, my son, involved in something sinister? *What was I thinking?* The feds are going after somebody named Nick Milligan. A total stranger.

"He goes by other names as well," Witten is saying now.

He takes a small pad out of his pocket and begins to read. "Burt Polley. Dennis Barton. Lou Corley."

I shake my head to all of them.

"Here's a picture of him," he says. He pulls out a mug shot of a nice-looking man in his forties. Front view. Profile. No. Can't be. This is clearly a picture of . . .

"Vincent Selko," he says.

And the earth opens up. I am sucked to the bottom. I know I am standing in the school parking lot, except I have fallen down into the very reaches of hell.

"Charming guy, from everything we hear," he says. "Able to con a lot of people into doing his dirty work. Down at headquarters, we call him the Suburban Manson."

He puts the picture away carefully in his wallet.

He keeps talking. I know, because I see his lips moving. But I'm only catching bits and pieces of what he says.

"Your family . . . tailor-made . . . husband in finance . . . teenage son who drives . . . and *you* . . ."

He doesn't have to say it: a lost, lonely housewife looking for love in all the wrong places.

Vince using Ned, using Jake, using Joey—maybe I can believe that.

But using *me*, after all the things he's said and done?

No. There's *no way* he could have made all that up.

"Why are you telling me all this?" I ask.

"Because . . . we need your help."

"No!" I say. I shake my head violently.

Witten pauses a moment. "Mrs. Sherman," he says,

very quietly, "we have your son on tape. Making deliveries, with Vince in the car." I can tell by the way he stares at me that he's telling the truth.

"And your husband has been laundering money for him. Several million dollars in overseas investments."

"What do you...want me to do?" I ask.

"We want you to wear a wire."

"I can't do that!" I say. He thinks it's because I'm frightened, or in denial. But that's only part of it.

If I'm wearing a wire, Vince will feel it when he hugs me.

"Well, here's the thing," Witten says carefully. "If you work with us—that'll go a long way toward helping your son and your husband. They're looking at jail time. *Serious* jail time. But if you agree to help us reel this guy in..."

"What you're asking me to...this is just too...I can't...I need to talk to...think about..." I say. It's more of a sputter than a sentence.

"Of course," Witten says.

This is all too much for me. I want to sit down but there is no place to sit. Instead, I lean against a car and put my head in my hands.

I start to sob.

"I know this is hard to hear," Witten says. His tone is so gentle, I expect him to put his arm around me. But he doesn't. "You need to know: The guy is dangerous. He's destroyed a lot of people who got in his way."

Destroyed? Does he mean blackmailed? Killed? Or just broke their hearts.

"And . . . he may know we're on to him."

"What do I do?" I ask.

"You'll hear from us. Meanwhile? Just stay away from him," he says as he heads back to his car.

Then he adds, as if he knew the truth: "*If you can.*"

CHAPTER 34

THE KIDDIE CARNIVAL MEETING. The other mothers look up as I enter. They stare. I must look even worse than I feel. I stumble through some lame excuses. A sudden emergency...a sick kid at home...my mother is ill. I'm babbling. Do they believe me? Who cares.

Then I run out. I dial Ned's office. I get his answering machine and leave a message: *Come home! Urgent!* I leave the same message on his cell as an email and as a text. Where the hell is he?

I call his secretary's cell, since it's after hours. She gives me a number where Ned can be reached. It seems familiar. But my brain is racing too fast to stop and sort it out. I dial it. And I hear a voice message: "You've reached the office of Dr. Maggie Treleven..."

Say, *what*?

Ned is in a session with Maggie? Ned, who hates therapy and was only going because I insisted?

Or—wait. Maybe it's a whole other scenario. Is he seeing her behind my back? Are they having an affair?

No. Impossible! But even if it's true—no time to deal with it now.

Somehow, I am able to drive back home. I send Ned more texts, more emails, more messages. Still no response.

All I can do now is wait. And wait. The clock is ticking.

Then suddenly, I hear a car in the driveway. Thank God! Ned is home!

But as I run to the window, I see it's not Ned at all.

It's Vince.

CHAPTER 35

TODAY, I'M FRIGHTENED. Does he know what's happened?

Just to be on the safe side, I grab my cell phone and press Video to start recording. I put the phone in the living room, on the table next to the lamp.

Vince rings the bell.

"Hi," he says. He smiles. "Okay if I come in?"

"Sure," I say. I try not to seem jittery. If he senses I am, he'll know something's up.

"Are you alone?" he asks. I nod yes. Then he leans in and hugs me. We stand that way for quite a while.

"I've missed you," he says. "Is everything okay?"

No.

I want to say: The FBI thinks you're a drug dealer. I think Joey is peddling drugs for you—unless he's not. My husband is somehow involved or having an affair with our therapist. Maybe both. Maybe neither. And the cops want me to wear a wire so they can reel you in.

But I say nothing.

"Something wrong?" he asks.

I try not to look at him. I don't want to get lost in those blue eyes.

"Tell me the truth," I say. "Did you do it?"

He looks—what? Confused? Frightened? In my state of mind, I can't quite tell.

"Do what?"

"All those things...they said you did."

Now he looks concerned. "Who have you been talking to?" he asks.

"The FBI."

"Whoa." He takes a step backward. "The FBI was here?"

"They arrested Jake," I say.

Now things are really beginning to spin out of control.

"Do you know anything about...any of this?" I ask. "The pills? The ones Joey has in his room? Are you involved...Is Ned...?"

I can't even get the words out. I'm sweating like crazy. How could I ever wear a wire? I'd electrocute myself.

But he seems relaxed. "C'mere," he says. He pulls me toward him and onto the couch. There's a part of me that really wants us to just dissolve into kisses.

But all the other parts are afraid.

As I pull away, I accidentally knock into the side table. My phone drops to the floor. Like the gentleman he's always been, Vince picks it up. He looks at it. He sees it's been recording. He frowns. Now what?

He slams the phone down on the coffee table, shattering the screen.

Then he slaps me across the face.

I cry out with shock and pain.

"You bitch," he says. "Were you trying to trick me?"

"Vince! No!"

He jumps up and grabs my arm. He's holding it too tight.

"That hurts!" I say. But he's dragging me to the front door. "Wait! Where are we going?"

He doesn't answer.

I try to pull away. But he's way stronger than I am. I scream.

"Shut up," he says.

He slaps me again.

On the way out the door, I stumble. I trip on the pavement, scraping my knees. They start to bleed.

But Vince is in a hurry. He picks me up by my hair and drags me toward his car. I'm trying to kick him and pull away, but he grabs my other arm and twists it behind me. He opens his car door and starts to push me inside.

Suddenly there's a loud horn.

It startles him. He lets go of me and I run in the direction of the horn. It's Ned! He's seen what is happening and drives up over our lawn. Frazzled, out of breath, I open the door and jump in.

"Drive!" I say to Ned.

Because there's no time to say anything else.

CHAPTER 36

NED PULLS OUT AS fast as he can...but Vince is faster. He gets in his car and zooms toward us. I feel a jolt and hear a sickening crunch. Vince has slammed his car into our rear bumper!

Even worse, he's backing up slowly. He's going to do it again!

"Drive, drive!" I scream, as if our lives depended on it.

Because right now, they do.

Vince isn't just trying to slow us down or even stop us.

Somehow, he's turned into a madman. And he's trying to *kill us*.

There's so much to ask Ned. So much to tell him. But for now we just need to get as far away from Vince as possible.

Ned floors the pedal. Our car screeches down our quiet suburban street.

My heart is racing. I look back. Vince's front bumper is smashed in. Smoke is seeping from under his hood.

But Vince quickly straightens out and accelerates directly toward us.

"Go faster, Ned!" I say. "He's still coming!"

"Laura, this is crazy. We have to call 911!"

He's right. But I realize with horror that my iPhone is still on my coffee table, where Vince smashed it. "I don't have my cell!"

"Take mine," Ned says, reaching for his front right pocket.

"No, *I'll* get it. You focus on the road. Just get us out of here!"

I grip the car door to steady myself as we make a squealing left turn at the end of the block. We're soon flying down another tree-lined street, passing station wagons parked in driveways, bikes strewn across lawns, children playing in front yards.

Vince is still on our tail—and getting closer.

I manage to pull Ned's phone from his jacket pocket and fumble to call the police...but I can't. There are no bars. No service.

"Look out!" I scream as a silver minivan starts backing out of a driveway right in front of us. I reach over and smack the horn as Ned swerves. We just miss it.

But so does Vince. Who's still coming for us.

"Let's head to a busy street," I say. "With lots of cars, people. *Somebody* will see us. *They'll* call the cops."

"I'll turn on Ridge Road," Ned says.

"No!" I say. "Take a left here! It'll be faster!"

"Here? That's a sidewalk—and a park, with a fence! And—"

"*Trust me!* Do it now!"

Ned cuts the wheel sharply and our car leaps up onto the curb. We both bang our heads on the roof as it lands.

"Go, go!" I scream.

Ned listens. We pick up speed...

And then we crash directly through a rickety chain-link fence!

Thankfully, the lawn is empty because the sprinklers are on. Our tires slip and slide like crazy when they hit the wet grass. The sprinklers pelt us with water like the inside of a car wash. I reach over and turn on the windshield wipers.

"Park Street is just on the other side," I say. "Once we get there—"

Suddenly two loud pops ring out behind us. They sound like fireworks, like on the Fourth of July. I'm confused, but only for a few seconds.

Because I hear a third pop—and our rear windshield shatters.

"Oh, my God!" I scream. "He's shooting at us!"

CHAPTER 37

I DUCK LOW IN my seat...*Bang!* Another shot. This one ricochets off our trunk.

I look in my side view mirror: OBJECTS IN MIRROR ARE CLOSER THAN THEY APPEAR. Vince's arm is sticking out the window, aiming a gun right at us.

Oh God. How close *is* he?

Ned zigzags back and forth, trying to dodge the bullets. We're like human targets in one of Ben's video games. I scream as Vince shoots twice more. Both shots miss us. Then we reach the end of the park.

There's another chain-link fence ahead of us. "Hang on!" Ned yells.

We crash through it and take a sharp right onto busy Park Street. Cars honk and veer out of our way.

Bang! Another shot hits us—this one on the side somewhere. Ned swerves across both lanes to avoid the next one—and into oncoming traffic!

This is crazy. I've been stopped on this street for a dangling license plate. *Where are the traffic cops now, when we need them?*

We smash into someone's mailbox. It goes flying, sending letters fluttering through the air like snow.

"Just keep going!" I plead. "We have to lose him, we have to—"

And then suddenly, I hear it.

"Aaagghhhh...!"

An animal cry. A sound filled with pain and fear. Half wail, half scream.

An inhuman sound.

Except...it's coming from Ned!

There's a giant red spot on his right shoulder, getting bigger and bigger. It looks like a large red corsage. But it's far worse.

He's been hit!

"Ned—are you okay?! Ned! Answer me!

CHAPTER 38

I CAN TELL HE'S in incredible pain. He's moaning in agony, maybe going into shock. Every instinct tells me to stop the car and help my husband before he bleeds to death.

But I know if I do, we'll *both* die.

"It'll be okay, Ned! It's going to be okay!"

I lean over and grip the wheel so we don't crash.

Vince's car pulls up next to us on the driver's side.

He rolls down his right window. And aims his gun at us.

Drenched in my husband's blood, my heart racing, I get one final crazy idea. I pray to God it works. I let Vince's car get a little closer...

Then I jerk the steering wheel to the left as hard as I can.

We crash into each other and we both go spinning like tops.

I hear metal crunching. Tires squealing. Glass shattering.

Ned and I are tossed around until finally our car comes

to a stop. I feel dizzy and dazed. My whole body aches, head to toe. But I'm alive.

Is Ned?

I reach over and take my husband's bloody hand. I give it a squeeze.

A few seconds go by. The longest in my life.

Then, weakly, Ned squeezes back.

Thank God!

I hear police sirens in the distance. I look out through my shattered window. Vince's car has rolled onto its side.

And Vince himself is slumped in the driver's seat. Not moving.

Am I in shock? I must be. Because I am about to do something crazy.

I push open my mashed car door and stagger out. Slowly, I start walking toward Vince.

Because there is something I need to ask him.

CHAPTER 39

A HALF HOUR LATER.

Ned is on a gurney. He is connected to tubes, with a mask over his face. Heavy bandages are wrapped around his shoulder. He is still bleeding, slipping in and out of consciousness...but alive.

I am on a gurney as well, lying quietly, a little woozy. They have given me a shot of something to stop the pain in my arm. My injuries are not life-threatening, they say.

So for the moment, all the available EMTs are surrounding Vince's Honda. It barely resembles a car at this point. They have been using a crowbar and a blowtorch to crack it open and get him out. I hear voices, noises, the whir of machines.

Vince is hanging upside down in his seat, still unconscious. The way he was when I first wandered over. He hasn't moved since his car rolled over onto its side.

Finally, the last piece of his car door crashes to the ground. They lift him out and put him on a third gurney.

There is blood in his hair, on his face. Blood is seeping from his ear. But then I see his lips move.

That means he's alive. Am I glad? Am I sorry?

No need to think about that now. I will have a long time—the rest of my life—to decide.

As I lie there, bits and pieces of the past few months with Vince float by me. The fancy French restaurant. Our first kiss. *I can see where she gets it from.* Darcy's early warning.

I think about that old parable of the man eating the apple. It is delicious—the best apple he's ever had. But just as he reaches the center, he finds a worm. Does this mean the apple wasn't wonderful? Does it negate every delicious bite that brought him joy up till then?

My family life is shattered. The two men I cared most about in the world lie broken and bleeding.

My life, with Vince in it, tasted wonderful.

But there is something I still need to ask him. Something I need to know, before I can ever move on.

CHAPTER 40

AGENT WITTEN WAS RIGHT. The surveillance tapes clearly showed Joey delivering drugs. So he agreed to testify against Vince. As a minor with a clean record and no "priors," Joey was given six months' probation, and was required to do community service for a year. The good news: he seems to enjoy it. I wouldn't be surprised if he winds up being a social worker someday. Well, maybe.

Jake never wrote fake prescriptions. He gave Vince blank pads, so his sentence was reduced to a misdemeanor. He lost his license for three years, and there's no guarantee the hospital will take him back. Darcy hasn't talked to me for quite a while. She still blames me for everything that happened with Vince. We're trying to ease our way back into some semblance of a friendship. But it will take time.

Vinny was sent to live with his mother. It turns out Vince had abducted the boy on one of his alternate custody weekends. The heartbroken mother had been searching for him all that time.

Ned was tried and convicted of laundering the proceeds from controlled substances—a Class B felony. He got two years in prison, plus a huge fine that wiped out most of our Roth IRA.

Vince's old house—the house next door—was sold to a young venture-capital couple who tore it down and are building a McMansion. I would be pleased by this, and what it does to real estate values, except I don't live there anymore. Once Ned was indicted, he lost his job at Reinhart. We sold the house soon after. No regrets there.

Well, maybe one: I would have wanted to move back into the city. But I promised the kids we'd stay in the suburbs till they all finished high school. I figure I owe them that.

Will I ever get over the guilt I feel, bringing Vince into our lives? I'm not sure. And I'm not sure what will happen once Ned gets out. It's clear to me now that our marriage had problems long before Vince entered the scene. Ned says he's willing to work on it. But I don't know if there's anything left anymore.

It's like that line from "The Gambler": "You gotta know when to hold 'em, know when to fold 'em."

So that kind of brings you up to speed on everybody involved.

Oh. Except for Vince.

EPILOGUE

FROM THE OUTSIDE, THE MacDougall-Walker Correctional Institution could pass for a Holiday Inn. But once you push your way through the heavy glass doors and walk through a metal detector, you know it isn't.

I put my pocketbook through an X-ray machine and submit to a serious body frisk. Then I fill out a bunch of papers, sign the visitor's log, and am sent to a waiting room. Along with many other visitors—family members, friends, clergymen, and attorneys—I wait.

Then I see him.

He is dressed in the classic orange jumpsuit, escorted by a prison guard who looks as if he doesn't know how to smile. I am seated at a wooden table. Vince sits down on the other side. He doesn't seem surprised to see me.

"They told me I had a visitor," he says. "I knew it would be you."

"How's it going?" I ask. I remember what I had read

in the local papers. In *Law & Order* terms: they threw the book at him. Forgery. Blackmail. Intimidation. Trafficking. Possession of controlled substances with intent to sell. Child abduction. Attempted manslaughter.

I think of the lovely afternoon he and I had on that park bench, a million years ago. He won't be seeing one of those anytime soon.

Vince looks older, tired, but as appealing as ever. That boyish lock of hair that kept falling into his eyes is gone—shaved away in a prison buzz cut. But he still has the same smile.

Here I am, seated across from the man who almost destroyed me and my family. Yet hard as I try, I can't hate him. We make small talk—the food there, his cell, what Joey is up to. And then I ask him the one question that's been burning in my brain.

"Did you ever care for me at all, or was I just part of the plan?"

He throws his head back and laughs.

"My God," he says. "All you women are the same!"

All you women...?

"A guy says a couple of nice things to a broad, and she's ready to follow him anywhere. You gotta learn to toughen up, Laura. Or else, the next guy who comes along..."

But I don't let him finish.

"Guard!" I call out. The guard comes over as I get up to leave.

"Laura, wait!" Vince calls out. But I'm already out the door.

The visit lasted six minutes. Just long enough to learn what a fool I've been these last several months.

And now?

These days, with Ned not there, I have a lot more time for myself. Time to figure out what makes me happy.

Maggie will be a help with that. And no, she and Ned weren't having an affair. He needed to come clean to someone; she was the perfect choice.

I joined a support group. That should help, too. Maybe I'll go back to acting, like I always wanted. Or maybe I'll write a play about everything that happened.

I think it would make a hell of a story.

THE KILLER'S WIFE

JAMES PATTERSON
with MAX DiLALLO

PROLOGUE

DETECTIVE ANDREW MCGRATH STANDS in front of his open liquor cabinet, shaking. Inside are just a few old bottles, most of them covered with a fine layer of dust. McGrath may have his share of vices, but booze has never been one of them.

Tonight, however, he's desperate to have a drink.

Partly it's to settle his nerves. But also because it's tradition. When McGrath first traded his patrolman's badge for a detective's shield nearly eleven years ago, his colleagues at the San Luis Obispo Police Department all pitched in to buy him a nice bottle of Scotch. A *very* nice bottle of Scotch. A Macallan 25-Year-Old Sherry Oak, which retails for about a thousand bucks.

The catch?

He was only ever allowed to drink it after he'd solved a murder.

Since then, McGrath has popped it open roughly once or twice a year. San Luis Obispo, a scenic town of about forty-five thousand tucked along California's hilly central coast, rarely sees serious crimes.

But tonight, the book has just been shut on the toughest, most taxing homicide case of McGrath's career. He's a veteran detective, but this pushed him to his limits—then *past* his limits. He is exhausted. Utterly drained. Shaken to his very core.

So once he unscrews the cap from the heavy glass bottle—after all these years, still about three-quarters full—McGrath doesn't pour a nip into a tumbler.

Instead, he takes a long, hearty gulp right from the source. Thick, amber rivulets trickle down his chin. The taste is rich and floral, sharp and smoky.

But the feeling is bittersweet.

Wiping his mouth on his sleeve, McGrath carries the bottle into his sparsely decorated living room. Nestled next to each other on the sofa, beneath a threadbare old quilt, are his elderly parents, Leonard and Evelyn McGrath. A late-night talk show is flickering softly on the TV, but both his parents' eyes are closed.

They look so calm, McGrath thinks. *So at peace.*

So different from how *he's* feeling.

With his free hand, McGrath gently lifts and retucks the blanket around their shoulders, careful not to disturb them. He turns off the television.

And, in the silence, hears something outside that makes him stop in his tracks.

The distant whine of a police siren.

Strange, given the late hour. To avoid bothering the

town's residents, police officers are instructed to use only their flashing lights between the hours of 10:00 p.m. and 6:00 a.m., except in extreme emergencies. So McGrath's curiosity is piqued.

But as he hears the siren getting louder, getting closer, he understands.

It's a professional courtesy. A friendly warning.

The cops are on their way for *him*—but he's been expecting them all night.

McGrath steps into his front hallway now. Without putting down the bottle of Scotch, he unholsters his sidearm, a jet-black Glock 22. He ejects the bullet cartridge, and places it and his gun side by side on the entry table.

Then he steels himself, and opens the door.

An unmarked white Chevy Impala and two squad cars are pulling into his driveway. Four uniformed male officers and a female plainclothes one—Detective Gina Petrillo, smart, feisty, ballsy, the only woman investigator on the entire force and therefore one of its toughest—exit their vehicles and approach.

"Evening, gang," McGrath calls to them. "Lovely night, isn't it?"

Gina takes a moment to try to control the storm of emotions raging inside her. Shock. Confusion. Fury. Betrayal.

Then she readies a pair of handcuffs.

"Detective Andrew J. McGrath," she says stiffly, "you have the right to remain silent. Anything you say can and will be used against you in—"

"Oh, Jesus, Gina, stop it." McGrath holds up the palm of his empty hand like a crossing guard. "Just tell me straight. What am I being arrested for?"

Gina responds with a vicious scowl. This was a colleague she once believed in. A man she once trusted. Once loved like a brother.

"Murder, Andy. But you already knew that, didn't you?"

With a resigned shrug, McGrath takes a final swig of the exorbitantly priced Scotch.

"Actually," he replies, "it's *worse* than that."

Without warning, he hurls the glass bottle to the ground, letting it shatter on his concrete front steps. Gina and the officers leap back, startled. But McGrath stays still as a statue.

"*Much* worse. Come on inside."

CHAPTER 1

Six weeks earlier

"KNOW THE THING I love most about this job?" asks Gina.

She's in the passenger seat to my right, rummaging through the plastic bag at her feet, which earlier held our grease-soaked KFC drive-thru dinner.

We've been sitting in this stuffy parked car together for the past five mind-numbing hours, so I answer sarcastically. "The nonstop thrills?"

Gina removes a crumpled paper napkin stained with barbecue sauce from the bag. She folds it inside out, then blots her glistening brow.

"You're close. The glamour."

It's true. Real police work *isn't* glamorous. Or very exciting. Definitely not how it's portrayed in the movies. Most of the time, our chosen profession is about as hip as digging ditches, as riveting as collecting trash—except that a hole in the ground won't ever lead you on a dangerous high-speed chase, and even the smelliest, foulest dumpster in the world won't ever pull a gun on you.

But real police work is what's required to catch a very real bad guy.

Like the one who's been terrorizing our quiet community on and off for nearly two years.

"Red Bull?" Gina asks as she reaches into a small plastic cooler behind her seat.

She already knows my response—*No, thanks. How can you even drink that crap?*—so I don't have to say it. Taking just one skinny, sugar-free can for herself, Gina holds it against her face for a few seconds, then cracks it open and gulps it down.

I admit I could use a little pick-me-up, too. After tailing and staking out our current person of interest for nineteen days straight—no breaks, no days off—I'm definitely feeling worse for the wear.

I can only imagine how Gina's holding up—my loyal partner of almost seven years, and my best friend for decades. We went to San Luis Obispo High together, if you can believe it, less than a mile down the road. Gina's a trooper: she and her girlfriend are raising two stinking-cute twin toddlers at home, and I don't know how she does it. Sure, I've got my aging folks I help take care of, but at least they can change their *own* diapers.

"Looks like another wild and crazy night in the Pierson household," she says.

Gina is peering through a pair of binoculars. I raise my own to look for myself.

Through the second-floor window of a modest Spanish-style bungalow down the block, we watch as

Michael Pierson and his wife, Ellen, get ready for bed. They change into almost-matching pajamas. They brush their teeth side by side at the bathroom sink in chilly silence. They exchange a chaste peck on the cheek. Then they slip under the covers and shut off the lights.

"That right there is why me and Zoe are *never* getting married," Gina says. "And they don't even have kids! I get depressed just watching."

"Well, your relationship's a little different," I say. "Neither of you is a serial killer. At least as far as I know."

"You really think he's our guy, huh?" Gina lowers her voice, adding somberly: "And you really think those poor girls are dead?"

I do. On both counts.

There's been only circumstantial evidence so far linking Pierson to the ongoing string of abductions. But after I interviewed him twice at the station, he just felt . . . *off* to me. I can't say why, but something deep in my gut tells me he's behind them.

For one, he's vice principal of San Luis Obispo High School, where all the young female victims were students, and he knew them fairly well. Two witnesses also put Pierson near Santa Rosa Park—where the most recent missing girl was last seen, out for a jog—on the night she disappeared, twenty-two days ago.

Like the three young women before her, she vanished without a trace.

But goddamnit, I'm going to prove Pierson is guilty!

That son of a bitch is going to pay, no matter what it takes.

And if by some miracle those girls *are* alive...I'll find them, too.

It's getting late, and I'm starting to feel a little foggy. I shut my eyes and rub my face, trying to fight it. Maybe I'll take a quick power nap. Maybe I'll have a Red Bull after all. Maybe I'll—

"Shit, Andy!" Gina exclaims, punching me hard in the shoulder. "Look!"

CHAPTER 2

GINA AND I WATCH with surprise as Michael Pierson exits his front door.

That might not seem like anything special. But over the past nineteen days we've spent surveilling this guy, his behavior has been so predictable, you could set your watch by it—as long as you didn't fall asleep first. Pretty much all Gina and I have seen him do is drive to and from school, drive to and from the supermarket, pick up some dry cleaning, do some yard work, and go to bed early. (As far as I can tell, he also hasn't made love to his wife once this whole time—which is criminal in *my* book, but not according to the California Penal Code.)

Tonight, Pierson has finally changed up his routine. In a very big way.

He was wearing pajamas less than an hour ago. Now he's got on jeans, a gray sweater, and a blue Golden State Warriors baseball cap, the brim pulled low. He's also carrying a small black duffel bag and speaking nervously on a cell phone, although we're much too far away to hear him.

"*That's* new," I say.

"Yup. I always thought he'd be an Angels fan."

I roll my eyes. My partner has two modes: sarcastic and *very* sarcastic.

"I mean his cell. Pierson has an iPhone. That's an old *flip* phone."

"Damn, you're right. Gotta be a burner. But who's he talking to?"

No idea. But the real question is, where's he going?

We watch as Pierson finishes his conversation, hangs up, then gets into his silver Honda Civic parked in his driveway. As he begins pulling out, I glance at my watch. It's 11:26 p.m. This is by far the latest we've ever seen him awake, let alone outside his house—let alone *going* somewhere. Something is most definitely up.

After his Honda passes us, I count to five, then start my engine. Keeping my headlights switched off, I pull a gentle U-turn. And follow.

San Luis Obispo—or SLO, as a lot of us locals call it—is a lovely place to live. But it isn't exactly a thriving metropolis. This late on a weeknight, the streets are empty, and I have to keep a good distance between my car and Pierson's. The last thing I want to do is spook him.

"He's making a left on Conejo Avenue," Gina says.

I don't tell her she's stating the obvious. If he continues straight, it's a dead end.

I simply nod and make a left up that hilly street myself, then keep an eye on the Honda as it continues to snake through this sleepy patch of residential homes.

Pierson soon makes a left onto Andrews Street, the road that leads into town...but then he hooks another left, looping back around.

"What's he doing?" Gina asks.

I have no idea. But soon, we find ourselves back on Pierson's block.

"Damnit!" I exclaim, pounding my fist against the steering wheel. "He's going home. He must've seen us. Shit."

"Or maybe he just wanted to take a little drive," Gina says. "Go in circles for a while. Clear his head."

"Or maybe...this is his ritual," I say. "He's psyching himself up before he strikes again."

Gina and I let that lie there as Pierson's car nears his driveway and starts to slow. It looks like he was taking a spin around the neighborhood after all. False alarm.

Except—he doesn't stop. He continues past it, then makes another left on Conejo, then heads down Andrews again.

And this time, he keeps going.

Gina rubs her hands together in excited anticipation. "Okay, we're back in business."

I'm a little antsy myself. This is uncharted territory— for Pierson and us, too.

The Honda heads east along Monterey Street, one of SLO's main thoroughfares. We pass a few shopping centers. A video rental store, shuttered long ago. A greasy taco joint right across from a hip new green-juice bar. (That's California for you.)

Pierson approaches an empty intersection with a stale

yellow light. Instead of slowing, he accelerates. It turns red—but he speeds right through.

"Let's pull this asshole over," Gina suggests. "Maybe see what's in that duffel."

I slow down but don't stop as I reach the same quiet intersection, to make sure the coast is clear. Then I speed through the red light myself.

"No, not yet. This is our chance. I don't want to blow it."

After a few blocks, Pierson turns off the main road and stops in front of a modest two-story apartment complex, the color of burnt coffee. I stealthily pull over about a block farther down, a discreet distance away but with a decent line of sight on him.

Maybe thirty seconds later, a woman exits one of the second-floor apartments and scurries down the stairs. She's wearing a baggy sweatshirt with the hood up.

"Here comes company," Gina says. "But I can't get a look at her. Can you?"

I can't, either. Not from this angle. *Damn.* Her face is totally obscured.

Until she opens Pierson's passenger-side door.

"Jesus . . ." I mutter.

As the woman turns to get in, the dome light casts an eerie glow across her face.

I see now that she's just a girl. A *teenager*. Bright-eyed and apple-cheeked.

I also get a glimpse of the writing on her sweatshirt.

SAN LUIS OBISPO HIGH SCHOOL

CHAPTER 3

"NOW WE *GOTTA* PULL this asshole over," Gina pleads. "She could be his next—"

"You don't think I know that?" I snap, surprised and a little embarrassed by the edge in my voice. "But if we collar him now..."

I trail off, because Gina knows exactly the classic police dilemma we're in.

A high-school vice principal picking up an underage girl around midnight looks sketchy as hell. But there might be a perfectly reasonable—and legal—explanation. They *could* be having an affair. Or Pierson could be helping her flee an abusive family and move into a shelter. Either way, it's not proof Pierson abducted or harmed any of those *other* poor girls. It won't bring them back. And it won't put him away.

"Run this address," I tell my partner. "Find out who she is. I won't let her out of our sight. I promise."

Gina gives me a troubled look, but agrees. She opens

the dashboard-mounted laptop between us and gets to work.

Meanwhile, I keep my eyes glued to the silver Honda, still just sitting there in front of the apartment complex. I'd give anything to know what's happening inside.

"Come on, *come on*," I whisper. "Get out of the damn car. Just walk away."

No such luck. The Honda shifts into drive and pulls back onto Monterey.

A few seconds later, Gina and I are trailing it again. Now I leave only about one block's distance between us. I'm not taking any chances.

"Okay, I think I got her," Gina says, her acrylic nails clattering across the laptop keyboard. "Brittany Herbert, age seventeen. Goes by Britt. She's a junior at SLO High. Lives in apartment 2C with her mom and stepdad. I found her Facebook page. Is this her?"

Gina flips the screen around to show me the profile picture of a teenager posing with some girlfriends, all puckering their lips for the camera, happy and carefree.

I'm positive that's the same young woman I saw get into Pierson's car.

This potential next victim has been identified. It just got *personal*.

"She lists her cell phone on her profile, too," Gina says. "Maybe we text it."

"And say what?" I ask. "'Hi, Britt, we're two undercover cops following the car you're in. Don't freak out, but your vice principal might be about to murder you'?"

"Fine," Gina says, exasperated. "We'll do this your way. But damnit, Andy, you're taking a major risk here. I'm warning you..."

I nod, stiffly. The pressure's on.

Pierson's Honda cuts through SLO's unimposing downtown, then heads toward the 101 freeway, which basically cuts San Luis Obispo in half. I start to worry that Pierson might merge onto it and try to spirit the girl out of town. I'd follow this bastard all the way to Canada if I had to, but the farther out they get from our jurisdiction, the tougher it will be to keep tabs on him and Brittany—and possibly call for backup.

Thankfully, the Honda cruises below the underpass and stays within the city limits. For now. But it keeps going, heading northwest, toward the town's hilly outskirts.

Soon, I can start to make out some tree-lined ridges off in the distance.

Which makes my stomach drop.

I know *exactly* where they're going.

CHAPTER 4

BISHOP'S PEAK. AT OVER fifteen hundred feet, it's the highest point in the region by far. With its stunning views of the city, it's a popular draw for hikers, picnickers, and bird-watchers alike.

It's also a *nightmare* for law enforcement.

The surrounding hillsides are rugged and treacherous. They stretch on for miles, a maze of winding trails and steep switchbacks. The tree cover is dense, the vegetation thick, the wildlife dangerous. And especially after sundown, the place gets darker than the North Pole during a lunar eclipse.

In other words, it's the perfect location to kill a teenage girl and dump her body.

"Relax, man," Gina says, touching my arm. After so many years of working together, she can practically read my mind. "This isn't his spot. We combed the peak for miles in every direction. Not just three weeks ago, but *every* time. Remember?"

I couldn't possibly forget. These hills are such an obvious choice to stash a kidnapping victim—dead or alive—that each time a girl has gone missing, the SLOPD pulled out all the stops. Most recently, we deployed multiple search parties, two circling rescue helicopters, even some K-9 units borrowed from the county sheriff. Officers worked around the clock for three days. We didn't find a thing.

Still, that's ice-cold comfort right now as the Honda reaches the end of the winding paved street...and rumbles onto a dirt service road.

If Pierson and Brittany just wanted to be alone for an hour or two, there are plenty of motels they could have gone to instead. What are they doing *here*?

I tighten my grip on the steering wheel and keep their car in my sights.

Up the hillside we go, higher and higher. Since my headlights are still off, it's getting almost impossible to see where the road ends and the steep ridge below begins. I have no choice but to drive even slower. If Gina and I crash, Brittany's all on her own.

We round a particularly steep bend. When I think I've steered through, there's suddenly a sick jolt—my front left tire is slipping off the road! Gina lets out a little gasp as I jerk the wheel to the right, barely keeping us from tumbling to our deaths. Cursing under my breath, I drive on.

"Hold up," Gina says, pointing her index finger to the sky. "I think they stopped."

Did they? I can't tell. The Honda is just around the next ridge, momentarily out of sight. But I do notice the glow of its headlights is gone.

Why here? Why now?

No clue. But if there was ever a time to make our move, this is it.

I shut off the engine. "Let's roll," I say to my partner, who is already quietly opening her door—and drawing her sidearm. I do the same.

Crouching low, we creep slowly along the side of the wooded hill separating us from Pierson and Brittany. Trying to move through the underbrush is like traipsing through quicksand. I feel the prickly brambles and cacti scratch my skin through my clothes, but I ignore them and keep moving.

Finally we reach the crest. I look down at the Honda below—*with horror.*

Pierson is standing by the open passenger-side door, heaving Brittany's limp body into his arms.

"Police! Don't move!" I shout as Gina and I charge down the hill.

Pierson looks genuinely shocked to see us, a real deer in the headlights. He immediately releases the girl's lifeless frame, letting her slump back into her seat.

Then he takes off running.

I nearly trip over myself rapidly changing direction downhill, trying to cut him off.

I'm no Usain Bolt, but thankfully neither is Pierson. I lunge for the son of a bitch and tackle him to the ground.

Shoving his head into the dirt, I quickly holster my service weapon and snap handcuffs on him in seconds.

I look back at the Honda, fearing the absolute worst.

"How is she?" I call to Gina, who is kneeling beside Brittany, frantically searching for her pulse, lifting her eyelids to inspect her pupils. "Britt, can you hear me?" Gina says. "You're safe now. Don't be scared, Britt. It's all over."

I look back down at Pierson, his face dirty and bloody, his expression stony.

"You piece of shit!" I shout. "Did you kill her? Like you killed all the others?"

Pierson spits out a piece of gravel. Then his lips curl into a chilling grin.

"Actually, it's *worse* than that. *Much* worse."

CHAPTER 5

"COFFEE, BLACK. ON THE HOUSE."

Gina thrusts a steaming Styrofoam cup of joe into my hands. I almost spill it all over myself, since my attention is elsewhere: I'm standing at the edge of a roped-off section of hillside, roughly fifteen feet by twenty, watching a team of crime-scene investigators wearing white full-body evidence suits carefully comb through it.

They're looking for a mass grave they suspect might be underneath.

What a goddamn world.

"Thanks," I reply, turning to face my partner. I have to squint a little, since she's backlit by the rising sun. We've been at this all night. "Except I take three creams and four sugars, Gina. You've only known that for years."

My partner shrugs. "I know your doctor wouldn't mind the change."

"Yeah, yeah," I mutter, and take a careful sip of the bracingly hot, bitter beverage. Like Gina's beloved sugar-free

Red Bull—another little can of which she's guzzling at the moment—I don't know how people can drink *this,* either.

"Speaking of white coats," I say cautiously, "any update on Brittany yet?"

"I just got off with the hospital. She's stabilized, resting comfortably."

Relief floods every cell of my body.

"Thank God. Okay. We need to get down there, talk to her as soon as she's awake."

"Doctors say it could be a while. Midday at least."

"That's fine. Have her labs come back?"

Gina tilts back her Red Bull can and drains the last few drops.

"Not yet. But based on her condition, they think Pierson slipped her some kind of sedative. Could be Rohypnol, maybe a ketamine derivative. My guess is, he hid it in that fifth of Smirnoff that was under the passenger seat, covered in her prints."

"Sick bastard," I mumble, simmering with rage. I bite down on my bottom lip, so hard it draws a few drops of blood.

"Detectives, a moment?"

The voice belongs to the bespectacled Dr. John Hyong, the SLOPD's chief forensic pathologist. He's walking toward us, peeling off his latex gloves. The way the rising sun reflects off his white jumpsuit and hood, he looks almost...*ghostly.* Which is grimly appropriate, actually. He's been leading the team of techs searching for bodies for the past six hours.

"Find anything?" I ask, almost afraid to hear his response.

Hyong shakes his head.

"No trace. Our subterranean sonar imaging has also been inconclusive. We're expanding the perimeter another ten feet all around. However, if we still don't find—"

"I appreciate the update, John," I say, deliberately cutting him off.

Because I know what this "expert" is going to say.

Hyong doesn't think we'll find *shit* buried in these hills. I practically had to beg him even to start a search. Hyong agreed only as a favor to me. He didn't think the rocky hillside would make a good burial spot in the first place—and the police had already combed this ground multiple times.

I can't say I blame him. There's no evidence that Pierson took any of the other four victims up here.

In fact, there's still no evidence linking Pierson to the other girls' abductions at all.

But damn it, I was right about that creep this time!

Would he really drive Brittany Herbert all the way to Bishop's Peak on a whim?

I don't think so. There's a method to his madness, and I'm going to figure it out.

And I'm going to find those girls. They've gotta be here somewhere.

Gotta be.

CHAPTER 6

I KNOW I SHOULD wait for my partner to do this, but I can't.

I should probably stop home first, too. Take a hot shower, grab a change of clothes, give my grimy teeth a quick brush. But I can't do that, either.

There's too much at stake. And no time to lose.

So while Gina swings by her place for a bit to help her girlfriend get their twins fed, dressed, and off to day care, I drive back to the Piersons' house.

I want to have a little chat with Ellen.

The woman I'm convinced is the killer's wife.

From our weeks of surveillance, I know Ellen usually gets up around six thirty. She goes for a quick jog around the neighborhood, has a light breakfast with her husband, then around eight heads to school—not San Luis High, where Pierson works, but Hawthorne Elementary, where she's the school nurse.

Sure enough, when I pull into the driveway a few minutes before seven, the kitchen light is on. I spot Ellen inside wearing workout clothes. She's holding a cordless phone to her ear and pacing anxiously.

Probably because she has no idea where her husband is.

On my way over, I spoke to the desk sergeant back at the station, who told me Pierson turned down the chance to make his one call. He hasn't spoken to his wife, to the high school, to a lawyer—anybody. He's just been sitting in his cell all night.

Does that sound like an innocent man to you, or a guilty one?

"Fine," I said to the sergeant. "His choice. Let him rot."

It feels a little strange to walk right up to the Piersons' front door and ring the bell. I'm so used to sitting in my car with Gina down the block, watching it from the shadows. Seeing the place up close like this, I notice a few details I didn't before. Like the mismatched screws holding the metal mailbox to the wall. The novelty welcome mat, old and fraying, with a yellow floral design around the word ALOHA.

The door opens, and Ellen stands there for a few seconds in stunned silence.

Up this close, I notice some new details about *her*, too. Like the dusting of freckles across the bridge of her nose. And her subtly mismatched eye color: the left one is a faint emerald, the right one aquamarine.

"Mrs. Pierson? I'm Detective McGrath, SLOPD. I, uh...do you mind if..."

I'm suddenly a little tongue-tied myself. Something

176

about this woman has caught me off guard. I always thought Ellen was nice-looking, if a little plain. But now I see there's a magnetism about her.

"Is this about my husband?" she asks. "He was gone when I woke up. His car, too. I called his cell, but it was charging on the kitchen counter. Is he all right?"

"He's fine. But he's…been arrested."

"Arrested?" Ellen covers her mouth with her hands as if she's just seen a ghost. "No. No, that's ridiculous. He didn't do it!"

I feel my right eyebrow arch of its own volition.

"I didn't tell you what he was arrested *for*, Mrs. Pierson."

Ellen looks rattled. Scared. Caught?

"Why don't we go inside and talk?" I say.

Ellen leads me into their quaint living room and right away begins nervously tidying the place up. Not that it needs it. In fact, the room is meticulously clean and orderly. Even the old magazines on the coffee table are in perfectly neat stacks.

"I—I'm sorry the place is such a mess. I had no idea anyone would be—"

"Please," I say, gently touching Ellen's forearm. Her skin feels clammy but supple and warm. "Let's have a seat. I'd like to ask you a few questions."

We settle next to each other on a sagging beige couch.

"Does the name Brittany Herbert mean anything to you?"

Ellen squints, thinking, then shakes her head.

"What about Claire Coates, Samantha Gonzalez, Maria Jeffries, or Patty Blum?"

Now Ellen shuts her eyes tight.

"Those names mean something to *everyone* in this town," she says. "They're the four girls who...who..."

Ellen can't finish the sentence. So I do it for her.

"Who all disappeared over the past twenty-two months. Presumed dead. Patty went missing just three weeks ago."

"I know. My God, it's so awful. Those poor girls. But what does this have to do with me and Michael?"

"We need your help finding the bodies, Mrs. Pierson."

"*My* help? What are you talking about?"

Ellen isn't making this easy. I have a feeling she knows a lot more than she's letting on. But I have to play this carefully.

"You and your husband have been married for six years. But tell me: How well do you *really* know him? Do you think he'd ever be capable of—"

"Absolutely not!" Ellen exclaims, springing to her feet. "You think *he*...? This is crazy! Whatever you think Michael did...he's a good man. He's innocent!"

Ellen glares at me with her bicolored eyes, now wet with tears.

Her emotion is so real, so raw, I almost want to believe her. Almost.

CHAPTER 7

I QUICKLY BACKPEDAL AND try to calm Ellen down. I assure her our investigation is ongoing and that no charges have been filed yet against her husband in connection with the four girls' disappearances.

But then I tell her about his arrest last night.

About the underage student he picked up around midnight. How he drove her to a deserted patch of woods and drugged her to near cardiac arrest. Whether Michael Pierson is involved in those other four abductions or not, he sure ain't a Boy Scout.

Ellen, her shoulders trembling, her voice cracking, sits back down on the couch and agrees to answer my questions.

We start with what she remembers about last night—which isn't anything out of the ordinary. She's just about done telling me what little she recalls about the nights the four *other* teens went missing, when I hear two vehicles pull up in front of the house.

I turn and look out the living room's spotless bay windows. Three uniformed officers are exiting a pair of squad cars. Gina is with them, clutching a trifolded sheet of paper.

"My partner's here," I explain to Ellen. "With your permission, we'd like to search your house and yard. You can wait right here until we're finished."

Ellen stammers a bit, then nods.

"If you think it might help, go ahead. Please."

"Thank you, ma'am," I tell her. "We appreciate that."

What I *don't* tell her is that I was asking simply as a courtesy, trying to curry a little extra favor with her. That document in Gina's hand is a search warrant, signed by a county magistrate.

I greet my partner and the officers at the front door and bring them up to speed on my dealings with Ellen. Then we divvy up the house and yard, snap on some latex gloves, and get to work.

But when I reenter the living room, I see that one of the bay windows is wide open.

And Ellen is gone.

"Shit, we got a runner!" I say, reaching for my service weapon. "Gina, cover the front. You two, the sides. I'll take the rear, see if she—"

"Are you looking for *me*?" comes Ellen's shaky voice from the kitchen.

I hurry in and there she is, innocently setting out a row of mugs along the counter. She looks both confused and embarrassed to have caused such alarm.

"It was getting stuffy in there, so I opened a window. And I thought I—I'd make some fresh coffee for you all if anyone wants some."

Ellen, the school nurse. Behind her, I see Gina step into the opposite doorway and roll her eyes.

"That's not necessary, Mrs. Pierson," I say, trying to control my irritation. "Why don't you wait in the living room. Like I *asked* you to."

Over the next ninety minutes, our search goes down without incident. Me, Gina, and the officers turn every square inch of the house inside out, looking for any clues that might link Pierson to Claire's, Samantha's, Maria's, or Patty's disappearance—or even better, that might lead to finding them alive.

We carefully bag and tag every possible piece of evidence, including Pierson's iPhone and laptop. An old paper datebook that may help reveal his whereabouts at the time of the crimes. Some unmarked bottles of pills in the bathroom. A stack of old SLO High School yearbooks filled with signatures—including one signed by Maria Jeffries, the third victim—that might shed light on the vice principal's relationships with the girls. One of the officers even finds a purple scarf that resembles the one Samantha Gonzalez, the second victim, was allegedly wearing the night she went missing.

All are tantalizing clues. But none is conclusive.

Then we do an additional search, a "structural sweep," pulling up rugs and carpets, moving furniture, checking every crack and crevice to make sure we didn't miss any hiding spots built into the house itself. Like a trick wall in the back of a closet. A secret nook under a staircase. A trapdoor that leads to a hidden soundproof room where four teenage girls have been locked away for two years.

Nothing.

I regroup with Gina in the attic, where it's stiflingly hot and muggy. My partner has just finished inspecting the roof and rafters and has come up empty-handed.

"I don't know whether to be relieved or pissed off," Gina says. "What a waste of time. We didn't find a damn thing."

"We still have to search the backyard," I say. "Could get lucky."

But Gina frowns. She pulls off her latex gloves with a snap and rolls them into little white pellets.

"You're really still convinced Pierson's our guy?"

I am. I can't say why exactly. Call it a hunch. Call it an instinct. Call it years of hunting down bad guys.

But I absolutely am.

"What's all that?" I ask, pointing to a little drafting table in the corner of the attic. On it are some wooden frames, glass panels, and a few small tools and tiny boxes.

"Apparently," Gina answers, "Mrs. Pierson is something of a lepidopterist."

"Huh?"

"A butterfly expert. A collector. Have a look yourself."

I head over to the workstation and see that pinned inside many of the framed glass panels are various preserved, drying butterflies. There must be dozens at least, each a different shape and size, every color of the rainbow, beautiful and delicate.

So Ellen Pierson collects butterflies.

And her husband collects teenage girls.

CHAPTER 8

ELLEN FELT LIKE SHE was living inside a terrible dream.

Her husband was missing. A detective was at her front door, sturdy and good-looking, but polite at first.

Yet his confidence grew as he explained the shocking reason he was there.

Michael had been arrested—for drugging a female student and attempting to dump her lifeless body in the woods near Bishop's Peak.

As if *that* wasn't hard enough to believe, the police also suspected he was behind the disappearance of those four *other* poor teenage girls who'd gone missing over the past two years, a crime spree that had set the entire town on edge.

Michael, a dedicated educator, her loving husband. Could it really be?

"He's a good man," Ellen insisted to the detective. "He's innocent!"

"We need your help finding the bodies, Mrs. Pierson," the detective said.

Ellen sent a hurried text to the principal of her elementary school saying she'd likely be coming in late, if at all, citing "personal reasons." Now she's gone numb from head to toe, watching the police tear her home apart, top to bottom.

This can't be happening…

Part of her wishes she could transform into one of her beloved butterflies, then float right out the open window, unseen.

Another part of her wants to scream and shout, flip over the sofa, hurl the coffee table clean across the room.

Instead, Ellen just sits there on her overstuffed couch, a human statue, forbidden by the police from even making a pot of coffee, praying that this all really *is* just a nightmare and she'll wake up any minute. That Michael will be snoring softly by her side, not sitting in a jail cell. That Brittany Herbert will be home, too, not lying in a hospital bed. That her husband's laptop, his anxiety medications, the purple scarf he bought her for Christmas four years ago, will all be in their proper places, not in plastic evidence bags on their way to a forensic lab.

The search finally ends, and the detectives and officers leave.

At least, Ellen *thought* they were leaving.

Instead, she sees they've simply relocated to outside, where they continue their invasive search in her backyard. Sifting through her rosebushes. Rooting through her vegetable garden. Poking holes in her lawn.

With the police outside, Ellen begins to clean up—

which will be a herculean task. Every room she walks through is an absolute mess. Every drawer and closet has been rifled through. Every single item she owns has been examined and moved out of place.

As her numbness begins to wear off, she starts to feel angry. Confused. Violated.

She knows what will calm her down: her butterflies.

So Ellen heads up to the attic, to the old desk in the corner where she stores and works on her collection. Of course the police rifled through her tools and framed glass shadow boxes. But they seem to have been gentle enough. Ellen notices a few of her colorful winged specimens have come unpinned, but thankfully none looks damaged.

Taking a deep breath, she selects a pair of tweezers and begins carefully restoring the butterflies to their proper places. She figures if she can reinstate some semblance of order to this tiny slice of her life, maybe the rest will follow.

She's wrong.

Barely five minutes have passed when she hears some kind of commotion out in her front yard. She peers through a tiny window overlooking her lawn and sees the two detectives and other officers buzzing around like bees on honey.

One of them is also yelling, barking orders. The words are faint and muffled, but Ellen can just barely make them out.

And they fill her with dread.

"We found something!"

CHAPTER 9

BONES.

Loosely packed topsoil.

The putrid smell of rotting flesh.

I know right away we've just stumbled on a shallow grave—right in the middle of the killer's backyard.

As Gina and the other uniformed officers start cordoning off the Piersons' backyard with yellow crime-scene tape, I'm already on my cell dialing Dr. Hyong.

"Hello, Detective, we're just wrapping up at Bishop's Peak," he says as soon as he picks up. "I'm afraid we didn't find anything. So I'm officially ending the search. I was going to call you this afternoon to tell you, after I grabbed a few hours of sleep."

"Sorry, Doc," I reply, "but no rest for the weary. I'm gonna need your team to pull a double shift. Because here at the Pierson place, we definitely just found *something*."

Within the hour, Hyong and a half dozen fellow white-suited crime-scene techs arrive and set to work. They carefully mark off the grave site, then begin to excavate, photograph, and catalog the brittle, buried remains.

Standing on the periphery of the property with Gina, I'm simmering with a mix of emotions. I'm glad my instincts were right. We finally have the proof we need to connect the other girls' disappearances to Michael Pierson. We can nail the bastard!

But seeing Hyong and his colleagues sift through the soil, I feel a well of deep empathy for the victims all over again. And fury that those poor young girls had their precious lives cut short.

"We're gonna have some new questions for Pierson after this," Gina says.

She offers me a pack of chewing gum, which I decline. She shrugs and folds a stick into her mouth, and the faint smell of hot cinnamon is soon tickling my nostrils.

Anything to replace the smell of death.

As we continue watching the forensic team, I get an odd sensation—like someone is watching *me*.

I turn and look back at the house. And what do you know? Ellen is staring down at us from an attic window. Her expression is cold, blank, like a mannequin's.

"I'm going to have a few more questions for *Mrs.* Pierson, too," I say.

"Detectives?" Hyong suddenly calls to us. He's heading our way, removing his face mask, and shaking his head.

With concern, Gina and I hurry over to meet him.

"John, what's wrong?" I demand.

"Those bones don't belong to any of our victims."

"What? But how do you—so you're saying—"

"No," he interjects. "They're just the remains of a dog."

CHAPTER 10

I'M BACK ON THE old beige couch again, sitting next to Ellen, who's twirling a fresh Kleenex in her hands. A tiny mountain of them has accumulated beside her.

"He told me...he told me Ruby ran away," she whimpers.

"And how long ago was that?" I ask.

"Four months, two weeks, and five days. I remember it perfectly. I'd just spent the weekend in Fresno. It was my nephew's third birthday. Michael had to stay here, catch up on some work. When I came home, he sat me down, right on this very couch, and broke the awful news."

I nod; her story checks out. Dr. Hyong isn't a forensic veterinarian, but he estimated, given the state of the dog's decayed corpse, that it was buried between four and six months ago.

With a gentle sniffle, Ellen adds, "She...she was such a good girl."

I want to give this woman a moment to compose herself. Her pain and shock seem genuine to me. But Gina, perched on a love seat nearby, interjects. Harshly.

"Wish you remembered the nights those *real* girls went missing half as well."

I know where my partner is going with this, so I shoot her a quick glance—*Hey, back off.* But she's on a roll.

"Chances are looking better and better that your husband killed them, too."

Ellen's bicolored eyes grow wide with horror.

"What do you mean, my husband killed them . . . *too*?"

Great. This was the other piece of info Hyong gave us about the dog's remains. I was planning on sharing it with Ellen later, when the time was right, or maybe not even telling her at all. But Gina just spilled the beans.

"Our forensic expert, Mrs. Pierson," I say delicately, "observed a prominent indentation on the left side of Ruby's head. He believes it was caused by blunt-force trauma."

"Hard enough to crush Ruby's little skull," Gina says, not helping.

"Her death was quick and painless," I add, possibly fudging the truth a bit. "But intentional. And cruelty to animals is often associated with cruelty to people. I know this is all hard to hear. But now do you see why it's so important you tell us everything you can about your husband?"

Ellen blinks a few times, processing this latest chilling revelation, but stays quiet.

Through the bay window facing the street, I see Hyong

and his team stripping off their white jumpsuits, packing up their response vehicle, and getting ready to leave.

It's a harsh reminder that after all this, we're *still* no closer to finding any evidence that links Pierson to the disappearance of Claire, Samantha, Maria, or Patty. And we're no closer to finding those girls, dead or alive. *Damn it!*

"*Mrs. Pierson,*" I snap, starting to succumb to my frustration, "we need your help. You're married to that man. Think. Hard. Talk to us. *Please.*"

Ellen stares right at me. Her lips part slightly, as if she's going to speak, as if she's finally going to give us something we can work with. I lean forward in anticipation.

Then Ellen leans forward, too. And bursts into heaving, ugly sobs.

CHAPTER 11

PRECISELY TWENTY-THREE MINUTES ago, Ellen pulled her Camry into the Hawthorne Elementary School faculty parking lot. She's been sitting in it ever since, willing herself to simply open the car door, get out, and head into the school that she loves so much, just as if it were any other day.

Of course, it's *not* any other day. Not even close. It's her first day back since that handsome detective knocked on her door last week and turned her whole life upside down.

Since then, Michael has been formally arraigned. But he is still refusing to speak to the police, to his court-appointed lawyer, or even to his own wife.

Detective McGrath is the opposite; he can't seem to talk to Ellen *enough*. He's been calling her every other day to check in, hoping she might remember some new detail that could help his investigation. But so far, she hasn't.

Reporters, too, won't leave Ellen alone. They've been

knocking on her door at all hours, trailing her everywhere she goes, begging her to break her silence and give an interview, which she has steadfastly refused to do.

But the damn press won't give up! Just this morning, to get to school unseen, Ellen slipped out the back door before dawn, hopped the fence on the far side of the yard, then sped off in her car, which she had deliberately parked a few blocks away from her home. And yet, Ellen could have sworn she saw one of them following her today. *No, I'm just being paranoid,* she told herself. *Or maybe all this stress is starting to play tricks on my mind.*

Ellen had wanted to come back to work to feel some semblance of normalcy in her life again. Just sitting around at home, helpless, was driving her nuts. But now she just feels foolish. And overwhelmed. She rubs her tired, bloodshot eyes. *Maybe this was a mistake,* she thinks. *Maybe I came back too soon. Maybe—*

"Good morning, Nurse Pierson!" comes a chorus of children's voices.

Ellen sees a gaggle of kids walking past. They're giggling and waving, tickled to see the school nurse outside the building and not wearing her trademark white coat.

Their laughter and innocence tug on Ellen's heart. Hard. It's an adorable reminder of why she became a school nurse in the first place: to keep these precious kids healthy. *They need you,* Ellen tells herself. *So quit wallowing and get moving!*

At last, Ellen does. She exits her car, approaches the building, and enters.

Walking through the halls to her office, however, is an unsettling experience.

Most of the students she passes greet her happily, like the ones outside. But the glares she gets from her fellow faculty members are fierce and unrelenting. Certainly they have all read the local papers and have been gossiping in the teachers' lounge for days. They all know Ellen's husband has been accused of some truly heinous crimes. But far from showing sympathy for their colleague, their expressions range from shock to judgment to horror.

Ellen shifts her eyes to the ground until she finally reaches the nurse's office. She hurriedly unlocks the door, then slams it shut.

The school day begins, and gradually Ellen falls back into the familiar routines of the job she loves, tending to student ailments large and small. She gently cleans and bandages the scraped elbow of a whimpering first-grader named Mackenzie, who fell while playing basketball. She "treats" a third-grader named AJ—who Ellen knows has a history of pretending—for his sore throat by giving him a couple of pieces of candy she's stashed in a cabinet. And she reassures a nervous fifth-grader named Carlos that the pimple on his nose might be a little embarrassing, but it's a perfectly normal part of starting puberty.

Ellen is a few hours into her morning, reorganizing the first-aid closet, when her cell phone buzzes. She's gotten a text. Pls see me asap.

Ellen's heart skips a beat. It's an unusual request, especially at this time of day. She starts to text back but decides it's better to simply do as she was asked.

After another long, even more unpleasant walk through the halls, Ellen reaches her destination. James Warrick, a distinguished and still nice-looking man despite his thinning hair and middle-aged paunch, is sitting in his office behind a messy desk.

"Ellen, hi," he says when he sees her in the doorway. "That was fast. Come on in. And why don't you shut the door, please?"

Ellen does both and tries to smile.

"I haven't been called to the principal's office since I was a little girl."

She waits for James to reply, but he doesn't. Normally they have a friendly, even flirty rapport. But Ellen quickly realizes this is going to be a very different kind of conversation.

"Look, this isn't easy for me to say," James begins. "I feel awful. And I can't imagine how *you* must be feeling. But given what's happened...on behalf of the school board...I'm asking you to take some additional time off. Indefinitely."

Ellen is too stunned for a few seconds to speak. Then she stammers: "You're *asking* me? Or...you're *telling* me?"

"Parents have been calling me all week. Teachers are worried, too."

"Worried about *what*?" Ellen demands, struggling to tamp down her rising anger.

"Ellen. Be serious. How would *you* feel if the nurse at

your child's school was married to a kidnapper and attempted murderer? How can I possibly—"

"My husband is innocent until proven guilty!" Ellen snaps. "And so am I, Jim! Isn't that how our system works?"

James sighs. "Please don't make this harder than it has to be. Listen..."

He reaches for one of her hands, which have involuntarily curled into fists—but Ellen angrily yanks it away.

"I can't believe you're doing this. After everything we've been through!"

James's face softens. He wants to do the right thing by her. But he has hundreds of students, parents, and teachers to think of, too.

"I'm sorry, Ellen. You know I am. But until this whole thing blows over, there's nothing else I can do. Except wish you good luck."

CHAPTER 12

SUSPENDED, FOR NOTHING!

Stumbling out of the principal's office in a daze, Ellen truly can't believe it. Another pillar of her life has just come tumbling down.

She shudders to think what might be coming next.

After the longest, most humiliating walk through the halls yet, Ellen returns to the nurse's office and begins to gather up her belongings. Pausing briefly to eye the rows of neatly organized translucent cabinets full of medications and first-aid supplies, she gets the sudden urge to smash them all to bits in a fit of rage.

But of course she controls herself. Ellen hopes to get her job back when all this drama blows over, and going postal is a surefire way to prevent that.

So instead, she swallows her shock and shame, scoops up her purse and uneaten lunch, and scrams. James told her the substitute nurse who covered for her over the past week would be arriving within the hour. Part of Ellen feels a pang of guilt about leaving the nurse's office unattended, even for such a brief time. Yet the thought of having to face her replacement is simply too much to bear.

Ellen scurries down the hall one final time, then pushes open the school's rear exit and steps outside. The bright midday California sun makes her squint, but its rays feel warm and soothing. Small comfort, but she'll take it

Ellen starts heading to her car in the faculty lot—when she sees something that stops her in her tracks. A man with curly black hair, wearing a wrinkled blue button-down, is leaning against her Camry, scanning his smartphone and smoking a cigarette.

He looks about forty. He looks familiar, too, although Ellen can't quite put her finger on how she knows him.

Then it hits her. He's a goddamn *reporter,* one of the many who have been knocking on her door for days. So she *was* followed this morning after all!

Ellen turns back, praying he won't notice her, but it's too late.

"Mrs. Pierson, wait!" the man exclaims, tossing down his cigarette and hurrying her way. "I'm Mike Curr, with the *SLO Tribune.* I'd just like to ask you a few—"

"I said *no!*" Ellen shouts, swatting the man out of her face. "Leave me alone!"

She nearly knocks him over as she plows past him, then slides behind the wheel, starts the engine, and screeches out of the parking lot, narrowly missing a gatepost.

Racing down San Luis's quiet streets toward home,

Ellen feels a growing knot in her stomach, knowing she'll have to face a phalanx of additional reporters waiting for her. It won't take long for them to realize she was suspended, either, and plaster that across every front page in town. She just can't handle that right now.

So instead Ellen pulls a U-turn. She takes South Street to Madonna Road, then hooks a right into Laguna Lake Park. It's a lush open space, one of her favorite spots in the city. The perfect place to unwind. To decompress. To think.

Ellen turns off her cell phone, then dons a floppy beach hat and a pair of oversized sunglasses—a crude disguise, but better than nothing—and spends a few hours ambling along the scenic lakefront and the park's gently sloping trails. She passes bikers, joggers, stroller-pushing parents, even a class of first-graders on a field trip—thankfully from a different elementary school, so she doesn't know any of them or their teachers. It's relaxing, but strange and painful, too, seeing all these other people carrying on with their lives while hers lies in tatters.

Finally, with the sun edging toward the horizon, Ellen decides she's ready to go home. All she wants to do is work on her butterfly collection for a bit, then curl up in bed—and not wake up for a very, very long time.

As she nears her home, in addition to the cluster of reporters still camped out in front, she sees an official-looking white Chevy Impala parked in her driveway.

And as soon as she pulls beside it, Detectives McGrath and Petrillo step out.

McGrath has been calling her fairly regularly since last

week, but he hasn't paid a house visit since the police searched her home and dug up her backyard. So Ellen immediately knows something is afoot. She watches them order the press to back off, which she appreciates. Then she steels herself as they approach her.

"Good evening, Mrs. Pierson," McGrath says with a rakish but polite smile.

Ellen struggles to keep her composure. "Hello again. Is something wrong?" Realizing the absurdity of her words, she backtracks. "I mean, something *new*."

"No, ma'am," McGrath answers. "We just have a few more questions for you. I was going to ask you to come down to the station. But I figured you'd be more comfortable in your own home."

Comfortable. That's not something Ellen has felt all week. And she probably never will again.

"Let me ask *you* something, Detectives," she says. "Do I *have* to answer these new questions? What would happen if I refused?"

McGrath sighs and runs his callused hand through his thick mane of hair.

"And here I thought we were becoming friends."

"Friends?" Ellen scoffs. She can't hold back anymore; she lets him have it. "You think my husband is a killer. And you think I'm involved. You're trying to cozy up to me so I let down my defenses. So I slip up and give you some clue or piece of evidence you can use against us. Well, if that's what you consider friendship, you might be stranger than I thought!"

McGrath looks irritated, but Petrillo cracks up.

"You're wrong about that, Mrs. Pierson," she says. "He's a *helluva* lot stranger."

But Ellen is in no joking mood. She promptly spins on her heel and marches into her house, slamming the door shut behind her.

CHAPTER 13

ELLEN DOES NOT OPEN that door for the next five days.

She has become a shut-in. A hermit. Too overwhelmed to venture outside her house. Too scared to confront the growing horde of reporters out front. Too despondent to even change out of her pajamas.

She's been spending her days in the attic, hunched over her colorful assortment of butterflies. Sorting and cataloging, cleaning and preserving, building and polishing their glass display cases.

She's been spending her nights in a haze of red wine and tears.

For food, Ellen has been subsisting on what was already in her cupboards, mostly staples like beans and pasta and cans of tuna fish.

For company, she's been rereading her favorite romance novels and streaming old sitcom reruns. Her friends have, by and large, abandoned her, so she's stopped reaching out and unplugged her home phone. Her jailed husband still refuses to speak with her, and she's begun to give up hope on that front as well.

Tonight Ellen is curled up on the sofa, wineglass in hand, watching an ancient episode of *Married...with Children,* thinking about how dumb and insignificant Al and Peggy's marital problems seem compared to her own— when her doorbell rings.

The sound startles Ellen out of her stupor. She pauses the show and checks the clock: it's after 10:00 p.m. She certainly isn't expecting any visitors at this hour. A few reporters still bother her from time to time during the day, but never this late at night.

It must be a prank, Ellen thinks. *Or someone trying to mess with me.*

So Ellen ignores it. She's about to restart the show when the doorbell rings again. It's followed by knocking, gentle yet firm. Then a familiar man's voice.

"Ellen? It's me. I know you're in there. Can we talk? I just—I want to know how you're doing. Please open the door."

Every muscle in Ellen's body tenses. She *definitely* wasn't expecting...*him.*

Ellen considers ignoring her visitor until he gives up and goes home. But it's been days since she's had any contact with another human being. And she's moved that he thought to stop by and check on her, even if it's mostly out of guilt. She decides seeing a semi-friendly face can't hurt. Right?

"Hi, Jim," Ellen says, opening the door for the same person who, just a few days earlier, had summoned her to his office via text message and suspended her for something her *husband* had done. Tonight James's tie is loosened. His shoulders are slumped forward. And his eyes betray a concern for her that was absent earlier in the week.

"This is quite the surprise," Ellen continues. Then, suddenly embarrassed by her makeup-free face and unwashed hair, she adds: "Clearly I wasn't expecting anyone."

James offers a tender smile. "Could've fooled me. I think you look lovely."

He's a terrible liar, but Ellen appreciates the sentiment.

"I just stopped by to see how you were doing. How you were handling it all. I tried calling, but there was never any answer. Your cell, too."

Ellen remembers that her phone died a few days ago and she never bothered recharging it. She shrugs.

"I'm fine, Jim. Considering."

"Listen. I feel awful about your job. I want you to know—"

"If you really felt that bad, you wouldn't have suspended me," Ellen says, deliberately putting him on the spot.

"That's not fair," James answers. "Parents, teachers, the board—you have no idea the kind of pressure I was getting. I tried to stand up for you as much as I could."

Ellen wants to believe him. She wants desperately to have a friend right now, an ally, when the rest of the world has turned its back on her.

"Why are you *really* here, Jim?"

"I told you. I wanted to apologize. Again. And make sure you were all right."

Ellen tucks a few strands of hair behind her ear. "Thank you. I appreciate that. More than you can know." Then she adds: "Does your *wife* know where you are?"

James looks down at the doorstep. He nervously shuffles his feet.

"Now, that's *really* not fair, Ellen."

With a coy smile, she reaches out and takes James's hand.

"You know I don't always play by the rules."

CHAPTER 14

ELLEN WAKES UP IN bed—alone. She feels a bit groggy. Her head is gently throbbing. She must have had more wine last night than she realized.

After taking a moment to steady herself, she hobbles into the bathroom and does something she hasn't done all week.

Ellen takes a good, long look at her reflection in broad daylight.

It practically makes her wince.

Her glassy eyes have plum-colored bags under them. Her skin is splotchy. Her hair is greasy, tangled. She knew she'd let herself go these past few days, but not *this* far.

Okay, she thinks. *Enough. No more wallowing. Time to pull it together.*

Ellen starts by taking a scalding-hot shower for almost thirty heavenly minutes. She briefly feels guilty for wasting so much water, knowing California has been suffering a major drought. But she hasn't bathed once in nearly a full week, so it's a reasonable indulgence.

Next comes vigorous brushing—both her sticky teeth and her knotty hair.

After that, it's makeup. Normally not a vain person at all, Ellen goes to town this morning. She dusts her cheeks with pink blush. Slathers her lips a shade of ruby red. Coats her eyelids a deep forest green, adding a Cleopatra-style flourish at the edges.

Lastly come clothes. By habit, Ellen begins to put on a variation of her typical school-nurse attire: sensible khakis, a simple blouse, a comfy pair of Keds. But no. Today that just won't do. After rummaging through her closet—and forcing herself to ignore her husband's clothes at the other end—she finds an old sundress, yellow with a red floral print. She hasn't worn it in years, and frankly, it's a little short and a bit too low-cut for a woman her age.

But what the hell? Ellen thinks. *I'm doing this for nobody but me.*

And it works. Striking a pose in front of her bathroom mirror again, Ellen can't believe the transformation. She looks a thousand times better. But more importantly, she *feels* better. She feels—almost—normal again.

Ellen pads down the stairs into the kitchen and puts on a pot of coffee. Through a side window, she glimpses a few reporters still camped outside along the sidewalk. She starts to grumble under her breath...until she sees them all move aside to let a car pull into her driveway.

It's a white Chevy Impala, which she recognizes right away.

Out steps Detective McGrath. By himself. And somehow, he's gotten even better-looking since the last time she saw him—the healthy amount of salt-and-pepper scruff he's sporting gives him an extra rugged, manly air.

Ellen wasn't expecting him today, but she's not upset to see him, either. She opens the front door for McGrath before his finger can even ring the bell.

"Mrs. Pierson, I—oh, wow," he says, clearly caught off guard by her appearance, and fighting the urge to glance her up and down. "You going somewhere? You're..."

"Like a human being again?"

McGrath smiles.

"Do you mind if I come in?"

"I could use the company. But I'm guessing this isn't a social visit."

McGrath shakes his head. Of course it's not. Ellen knows *exactly* why he's here. To ask her more questions. To gather more evidence against her husband.

Ellen is soon pouring two cups of piping-hot coffee. Once again they're seated beside each other on her couch. But this time, she feels...different. She's less shell-shocked. More comfortable.

But more tingly, too.

"It's good to see you again, Detective," she says, "but I'm afraid you're wasting your time. As I've been telling you for weeks, I don't remember anything more about—"

"No, I get that, Mrs. Pierson. And the details you *have*

been able to remember about the nights of the disappearances—they've been very helpful. But today..."

McGrath takes a careful sip of his coffee, then gently sets it back down.

"...with my partner working another case, I'd like you to tell me more about your husband *generally*. The kind of man he is. How you met. The state of your marriage. That kind of thing."

"How we met? Our marriage? I don't quite see how that—"

"I don't mean to pry. I'm just trying to get a fuller picture of our suspect. Because to be frank with you, ma'am..."

McGrath leans in a bit and gives Ellen a smoldering gaze.

"...I can't for the life of me figure out why any man would ever go after a couple girls when he's got a *woman* at home like you."

Ellen shifts on the sofa. She tugs at the hem of her sundress. She doesn't know if McGrath is using his sex appeal as a new tactic, or if he's hitting on her, or both. Part of her is offended by this approach. But part of her—fine, *much* of her—is flattered.

"Well, to be honest," she says, "Michael is...a lot like *you*, Detective. Not on the outside. But he's very loyal. Focused. And determined. We met about seven years ago at a California state teachers' conference. In Sacramento. We couldn't believe we had both been living in San Luis Obispo—and working in education—for so long and hadn't met. He asked me out that night, but I said no. I had just gotten out of a rocky relationship and wasn't interested in dating yet. But Michael persisted. He kept calling me and calling me. Sound familiar? Anyway. Finally, I said yes. And I'm glad I did."

McGrath now looks at Ellen a little icily.

"You're 'glad' you went out with, then married, a serial killer?"

Ellen blushes. "You know what I mean."

"And how has your marriage been recently? Specifically, the past two years. Since the abductions began."

Ellen's eyes fall to her mug. She stares at the milk and coffee swirling together, like mini storm clouds brewing on the horizon. She begins to choke back tears.

"Every relationship has its ups and downs. But my husband always seemed like such a sweet, caring, wonderful man. I loved Michael. Even now, a tiny piece of me . . . still does. And maybe always will."

McGrath rubs a callused hand over his scruffy beard, thinking.

"Has he still not talked to you since he was arrested?"

Ellen nods, almost embarrassed.

"In that case, I have some news about him you might want to hear."

CHAPTER 15

I WONDER SOMETIMES WHAT'S really going on in their heads.

What they're really thinking about when they look up at me with those puppy-dog eyes but are so clearly talking nonsense that I can see through it a mile away.

"The turkey is burning!" my mother, Evelyn, is exclaiming.

She's rocking her ninety-five-pound, eighty-six-year-old frame back and forth in her easy chair, flailing her arms and struggling to get up.

"Ma, shhhh, relax," I coo as gently and sweetly as I can.

"And the stuffing, too! And the sweet potatoes and, and— oh, Andy, Thanksgiving is ruined, and it's all my fault!"

I place my hands on her shoulders and guide her back into her chair. I do so as delicately as if she were an antique porcelain doll.

"It's all gonna be fine, Mom. I'll take care of it, I promise. Don't worry."

This seems to settle her. It usually does.

As she and my dad have both gotten worse over the last couple years, I've found that responding to them with facts or logic or reason doesn't work. The actual words I say basically don't matter at *all* when either one of them gets like this. As long as my tone is tender and my energy is calm, I could recite the Gettysburg Address to my parents and it would chill them out and bring them back to reality.

I've just about gotten my mom soothed when I hear the toilet flush in the bathroom down the hall. Then comes my father's booming voice.

"Snap out of it, Evie!" he barks, shuffling into the living room still rebuttoning his pants. "Thanksgiving? It's March. Do you hear me? It's springtime!"

"Oh, of course it is, Leonard!" my mother snaps, waving her hands in the air like she's at a revivalist church service. "I know that. I'm talking about *next* year!"

I let out a long sigh, my patience wearing thin.

"Let's all stop with the yelling, huh?"

I love my parents. I really do. But dealing with them isn't always easy.

They refuse to move to an assisted-living home, so I'm the one who has to do the assisting in *their* home. I try to swing by as much as I can, but working overtime these last few weeks on the Pierson case has mostly kept me away. But now, here I am.

"Andy, tell your father and me more about that nice girl you met. She worked in real estate, didn't she?"

Ugh. This time I have to grit my teeth as I speak patiently and pleasantly.

"Mom, you're thinking of Kelly. We broke up two years ago. Remember?"

My mother's expression gets spacey for a few seconds as she processes this.

"You know I just want you to be happy is all."

"You deserve to have a special woman in your life, son," my dad chimes in. "Just like I do."

My mother warms and puts her bony hand on his.

"Her name is Gloria," he says. "She's a real doll. I'll introduce you sometime."

With a laugh, my mother playfully swats him. Despite myself, I chuckle, too.

But the thing is, lately, I *have* been thinking about a special new woman in my life—a helluva lot more than I thought I would be.

Her name is Ellen Anne Pierson. She sure is an intriguing creature. Married to a psychopathic, pedophilic serial killer for years and never had a clue.

Or so she says.

Except more and more, I'm really starting to believe her.

And if she *is* telling the truth, just think about what she's going through! The shock. The denial. The loneliness. The pain.

For a sweet, attractive, bighearted woman like that—a school nurse, for God's sake—it's gotta be overwhelming.

I guess I've been starting to feel sorry for her.

And maybe—Jesus, I can't believe I'm even saying this—maybe I've been starting to feel something *else* for her, too.

CHAPTER 16

"**SIR, I WILL ASK** you one more time. Do you fully understand the severity of the crimes of which you have been accused?"

When facing the formidable, no-bullshit superior court judge Linda Knier, plenty of suspects tremble in their shackles. But not Michael Pierson. That smug son of a bitch is just standing there in his orange jumpsuit, saying and doing nothing.

Hang on. Scratch that. I'm wrong. Even though I'm sitting in the very back row of the courthouse, I can make out that he's literally twiddling his thumbs.

"He does, Your Honor," answers John Kirkpatrick, Pierson's rumpled, perpetually disheveled lawyer. "And my client strongly denies any and all allegations. Furthermore, given that so much of the evidence the State has outlined against him is circumstantial at best and mere conjecture at worst, we urge the court to toss out each and every count with prejudice."

I shake my head. *Defense attorneys.*

I've encountered Kirkpatrick a few other times. He even cross-examined me once on an assault-and-battery case. By all accounts, he's a good and decent man. And I know it's wrong to condemn attorneys—especially public defenders, who don't have much say in it—for the clients they represent. But the fact that the guy can stand up there with a straight face and say Michael Pierson should walk free makes me sick to my stomach.

And apparently, most of the spectators feel the same way. His comments trigger a chorus of groans and boos from the packed gallery. These onlookers include Brittany Herbert's mother and stepfather, of course, as well as the parents of Claire, Samantha, Maria, and Patty. Black, white, Hispanic, rich, poor—the families of Pierson's victims represent a cross section of San Luis's diverse community, united in their shared grief and desire for justice.

Judge Knier holds up her hand, and the commotion simmers down.

"Thank you, Counselor," the judge responds. "But the court disagrees. I will take under advisement your motion to dismiss the ancillary counts against your client. But the primary charges against him very much still stand. A jury of Mr. Pierson's peers will decide his guilt. Your motion for bail is also denied. Defendant is to be remanded into custody until the start of trial. We are adjourned."

Crack-crack-crack goes her gavel. And just like that, the hearing is over.

Kirkpatrick tries to hastily confer with his client as a

burly bailiff cuffs Pierson and starts to cart him off, but the bastard couldn't seem to care less.

Instead, he looks back at the gallery and makes eye contact with Ellen. She's been sitting in the third row on the far left side, as still and silent as a statue. He gives her a solemn nod, and I see her quickly mouth something back to him.

Wait—that was the first time they've made contact since his arrest.

What did she say?

It looked like "Good-bye."

But it also kind of looked like "You'll die."

Or maybe: "Should I?"

Shit. This could be important. I gotta find out. Fast.

CHAPTER 17

"MRS. PIERSON, HOLD UP!"

I'm racing through the courthouse hallway after Ellen, my boots slapping against the white marble with every step. I'm already feeling out of breath, but I'm very happy I found her.

Just after Pierson was led away, Samantha Gonzalez's mother, Maria, buttonholed me and asked if there was any new evidence in her daughter's case. In the approximately 3.2 seconds it took me to politely say, in my badly broken Spanish, *"No, señora, now excusa-me,"* Ellen is gone.

Now, scurrying down the hallway, Ellen glances back at me, but she doesn't slow down. In fact, she slips on a pair of sunglasses, ties a white scarf around her head, and quickens her pace.

Is she *running* from me?

"Mrs. Pierson," I call out again, "I just wanna talk to you!"

But still she pretends to ignore me and keeps moving. Damn it!

She's pretty fast, too—until she gets caught up in a gathering crowd of reporters all hollering questions at her. In no time, they've practically got her surrounded. Poor Ellen tries to snake her way through, but she can't.

Which gives me the opportunity to snap into action.

"Police! Everybody step back!"

Hurrying over, I wave my silver badge in the air with one hand while moving the reporters aside with the other until I reach Ellen, who's now cowering, practically frozen.

"Mrs. Pierson will not be answering any questions!" I bellow. Then I drape my arm around Ellen's slender shoulders and start pushing our way through the horde like a human snowplow.

"And if any one of you keeps giving her a hard time, now *or* at her house? I will *personally* arrest you for aggravated harassment and disturbing the peace, and you will *never* get another quote or tip from the SLOPD until I retire. Anybody wanna test me? Go right ahead!"

That does the trick, all right. Even though most of these reporters are smart enough to guess I'm probably bluffing, they back off anyway and let us pass.

Once we're out of the thick of it, I steer Ellen away from the main entrance and down a side hallway.

"Wait . . . wh—where are we going?" she stammers, still overwhelmed by it all.

"I know a side exit," I tell her. "It'll spit us out right

next to the employee and law-enforcement parking lot. I'll drive you home, Mrs. Pierson, okay?"

"What about...my car?"

"I'll have it towed." With a smirk, I add: "To *your* place. It's no sweat. I'm a cop, remember?"

Ellen gives me a grateful look, along with a smile.

It's only then that I realize, even though we're far from those crazy reporters now, I've still got my arm wrapped around her.

CHAPTER 18

NOT TWENTY MINUTES LATER, I'm turning onto
Ellen's street. Her house comes into view. And she gasps.

It's an unbelievable sight.

There isn't a single reporter or news van out front anymore.

"I...I don't know how to thank you, Detective," she
says as we pull into her driveway. "They were *monsters.*"

"They just want to find the facts. Know the truth. Can't
say I blame them."

Ellen seems to get my message. When I shut off the
engine, she finally takes off the sunglasses and scarf she's
been wearing since the courthouse and turns to me.

"Is this the part where I invite you inside, and since
your partner is still working that other case, you ask me
some even *more* probing, personal questions?"

"Maybe. But let's start with one you *do* know the answer to."

"I'll try," she says moments later as I follow her into the kitchen. "That's what I mouthed to him as he was led off. *I'll try.*"

Ellen heads straight for the sink and pours herself a tall glass of water. She drinks it down in a few big gulps. She starts to fill the glass up again, then stops and opens the freezer. From the back she pulls out a half-empty bottle of Grey Goose vodka. Fancy stuff. She pours a healthy amount of *that* into her water glass and guzzles it just as fast. It seems to settle her nerves almost instantly.

"You'll try *what*?" I finally ask as she wipes her mouth with her forearm.

"To survive. To get through this nightmare. To stay strong. To move on. I think that's what Michael was trying to tell me with his look. I wanted him to know I would."

As I watch Ellen put away the vodka and rinse out her glass, I can't help but be fascinated by this strong, beautiful woman.

"Detective," she says softly, "do I ever get to ask *you* any questions?"

"You can ask me anything," I answer. "If there's something you want to know about the investigation, or police procedure, or—"

"That's not what I'm talking about. I mean, questions like . . . 'With so much crime and hate and ugliness in the world, how do you get up every morning and still do your job?' Or, 'Is there any line you *wouldn't* cross if it meant solving a crime?' "

Ever so slightly, Ellen pouts her lips.

"Or . . . 'Is there a special someone in your life?'"

This woman! If she's trying to throw me off, I will not let her succeed.

Breaking the tension, I say: "Your butterfly collection, I presume?"

I've just spotted a couple items sitting on the table on the back porch. They look like frames of some sort, beside a few bottles of paint and brushes. Without letting Ellen answer, I head out to get a better look.

"After I've cataloged and filled a new shadow box with specimens," she explains as she follows me, "I like to stain the frame. I use different colors for different woods. It's too stuffy to paint up in the attic. All the fumes. So I do it out here."

I glance out at the backyard now and see all the uneven mounds of dirt where Dr. Hyong and his team dug up the dog grave we stumbled on. It was just a few weeks ago — but it feels like ages.

Then I look back at all the colorful butterflies in their freshly stained frames.

"It really is a wonderful collection, Mrs. Pierson."

I turn to face her and look directly into her sad, tired, but still entrancing bicolored eyes.

What kind of woman, I wonder, takes pleasure in collecting dead things?

CHAPTER 19

SOMETIMES I WISH I was one of those cops who drink.

Watching Ellen chug that vodka the other night—and seeing her flooded with such instant relief—actually made me a little jealous. Sure, I'll have a beer or two or four with some pals once in a while, but the hard stuff just isn't my style. Which is why my liquor cabinet looks so pathetic. Rifling through the couple of dusty bottles in it from God-knows-when, none of them really appeals to me.

Except that Macallan 25-Year-Old Sherry Oak. It's the gift all the guys in the department got me years ago, right after I got my detective's shield. It's the extra-extra-good shit I'm only "allowed" to pour after I've solved a murder case.

That's the drink I'm dying to have right now.

After almost five weeks since Pierson's arrest, I'm more convinced of his guilt than ever...but I'm still no closer to finding those other girls.

I know I should be focusing more on the case. Me and Gina should be out there hunting down more leads. Scouring the town and woodlands for more clues.

But instead, all I can think about is Ellen.

The goddamn killer's *wife*.

She's such an enigma. The more time I spend with her, the less I get her.

Most of the time, she seems like an open book. But every once in a while, I feel like she's hiding something, even though I can't put my finger on it. I can't tell if she's as steely as she seems, or as delicate as one of her butterflies.

But either way, there's something about her that's simply...intoxicating.

Jesus, McGrath, stop it. You're talking crazy!

I finally cave and grab a grimy old bottle of Jack Daniel's that's probably been sitting in my cabinet since the first George Bush administration. I slosh a bit into a tumbler and shoot it back—and nearly gag.

Can hard alcohol go bad?

Can an *innocent woman* go bad?

CHAPTER 20

AFTER HER SCUFFLE WITH that horde of reporters outside the courtroom—which ended only thanks to her white knight, Detective McGrath—Ellen thought her war against the press was over.

She had no idea it was about to get worse.

By the following morning, even *more* members of the media appeared in front of her home. The courthouse episode seemed to energize them, not discourage them. They took to knocking on Ellen's door at all hours of the day and night, preventing her from getting any decent sleep. (Maybe this was a deliberate tactic to wear her down.) Even just opening the blinds to peek outside for a few seconds subjected her to a hail of screams and taunts.

If Ellen was afraid to leave her house before, now she was terrified.

On more than one occasion, she thought about calling McGrath. She assumed he hadn't been serious about his threat, but she figured he would at least keep an eye on her place. Come to think of it, she hadn't heard from him since that day. Had he gotten too busy? Had he lost interest in her as a source of information? Or had the unexpected intimacy of their last conversation spooked him and pushed him away?

It doesn't matter. With or without him, Ellen knows she can't keep living this way, a prisoner in her own home. And as the start date of her husband's trial draws closer, this hell will only get worse—unless she puts an end to it now. Herself.

Standing in her kitchen, so bone-tired that she's brewing a rare pot of midday coffee, Ellen knows what she has to do. A simple act of defiance to show the press who's boss. She flips off the gas, opens her freezer, and downs the remaining few gulps of Grey Goose straight from the bottle—a little liquid courage that she very much needs.

Then she unlocks her front door and steps outside.

"Mrs. Pierson! Any comment on your husband's charges?"

"Will you ever apologize to the families of his victims?"

"Do you plan to stand by that monster's side at trial or divorce the bastard?"

The questions come fast and hard, hurled like rocks and glass bottles by an angry mob. Ellen's instinct is to duck and hurry back inside, but she resists it with every ounce of her strength.

"Will your husband be mounting an insanity defense, Mrs. Pierson?"

"Can you confirm reports he's been put on suicide watch?"

"How could you live with him for so long and have no idea who he really was?"

Ellen still refuses to take the bait. *I can do this,* she thinks.

Keeping her head held high, she walks calmly down her driveway, past her car, then steps onto the sidewalk. Now that she's on public property, the reporters swarm around her like vultures, surrounding her on all sides.

Still, she forges on, moving slowly and steadily down the block. But then the questions begin to get even worse. The reporters are growing frustrated by her silence and are desperate to get a rise out of her.

"How do you respond to claims that you knew about your husband's crimes and kept quiet?"

"If you're really innocent, why won't the police leave you alone?"

"Is it true you helped him pick his victims out of the yearbook and were there when he killed them?"

Ellen feels her lip start to quiver now. Her hands ball into fists. The notion that she had *anything* to do with what happened to those young women is sickening. Humiliating. And infuriating.

She feels the urge to start screaming at those vicious reporters to be quiet, to leave her alone, to show a little human decency. But making a scene when a dozen cameras are rolling is the *last* thing she needs.

Ellen walks faster now, keeping her eyes straight ahead. *Let me just make it once around the block,* she thinks. *Just give me that tiny victory. Please.*

But the reporters smell blood in the water.

"Did you and your husband get off on hearing those poor girls scream?"

"Where the hell are the bodies, Mrs. Pierson? Where did you bury them?"

And that's it. All Ellen can take. The final straw.

But instead of having a meltdown in the middle of the street, she turns and starts to run. Shoving the reporters out of her way, she races back home.

Once back inside, she slams her front door, locking and bolting it. Then she collapses in a heap of tears right there in her entryway.

McGrath. He's the only one who might even begin to understand what she's going through. He's the only one who'd listen if she called him. Ellen crawls toward her kitchen, toward her cell phone, resting on the counter. All she has to do is pick it up and dial to hear a friendly voice, to see a friendly face, to—

No. She can't. She won't.

At least not yet.

CHAPTER 21

NIGHTFALL IN THE HILLS of San Luis Obispo is a quiet, peaceful time. It's one of the things Ellen has always loved most about living here.

But tonight, she finds the silence outside her home deafening.

She's been tossing and turning for hours. The two tall tumblers of Scotch she had made her fuzzy but not sleepy. The old sitcom reruns she tried watching were agitating, not distracting. And now, a few minutes before 3:00 a.m., Ellen feels the walls of her little home closing in on her. She can't breathe. She needs to get out. Get some oxygen. This instant.

Those damn reporters camped outside can go to hell.

Ellen bolts out of bed. She throws on a pair of jeans and a black sweater. She ties her wild mane of hair in a sloppy bun. Then she grabs her car keys and, before she has time to change her mind, bursts out her front door toward her Camry.

This unexpected development clearly catches the sleepy press off guard. Which was exactly Ellen's intent. "Hey, she's going somewhere!" one of them shouts as Ellen starts her engine and peels out, the squeal of her tires piercing the quiet night.

Free at last!

Ellen tears down her street, blowing past the homes of all her dozing neighbors, who have long since shunned her. She rolls down all her car's windows and lets the cool air hit her face from every side. It's exactly the kind of refreshment she needs.

Ellen applies the brakes as she approaches a yellow light at the intersection of Andrews Street and Monterey. She flips on her turn signal to make a left, even though she doesn't know exactly where she's going. For now, she just wants to drive and enjoy the freedom of the open road.

After a few seconds stopped at the red light, however, that freedom disappears.

In her rearview mirror, Ellen spots a small caravan of cars and news vans speeding toward her. Those goddamn reporters are following her!

Ellen furiously pounds her steering wheel. *Come on!*

But no. This time, she is *not* going to give in to them. Not a chance.

Making sure the intersection is clear, Ellen blows right through the stoplight, crossing Monterey Street and heading onto Grand Avenue. Most of the press is still stopped at the red, but damn it—a few run the light, too, and keep following!

Gotta get away, Ellen thinks as she barrels along this four-lane thoroughfare. *Gotta shake them!* But how?

Up ahead, Ellen sees signs for on-ramps to the 101. Which gives her an idea.

She knows it's crazy... but she also knows that at 3:00 a.m. on a weeknight, the freeway should be practically empty. And if she happens to get pulled over, well, she's been growing chummy lately with a certain SLOPD detective who could probably help her get off with just a warning.

Ellen takes another look behind her and sees two local news vans and three other cars on Grand Avenue, coming up fast. So she decides it's worth a shot.

Making a wildly sharp left to head southbound—via the *off-ramp*—Ellen is soon racing down the freeway... in the wrong direction!

Honk-honk-hoooooonk!

Horns blare and tires screech as the few cars that *are* on the freeway at this hour brake and swerve like crazy to avoid plowing into her.

Ellen quickly gets over to the shoulder. She flashes her brights and honks her own horn as a warning to other oncoming vehicles, but she doesn't slow down one bit.

Soon she's pushing forty-five miles per hour, which is about as fast as she feels safe driving in this insane condition. But she knows it will be only a matter of minutes before one of the stunned drivers she passes calls 911. So she'll have to get off the freeway as soon as possible.

The hard part, though, is over. She checks her rearview

mirror. Not a single news van or reporter's car is following her! None of them had the balls, which fills Ellen with a burst of pride.

She keeps driving, the wind roaring through her Camry, the cacophony of horn-honking never stopping.

Up ahead, finally, Ellen sees an exit. The sign is facing the other direction, of course, but she knows it's for California Boulevard. The off-ramp gets closer...closer...

But Ellen steers clear of it. It would spit her out too close to the Grand Avenue off-ramp she used. And the press might be expecting her to do that. They might very well be there waiting for her. Definitely not worth the risk.

So Ellen continues speeding along. Her sweaty hands stay glued to the wheel. Her steely gaze stays fixed straight ahead. Her icy resolve stays as strong as ever.

She passes another exit, Santa Rosa Street. Then a third, Osos Street. Ellen considers driving even farther this way, possibly out of town—

But then she hears a distant police siren.

Shit!

Okay. No more time to mess around. The next exit is for Broad Street, and Ellen decides she has no choice but to take it.

Pumping the brakes as she nears it, she pulls a wide, insanely dangerous U-turn across the two right lanes. Scraping the side of her Camry against the guardrail, she accelerates down the off-ramp and onto this sleepy residential street.

Ellen heads a few blocks down, then finally pulls over,

stopping under the cover of a giant oak tree. She shuts off her engine. She leans her head back.

And she lets out a long, guttural scream.

Adrenaline is surging through her body. Tears are leaking from her eyes.

How the hell did this happen to her life?

But for right now...what the hell does she do next?

CHAPTER 22

SLEEP. BLESSED SLEEP. That's what Ellen needs most right now.

As if she weren't exhausted enough from the stressful hell of the past few weeks, her pulse-pounding drive the wrong way down the 101 has left her drained, both physically and emotionally.

And now, the sound of that faraway police siren seems to be drawing closer.

Ellen holds her breath. She clenches her fists. She says a silent prayer.

Finally, the siren passes, fading into the quiet night.

Ellen exhales in relief, then starts to consider her next move. She *could* get back on the freeway—heading in the right direction this time—and keep going, out of SLO. But where? And what would that accomplish? If anything, it would look like she was running away, and that would give the press even more reason to hound her.

"Those bloodsucking creeps!" Ellen screams out loud inside her car.

A small army of them are certainly still camped outside her house, waiting to pounce. If she dared go home now, especially at this ungodly hour, after leading them on that high-speed chase? The scene would be sheer chaos. Not very conducive to a good night's sleep.

So if Ellen can't skip town but can't go home yet, either, what now?

She gets an idea and shifts her Camry back into drive.

A few turns later, she's cruising in the direction of the freeway again, more or less retracing her path, but on surface streets. Eventually she starts driving through a residential neighborhood, nestled in the foothills, where there isn't another car or person on the road at all. The solitude is calming but also eerie. Unsettling.

Ellen glances down at her dashboard clock: 3:51 a.m. With a shake of her head, she tries to remember the last time she was out and about this late. Even when she and Michael used to celebrate New Year's Eve together at the old Moonbeam Lounge downtown, their one big night a year to let loose and drink and dance and act like kids again, they were always back home and in bed by one o'clock at the very latest.

Tonight, Ellen has been *run out* of her home. And Michael's bed is a cot in the county jail. How quickly life can change.

After passing a block of modest adobe-style houses, Ellen pulls into the driveway of an old-fashioned motor inn, the El Toro Motel, the building small and quaint and painted a light cantaloupe. Seeing a flickering neon sign out front advertising VACANCY, Ellen parks her car in one of the many open spaces and heaves her tired body out.

She pushes open the lobby door. As it swings shut, a set of old sleigh bells attached to the knob jangles. Inside, the air is air-conditioned cool, but smells faintly of marijuana. Ellen immediately spots the likely source: a young man slouching behind the front desk, his nose buried in his smartphone, his eyes at half-mast and bloodshot.

Ellen has a hunch this twenty-something stoner— CARSON C., according to his name tag—isn't about to give her a world-class customer-service experience. But that's just fine by her. Better than fine, actually. Between his youth, his slovenliness, and his likely altered state, the chances of him *recognizing* her are slim to none. Which is something Ellen definitely doesn't want right now.

"Excuse me, Carson?" she asks, after standing there unseen by the man for nearly thirty whole seconds.

"Oh, sorry . . . can I, uh, help you?" he finally mumbles.

Ellen requests a room for the night. Carson tells her that checkout is at 10:00 a.m., meaning she'd have it for only about five and a half hours. Ellen thinks about that and changes her request.

"Two nights, then, please. Under the name Judith Hayes."

Using an alias gives Ellen a quick shiver of excitement, as if she were a spy or undercover agent. But that was the name of her maternal grandmother, a woman she loved dearly, and using it now also provides her a tiny bit of comfort.

"Sure thing, ma'am. I just, like, need a credit card?"

Ellen opens her purse and removes a thick wad of bills instead.

"How about cash?"

Key in hand, Ellen shuffles down the walkway to room 4.

Four—oh, great, Ellen thinks. That's the number of girls who have gone missing. The number her husband stands accused of kidnapping and murdering.

Ellen hesitates before unlocking her room. She debates whether to go back and ask Carson for a different one, one that won't remind her of—

No. Forget it. She's just seconds away from passing out anyway, so Ellen opens the door, locks the bolt behind her, and without even turning on the lights, literally collapses face-first onto the queen-size bed.

In her final few moments awake, an image of Detective McGrath flashes through Ellen's mind. He'll probably be waking up soon for work, she thinks. He'll be told about her daring late-night "escape" from her own home, and her reckless driving down the freeway, too. He might even guess her alias and figure out what motel she's staying at.

McGrath might then pay her private room a visit.

And maybe a part of Ellen wants him to.

CHAPTER 23

ELLEN WAKES UP IN the exact same position: face-down on the bed, arms slightly akimbo, feet and calves dangling off the edge. Only now, her sparse little motel room is flooded with morning sunlight.

Ellen peels herself off the itchy maroon bedspread and looks around, squinting, and fighting off the faintest feeling of nausea. Just like the outside of the motel, the walls are painted a pale orange. *The color of vomit,* Ellen can't help but think. And although San Luis Obispo is land-locked, the room is decorated with a maritime theme. A bland watercolor of an anonymous beach is over the bed. A cheap print of a nineteenth-century whaling vessel hangs next to the dusty TV, slightly askew.

Ellen stumbles into the bathroom and splashes her face with cool water. She gargles some, hoping to flush the sour taste from her mouth. In the process, she gets the briefest glimpse of her ghostly appearance in the mirror—and quickly looks away.

Debating what to do next, Ellen gives her motel room

a once-over. Other than a few creases in the bedcovers, it looks completely untouched, as if she'd never been there at all. As if all the pain and stress and anger she felt last night never even existed. As if it *were* all right to head back home—which is what Ellen decides to do.

Next to a decorative glass starfish paperweight on the nightstand sits an ancient clock radio. The time is 10:05 a.m. Which makes Ellen grimly chuckle. She paid for this room for a whole extra night and has ended up needing it for only an extra three hundred seconds.

Maybe I'll keep it anyway, she thinks. *Just in case.*

Ellen locks the door behind her, then gets into her Camry and pulls out of the El Toro's parking lot. Some twenty minutes later, she's rounding the corner onto her block. And the scene is an absolute zoo, the street and sidewalk in front of her home crammed with more reporters and news vans than ever before.

Just as Ellen starts considering making a U-turn and heading back to the motel, she sees a familiar white Impala parked in her driveway. And there's good old Detective McGrath again, leaning against the hood, talking on his cell phone. When he spots Ellen's approaching car, he quickly hangs up. Ellen knows she can't turn around now. And part of her doesn't want to anymore.

"Mrs. Pierson, where did you go last night?"

"Were you thinking about running away because you're guilty?"

The reporters' questions again come flying at her fast and hard the moment Ellen steps out of her vehicle. But just as fast, McGrath is next to her. He lays a comforting hand on her shoulder and draws her close to him, shielding Ellen from the verbal assault and speaking softly into her ear.

"Hey...you doing okay?" he asks.

"Yes, I suppose. I've been running errands all morning, just trying to—"

"Because I was having some trouble sleeping last night, not an uncommon problem for me, either, when I heard a call come over the radio. A car was spotted driving wildly down the 101, the wrong way. Female driver. The descriptions of both sounded familiar. But she somehow slipped away. Crazy, huh?"

Ellen nods solemnly, realizing now why McGrath is there. She braces herself for what will be coming next: handcuffs and further humiliation in front of the rabid press.

"If you're here to arrest me, Detective, just go ahead and—"

"Arrest you?" McGrath asks, the faintest twinkle in his deep-set eyes. "For what? I just swung by to make sure you are okay."

Ellen flushes with relief—and decides to extricate herself as quickly as possible.

"I'm fine, Detective. Thank you. No need to worry. Now, if you'll excuse me..."

Ellen shrugs off McGrath's touch and starts to hurry inside, averting her gaze.

She doesn't want the detective to know how she *really* feels.

CHAPTER 24

"WAIT," I CALL OUT to Ellen as she rushes past me toward her front door. "Just promise me you won't ever do anything that stupid again."

Ellen stops and spins around to face me but still won't look me in the eye.

"Why? Are you afraid I might die, and you'll lose all that precious evidence in *here*?" She taps the side of her head, a little tauntingly.

Despite the crowd of reporters at the end of the driveway, their cameras watching our every move, I feel the sudden urge to grab Ellen's shoulders and give them a violent shake. *Of course that's what I'm afraid of!* I want to shout. *What the hell are you hiding from me?*

But instead, I say gently, "I want you safe, Mrs. Pierson. For a lot of reasons. Is that so hard to understand?"

Ellen nods and finally looks me in the eye.

"I do understand," she says. "I'm just not sure if I believe you. Or if I trust you." She pauses, then asks, "I *want* to trust you, Detective McGrath, but should I?"

I've had similar doubts about Ellen's honesty since the moment we met. I'm usually damn good at reading people, too. But these past few weeks, the more I've gotten to know the intriguing, alluring Ellen Pierson — the low-key wife of one of the most despicable killers I've ever put away — the more mysterious she's become.

"For someone with those kinds of doubts," I say, "you seem pretty willing to keep talking to me."

Even though you never actually say a damn thing, I think.

Ellen smiles and tucks a few errant strands of hair behind her left ear.

"Maybe... maybe that's because I *like* talking to you."

I look back at all the reporters crowded up and down the sidewalk, jostling to get the best position, their cameras and microphones pointed at us like weapons.

"There's another pretrial hearing today in your husband's case. Starts in less than an hour, actually. I guess you're not going?"

Ellen bites her lip. And shakes her head.

"Just take care of yourself, Mrs. Pierson. Okay? No more late-night joyrides on the freeway. No more disappearing on me. I need you to be—"

Ellen takes a sudden step toward me, getting right up in my face.

I flinch, caught off guard—and reach for my sidearm. But Ellen is too fast.

She leans in and plants a kiss on my cheek.

I'm too startled to pull away. But I hear the reporters

going wild, hurling questions at us, their cameras *click-click-click*ing like a swarm of angry cicadas.

"I—I'm sorry, Detective," Ellen says, backing away now. "I don't know what came over me."

I'm feeling equally flustered. Maybe more so.

"Bye, Mrs. Pierson," I mutter, and get back in my car as quick as I can.

CHAPTER 25

THIS TIME, I REALLY stepped in it.

After leaving's Ellen's place, I decided to skip the hearing, drive around town for a little while, then head back to the station. I was feeling so...*thrown* by the whole episode. So confused. Pierson wasn't going to be in court today anyway—just his public defender, Kirkpatrick, and the state prosecutor squabbling over some pretrial motions. I could use that extra time to catch up with my partner, get ahead on some paperwork, and think.

But as soon as I step into the bullpen, I realize I've made a big mistake.

Nobody says a word, but I can feel the judgmental glares of every officer, sergeant, and fellow detective I pass boring right through me.

"What the hell were you thinking, man?" Gina demands before I even sit down at my desk. "You see the *Tribune* yet?"

With dread, I fire up the website of San Luis Obispo's local paper.

Sure enough, the home page's lead headline reads: SLO COP LOCKS UP SUSPECT, LOCKS LIPS WITH SUSPECT'S WIFE.

And below it, in full color, is a giant picture of me and Ellen caught in the act.

"She kissed *me,* okay?" I insist to my partner, who's more pissed off than I've ever seen her. Not that I can blame her. "And it was on the cheek, for godsakes. You can see it right there in the photo."

"Tell me *why,* Andy," Gina says. "Is there something going on between you two? Something I gotta know about? Are you sleeping with this woman?"

"Christ, no," I answer. "She's lonely is all. Scared. Confused. And I'm the only one in this town who's still willing to talk to her. Maybe Ellen's developing a...a little *thing* for me. I don't know. I can't help the powerful effect I have on women sometimes."

Gina smirks and tosses one of her empty Red Bulls into the trash.

"This could actually be a blessing in disguise," I continue. "Think about it. The more she trusts me, the more she might tell me. Might be the only chance of finding those girls alive that we've got."

Gina is about to respond when her cell phone rings. She checks the ID.

"Hmm. It's my guy at the courthouse. Hold that depressing thought."

Gina picks up. She listens. She shakes her head with quiet fury. She hangs up.

Then she shares the terrible news she's just learned.

Son of a bitch!

Now it's my turn to place a call. To Ellen Pierson.

The line rings and rings. It goes to her voicemail, which an electronic voice informs me is completely full. I angrily hang up and dial again. This time she answers.

"Detective McGrath, I'm glad you called. What happened earlier, I—"

"That's not what this is about," I snap, struggling to control my simmering rage.

I don't want to push Ellen away. I need her on my side right now more than ever.

"They just threw out all four murder charges against your husband."

"Wait...what?"

"Without a murder weapon, without any eyewits, without the girls' *bodies,* Judge Knier ruled that there's not enough evidence. Michael's only going be tried for Brittany Herbert's abduction and *attempted* murder. That's it."

I pause for a moment to let that sink in and to hear Ellen's response.

"Well...at least he'll go to prison for *something.* That's good, right?"

"No, Mrs. Pierson, it's *not* good!" I explode. "He's a cold-blooded killer. I want justice for Claire, Samantha, Maria, and Patty. I want your husband to pay!"

There's an even longer pause on the line now. I use it

to try to slow my sharp breathing and lower my soaring blood pressure.

After what feels like an eternity, Ellen finally speaks again.

"Come over again tonight," she says. "Anytime after sunset. Use the back door. Not the front. There's something I want to give you."

CHAPTER 26

ELLEN WOULD BE HARD-PRESSED to name her favorite butterfly. She admires every species and type. But there are some in her vast collection that she particularly cherishes. Like her rare Kaiser-i-Hind, native to India and Nepal, with its brilliant green-and-gold coloring. Or her South American glasswing, whose delicate wings are literally translucent, like tiny panes of glass.

But it's her European peacock that Ellen has always felt a special kinship with. Seen from below, its wings look as boring as tree bark: speckled, rusty brown. Yet viewed from above, they are a stunning pattern of red, yellow, and blue.

Which side is the "real" one? They both are. Which is what Ellen likes so much. It's all a matter of perspective. The butterfly possesses some strange contradictions.

Just like she does.

Ellen is currently using a pair of tweezers and a magnifying loupe to inspect this beloved specimen. Outside, the sun is going down; it's starting to get dark. So with her free hand, she flips on the lamp beside her attic workstation to get a better view.

When suddenly, she hears a faint knocking.

It's coming from downstairs.

And not from the front door, but the back.

A shiver of anticipation buzzes through Ellen's body. She carefully sets down her European peacock and shuts its glass case. Then she goes to greet her visitor.

Detective McGrath is standing on the rear patio, fidgeting slightly, backlit by the setting sun. The sky behind him is a blend of lavender purple and bubble-gum pink.

Ellen takes a moment to compose herself. She smooths down her hair and flattens the imaginary wrinkles in her simple blouse. Then she opens the door.

"Well, I'm here," he says. "Wanna tell me what this is all about? I really don't like surprises."

"Good evening, Detective," she says. "Thank you for coming. Would you like to come inside?"

"I don't know, Ellen," he huffs. "Would I?"

Ellen smiles demurely, but on the inside she's burning up. In all the weeks they've been getting to know each other, McGrath has always called her Mrs. Pierson. Ellen takes his casual use of her first name as a very good sign.

"I think you *do* want to come in," she replies. "Very much."

Growing hesitant, McGrath checks behind him and looks around, making sure the coast is clear. Unless a reporter is hiding in her bushes, it seems that they're alone.

At last McGrath steps inside. He shuts the door behind him.

Then he turns back to face Ellen. Stares into her eyes.
And suddenly, they're kissing.

It's so much more this time than just a quick peck. It's
deep. Raw. Electric.

Passionate.

It goes on for quite some time, their hands clawing at
each other, their breath quickening—until it becomes too
much. Certainly for McGrath. Maybe Ellen, too.

Just as suddenly, they both pull away, shocked and
bashful.

"I—I'm sorry," McGrath says. "That was completely
unprofessional."

"It's all right, Detective. I don't know what came over
me, either."

McGrath rubs a shaking hand over his scruffy cheek.

"At this point," he says softly, "you can probably start
calling me Andy."

"Okay, then . . . *Andy*," Ellen replies a little playfully, en-
joying how the name rolls off her tongue. "Here's what I
wanted to give you, *Andy*."

From her back pocket she removes a blank, sealed envelope and holds it out to him.

"What is it?" McGrath asks.

Ellen says nothing, so McGrath snaps on a pair of latex
gloves and plucks it from her grasp. He can feel that there
isn't a letter inside, but something else. Something small.
Pointy. Heavy for its size. McGrath begins to tear the envelope open when Ellen touches his gloved hands.

"No," she says. "Later."

CHAPTER 27

"DON'T PUT THAT SHIT in my mouth—it'll kill me!"

"It's applesauce, Pop, not arsenic," I say, clenching my jaw so tight that I'm afraid my jugular is about to burst. "And I'm a homicide detective, remember? If and when the day comes that I decide to put you and Ma out of your misery, I know about a hundred better ways to do it than hiding poison in your dessert. Okay?"

My father's flash of anger slowly disappears and turns into dark laughter. He gives me a good-natured jab to the shoulder as I finish spooning the yellow mush into his toothless mouth.

"Now let's get you ready for bed, huh?"

I lead my old man up the stairs and into the bathroom. I help him change into his pajamas, wash his face, moisturize his skin, and take his evening pills. Then I lead him into his bedroom, where my mother—always much more of a morning person than my night-owl dad—has already been asleep for over an hour.

I pull back the covers on my father's side and start to guide his frail frame into bed, when he suddenly reaches out and grabs my arm.

"Thank you, son," he whispers. "Andy...what would we do without you?"

"Aw, Pop. Let's hope we never have to find out. For both our sakes. G'night."

I pad softly back down the stairs. In the kitchen, I load my parents' dinner plates into the dishwasher. In the living room, I straighten up the throw pillows on the couch.

In the entryway, I reach into my pocket and pull out the envelope Ellen gave me, which I tore open the second I got back to my car.

Inside was a single metal key attached to a fob with the words EL TORO ~ RM 4 printed on it in faded, old-fashioned lettering.

First I make out with her...then she slips me the key to her motel room?

Jesus, what the hell am I doing?

I hold the key in my hand, feeling the cold, hard metal against my palm—and remembering Ellen's warm, soft lips against my own.

There's a chance I'm misreading this whole situation. A small one, but still. Ellen could be trying to tell me that the El Toro played some role in Pierson's crimes. Maybe room 4 is where he took those girls and killed them. Maybe their bodies are buried under the floorboards. Maybe Pierson had an accomplice, and the guy is holed up there right now, waiting, armed and dangerous.

Oh, come on. Who the hell am I kidding?

This has nothing to do with the murders at all. It's strictly personal.

If I were smart—and if this were a more typical case—I'd ask the San Luis County SWAT team to set up a perimeter and breach the El Toro, just to be safe. At the very least, I'd tell my partner about the key. Log it into evidence.

What I wouldn't be doing is going to the motel alone and actually *using* it.

Which is what I'm seriously considering. I know I shouldn't... *but should I?*

My cell phone suddenly rings, startling me out of my deliberations. I check the ID. *Great.* I can't dodge this call any longer. I have to take it. So I do.

"Well, shit, man, forget you have a partner?" Gina says. I can hear her sarcasm has a slight edge to it tonight. "I've been calling you for the past three hours."

"Yeah, right, sorry," I say. "My phone died, then I had to give my folks dinner, then I—"

"Whatever, it's fine. Your visit with Pierson's wife—don't leave me hanging. What did she wanna give you? And I just ate, so if it was some kind of freaky sex act, keep it G-rated, please."

"Funny," I say—with a gulp.

I look down again at the old key in my hand. In all the years I've known my partner, I've never lied to her. Not once. Honestly, I trust this woman with my life.

But can I trust her with *this?*

"Nothing," I finally say. "Ellen was full of it. Maybe the charges being dropped against her husband rattled her. I don't know. She just wanted somebody to talk to."

"Hey, Andy, are you okay? You sound distracted or something."

"Me? I'm good, Gina. Just tired. Thanks. Let's talk in the morning."

I hang up, feeling like a total piece of shit. But I've made my decision.

Now I gotta live with the consequences.

CHAPTER 28

MY IMPALA'S HEADLIGHTS ILLUMINATE the El Toro's peach-orange facade as I pull into the parking lot. I take a spot on the far end of it, cut my engine, and pause to think.

I still have a chance here to back out. To go home.

To *not* sleep with the goddamn killer's wife!

Instead, as if my body is on autopilot, I get out of my car and march up to 4.

I knock, then wait for a reply. Which never comes. So I try to turn the key—but the lock sticks. Shit. Is this the right place? The right door? The right move?

I try the key again. This time, the lock clicks open.

Stepping into the dark little room, I can sense it's empty even before I flip on the lights. It's cozy in here, but creepy, too. The nautical artwork on the walls is plenty tacky. And the maroon bedspread is plenty ugly—and the color of dried blood.

As I wait for Ellen, my mind starts trying to work

backward, posing way more questions than I can answer. When did she book this place? Last night, when she went for that crazy drive down the freeway? Or earlier? And at what point did she decide to give me the key? I called the motel from the car, but the guy at the front desk told me no one by the name of Ellen Pierson had checked in recently at all. Makes sense she'd want to use a pseudonym. But what else is she hiding from me?

And where the hell *is* she, anyway? What kind of one-sided rendezvous is this?

I pull my cell from my pocket and start to dial Ellen's number—when I stop myself. Come on. It's not like she *forgot*. If she's coming tonight...she'll be here.

I wander around the room a bit, looking for any tiny details that could prove helpful, treating it like a possible crime scene, not a love nest. At least for now. This also helps occupy my mind and ease the butterflies in my stomach. But the room looks so untouched, I wonder if Ellen has even stepped foot in here before.

I adjust the crooked whaling-ship painting near the TV. Then I check my watch. It's nearly eleven; I've been waiting for almost half an hour. And I'm starting to get a little sleepy. So I sit down on the bed. Ellen could walk in any minute, and we'll probably end up on the bed anyway...

Jesus, this is so wrong!

A few more minutes pass. I lean back against the headboard, propping myself up with a few pillows. My eyelids are getting heavier, so I rest them for just a moment.

Next thing I know, I'm startled awake by my ringing

cell phone. I fumble to answer it—noticing some predawn sunlight peeking in through the curtains.

"Gina, hey," I say groggily. "Everything okay? What time is it? You're calling so early."

"It's me, Detective. I mean...*Andy.*"

Ellen's voice hits me like a shot of espresso. I'm instantly wide awake.

"Where are you?" she asks. "I need to see you. Right away."

I can't help but scoff, feeling stood up.

"I thought that was the plan last night," I answer.

"I'm sorry. I lost track of the time. I never—"

"And I think you know exactly where I am. Where I *still* am."

I can tell that Ellen is trying to stifle a big smile.

"You...you really waited for me? The whole night?"

I don't tell her that most of the night I was fast asleep.

"Look, it's probably for the best this way. What's up *now*?"

Ellen takes a deep breath. "I have something else I need to give you."

This freaking woman! Messing with my head. Toying with my heart.

"Tough shit, Ellen. You had your chance. I'm not falling for that again."

"Please, Andy," she begs. "This is different. I was up all night going through my husband's things. I think it might be important for your case. *Very* important. I swear."

I hate these kinds of games. And I'm quickly running out of patience.

But I need this woman. To put Pierson away.

And I *want* this woman. And Ellen knows it, too.

"Tell me what it is first. Then I'll decide."

"I would, Andy," Ellen replies. "But you wouldn't believe me."

CHAPTER 29

HERITAGE OAKS BANK: a squat, redbrick building in the middle of downtown San Luis Obispo. If Ellen's hunch is right, this unassuming spot might be where this whole case is finally blown wide open.

I swung by her house again after we hung up. Like she asked, I didn't bother getting out or even turning off my engine. She hopped right into my car and said, "Just drive," hoping to throw the press off our tail.

Once we were a few blocks away, she handed me what she'd found.

Another key.

"For crying out loud, Ellen!" I snapped. "I thought we were past this."

"Look closer," she said. "It's not a motel room. It's a safe-deposit box."

Ellen explained that right after they got married, she and Pierson rented a box together at Heritage Oaks to store their marriage license, various other documents, and a couple pieces of jewelry she'd received as wedding presents. A few years later, after they bought a locked filing cabinet for the house, she and her husband gave the box up.

At least, Pierson *told* her they gave it up.

Ellen was moving a pair of her husband's shoes that night when she heard something rattling around. She grabbed a screwdriver, pried off the sole, and hidden inside the hollowed-out heel was the old, familiar key.

I have no way of verifying a word of that story, of course. And after last night, I don't exactly trust Ellen much anymore. But an opportunity like this—I can't pass it up.

We're sitting in silence together, parked across the street, waiting for 9:00 a.m. to strike and the bank to open up. From the corner of my eye, I watch as Ellen takes a dainty sip of the steaming cup of coffee I bought her. Stood up or not, I'm still a gentleman.

"That looks like the manager," I say, noticing a comely middle-aged woman with jet-black hair unlock the front door and roll up the metal gate. "They're open. Let's go."

Ellen and I head into the bank so fast, the manager has barely had time to sit down at her desk. Noticing a name placard on it—ALEXANDRA GARCIA—I hold up my badge and call out: "Excuse me, Ms. Garcia? Urgent police business, please."

I bring her up to speed on our situation. But this lady is smart. The moment I mention Pierson's safe-deposit box, she shrugs apologetically and says, "I'm afraid you'll need a warrant to access it, Detective."

"Not if I've got the consent of one of the box's co-lessees," I reply, gesturing to Ellen. Reluctantly, Garcia looks up the agreement on her computer. Sure enough, it's still in both Michael Pierson's *and* Ellen Pierson's names. Bingo.

Garcia leads us into the main vault room, a claustrophobic space lined with metal boxes from floor to ceiling. She inserts her manager's key into one slot, I put Ellen's into the other, and the shoebox-sized steel container slides right out.

"I'll leave you two alone," she says, and does just that.

Snapping on a pair of latex evidence gloves, I consider asking Ellen to scram as well. But I can see she's just as eager to see what's inside as I am.

Carefully I lift up and remove the top.

Inside is an old cigar box, the kind I used to keep my baseball-card collection in when I was a kid. But the lid is sealed shut with duct tape. Great. Using a different key from my own keychain—the house key to my parents' place—I slice through the tape.

And I open the cigar box.

"Oh, my God!" Ellen gasps. "No, no . . . no!" She covers her face with her hands and crumples to the floor in sobs. "I didn't want to believe it. It can't be true!"

My reaction is far more controlled, but I'm just as stunned as she is.

Inside the box is a small stack of pictures. They look

like they were taken on a cell phone or digital camera but printed out on typing paper from a personal printer.

I sift through them, delicately, almost numbly.

The terrified, bloodied faces of those four missing girls—Claire, Samantha, Maria, and Patty—are staring back up at me.

CHAPTER 30

KEEP IT. MAYBE I'LL *take another drive tonight.*

Those are the words Ellen leaned over and sensually whispered to me as I dropped her at home and tried to give her back her motel-room key a few hours after the bombshell discovery at the bank.

As Gina and I continue dealing with the pictures' fallout all afternoon, they're the words that keep echoing inside my head. "Hey, Andy, focus here," my partner snaps at me as we comb through old security footage in the bank manager's office. Eventually we find a tape showing Pierson entering the vault and presumably accessing his safe-deposit box, just two days after Patty Blum, the most recent victim, went missing.

Oh, Ellen. How could you not have known you were sharing your bed with a monster? And are you really inviting *me* to share it again? Are you actually going to show up tonight? Am *I*? I swore I wouldn't go near this mess a second time, but—

"Sorry, uh, say that last part again?" I have to ask Dr. Hyong as he shares his lab's analysis of the photos of Patty and the other four young women. I want nothing more in the world than to find these girls and punish the bastard who did this...but all I can think about right now is the bastard's irresistible wife.

Hyong clears his throat. "What I said was, it's impossible from a few grainy photographs to know any of the victims' past or present conditions for certain. The images could have been altered. The victims *themselves* could have been altered—their appearances degraded, for instance, with makeup or fake blood to make us think they were killed and discourage us from actively searching for them. However..."

Hyong removes his tortoiseshell glasses and lets out a sad sigh.

"If the photos are real, I believe the four victims...are long since deceased."

That statement literally knocks the wind right out of me. It's all I can do to whisper "Thanks, Doc" as Gina and I leave his cluttered office.

"Just got a message from the District Attorney," my partner says, lowering her cell phone from her ear as we climb back into my Impala. "If there's any silver lining in all this, the DA is going to refile the abduction and murder charges against Pierson. The photos plus the bank security tape—they're confident they can make a case now."

"That's great news," I say. "Will Ellen have to testify?"

"Shit, I hope not. No way a jury buys a word she says. I haven't trusted that bitch since the moment we met her."

I feel the urge to push back. To defend Ellen. To explain to Gina that she has it all wrong. That the woman I've been getting to know all these weeks is kind and decent and gentle and good. Instead, I keep my mouth shut. At least for now.

After a few more hours back at the station, Gina decides to head home. "My mom's taking the twins," she explains, "and me and Zoe have date night. I'm not feeling too frisky after the day we just had, but hey."

If my partner knew I *also* might have a date tonight— and with whom—she'd blow a gasket. Disown me. And I can't say I'd blame her.

I hang around the station for another few hours, catching up on paperwork, dodging calls from the press asking me to comment. But mostly I stare at those grisly photos, which are now all over the news. I keep scanning them for clues. Praying that Dr. Hyong is wrong. Wishing I had the willpower to not do what I'm considering.

It's after nine o'clock when I finally leave the station. I swing by Noah's Bar & Grill, a quiet neighborhood spot with the best burgers in town. I wash one down with an ice-cold beer. Then a second beer. Then a third.

It's half past ten when I pay the bill. *Okay, decision time.* I sit behind the wheel for a good ten or fifteen agonizing minutes, twirling the cool metal motel key in my hand. My brain is screaming *Go home, you moron!* But I can't. I just can't.

Soon I'm pulling into the shadowy El Toro parking lot, scanning for Ellen's car—but I don't see it. I shut off my engine, get out, and approach room 4. The front window's curtains are drawn, but the inside looks completely dark. Before I can change my mind, I give the door a quick knock. I wait. I listen.

No response. I guess Ellen must not be here yet. It's only eleven, still fairly early. After glancing around to make sure the coast is clear, I unlock the door and enter, shutting it quickly behind me.

I flip on the lights—and there she is.

Ellen is lying on the bed, wearing nothing but a sheer black bra and red lace panties. The sight stops me in my tracks. I open my mouth to speak, but no words come out.

"Hello, Andy," she says. "I'm glad you came. You look a little nervous. Why?"

Gee, maybe because I'm alone in a motel room with the killer's half-naked wife?

"To be honest, I'm nervous, too," she continues. "Because the truth is . . . I'm falling in love with you, Andy. But I'm afraid. That you're just using me. The way my husband did."

Ellen looks so vulnerable right now. So innocent. And yes, so unbelievably sexy. Her pouty lips, her porcelain skin, her firm breasts. It's all making my head spin.

"Of course I'm not using you," I answer. "I would never. That's not who I am. I really care about you, Ellen. I think I . . . I think I'm falling in love with you, too."

Ellen smiles and slowly sits up. "Then what are you waiting for?"

I approach the bed—and we *pounce* on each other. Kissing ferociously. Pawing at each other's clothes. Releasing weeks of pent-up tension. Ellen is soon moaning and trembling in my arms, digging her nails into my back, drawing blood.

I know this is so, so wrong... *but it feels so, so good.*

CHAPTER 31

WE MAKE LOVE THAT night for hours. We're both so drained afterward, we can barely speak. We just lie there, holding each other, exhausted but exhilarated. Then we get dressed and, without exchanging a word, part ways.

It's almost 3:00 a.m. when I finally get back home. Nearly dawn. I stumble into my bedroom to try to steal a few winks of sleep before heading in to work.

But then my cell phone starts ringing. My head's barely touched the pillow, so I let it go to voicemail. It rings again. I roll over and check the ID. It's the San Luis Obispo area code—805—but I don't recognize the number. I decide I should probably answer it.

"Detective McGrath? This is Sergeant Matt Kerr with the SLO County Sheriff's Office. I'm calling regarding an inmate in our custody, Michael F. Pierson..."

The news makes me leap right out of bed.

No...I can't believe it...those fools—how could they let this happen?

After I hang up with the sergeant, feeling a little dazed and hoping it was just a bad dream, I dial Gina. But my partner says she just got a similar call from the jail. Next I phone the county lockup myself and confirm the news a second time.

So much for getting any sleep tonight.

I throw some clothes on and speed to the station. I request urgent copies of the correctional officers' incident reports and the deputy warden's preliminary assessment. When they arrive, I read the few dozen pages of documents as fast as I can. Soon my desk phone starts ringing with reporters asking for comment—until I literally yank it from the wall. When bleary-eyed, Red Bull–chugging Gina arrives an hour later, I tell her to hold down the fort for me here while I step out for a little while.

There's something I have to do.

I turn onto Ellen's street and see that the reporters camped outside her home have been whipped into a frenzy. I'm not surprised. As I pull into the driveway and get out, they swarm my car, shoving their cameras in my face, shouting questions like:

"Detective McGrath, how will this impact the search for the missing girls?"

"Do you believe it was triggered by the discovery of those photos?"

"Was justice done today—or now can it never be done?"

"Jesus Christ, you people are vultures!" I exclaim as I march up the path to Ellen's house. I pound the door, calling out her name. No answer. I keep knocking, louder, rattling the doorknob. Maybe she's not here. But finally, she opens it.

"Sorry, Andy," she says, quickly ushering me inside. She's wearing a simple tank top and baggy sweatpants, but still looks incredible. The tension between us is suddenly so charged, I half expect her to push me against the door and kiss me.

Instead, Ellen holds up a pair of tweezers and a magnifying loupe.

"I was in the attic, working on my butterfly collection."

"I wish *I* had a hobby like that to distract me at times like this," I answer. "I'm not sure if you heard the news, but—"

"Of course I did. In the middle of the night, while you and I were at that motel together...while I was *cheating* on him...Michael hanged himself inside his cell."

Ellen's bottom lip begins to quiver, and she starts fighting off tears.

"I know you used to love him," I say tenderly. "You have every right to be upset."

But Ellen shakes her head. "The case is closed now. Those girls are dead, and so is their killer. You don't need me anymore." Then she adds, softer, "I lost *two* men I cared about today, didn't I?"

It's breaking my heart how sad and helpless Ellen looks. I know the decent thing to do would be to take her in my arms and try to comfort her. Tell her it will all be okay. That maybe we *can* still be together.

But we both know that's a big, fat lie.

CHAPTER 32

ELLEN TURNS AWAY FROM McGrath. She has to. It's simply too painful to look him in the eye. She's hoping against hope that he'll step up and embrace her, or fight with her—fight *for* her—but she isn't surprised when all he says, weakly, is "Oh, Ellen."

She hears him place something small and metallic on the entry table as he leaves: her motel-room key, no doubt.

And just like that, the dreamy detective is gone.

From her house. From her life.

Forever, Ellen thinks.

She listens to the legion of reporters outside shout another round of questions at McGrath as he exits and heads to his car. But once he drives away and the journalists stop yelling, Ellen's home falls instantly, eerily quiet.

Ellen looks down at her hands, still holding the tweezers and magnifying loupe. Her husband is dead, and she has a million things to take care of. Forms to fill out, calls to place, arrangements to make. And yet, in this moment, there is nothing in the world Ellen wants to do except get back to her beautiful butterflies. Tinkering with her collection has always helped soothe her. And right now, a little comfort is what she craves most. So she heads back up to the attic to get to work.

Many hours later, in the middle of the night, Ellen wakes up slumped forward across her worktable. She was up until God-knows-when arranging a display box with some of her newest specimens and must have dozed off.

To her great horror, she sees she fell asleep directly on *top* of an uncovered case—crushing the butterflies' delicate bodies and wings.

"Oh, no...no, please..." Ellen mutters, frantically inspecting the damage in a state of disbelief. She might be able to fix a few of them with glue and patience, but most of the butterflies are mangled beyond repair.

"No, no!" she exclaims, louder now.

Ellen did not cry when she heard her husband had taken his life. Or when McGrath silently confirmed that their relationship was over.

But now the sobs come heavy and ugly.

When she finally calms down, Ellen blots her puffy eyes. She blows her runny nose. Then she stands and heads downstairs. She knows what she has to do.

Dreading it, she approaches her front bay window and pulls back the curtains just a hair to check the size of the mob of reporters camped outside.

Ellen is stunned. She can't believe it.

Every last one of them—they're gone!

True, it's almost one o'clock in the morning, but they've

been spending nights out front for weeks now. With Michael dead, apparently they've abandoned her, too.

Just like McGrath.

It feels a little strange to Ellen to be able to walk calmly out her front door and down her driveway without two dozen rabid journalists clamoring at her and recording her every move. She gets in her car, slowly pulls out, and heads down her quiet street, bound for her destination. She checks her mirrors multiple times as she drives. It feels even stranger not to be followed.

Ellen takes a spot in the El Toro Motel parking lot. Not one near room 4, but the closest available to the front desk. She leaves her engine running; she won't be long.

Pushing open the lobby door, she hears that jangle of the sleigh bells hung from the handle again, followed by "Hey there, Mrs. Hayes."

It's Carson, the stoner twenty-something who works the night shift, who knows Ellen only by her alias. "Is everything, like, cool with your room?" he asks.

"Yes, yes," Ellen assures him. "And I know I've prepaid for it for a few more days, but I won't be needing it any longer."

Before she can change her mind, she places her room key down on the desk.

"Uh, okay, sure," Carson replies. "You're all set, then, Mrs. H. Hope you'll stay with us again soon."

Ellen smiles, a little sadly.

"I'd like that. Very much. But, Carson? I wouldn't count on it."

CHAPTER 33

BACK IN HER CAR. Back on the road.

Ellen heads along Santa Rosa Street, then takes the on-ramp for the 101, the same freeway she sped down the wrong way just a few days ago, which feels like another *lifetime* ago.

Merging into the middle lane, she settles in for a long drive.

Again, this late at night, the freeway is nearly deserted, and the hum of the road is almost hypnotic. Most people driving at this hour on so little sleep might worry about nodding off, but Ellen is wide awake. Jittery with nerves. Jumpy with anticipation.

The minutes tick by, turning into hours. Ellen finally exits the freeway at about half past two. She's soon cruising through the sleepy town of Landor, California, such a dusty, tiny speck of a place that it makes San Luis Obispo look like San Francisco.

Ellen turns left off the main drag and onto Sheridan

Road, which leads out of the town proper and up into the adjacent hills. Knowing there will be no streetlights for miles, she flips on her high beams, but the winding road is still dark and treacherous.

After a good fifteen minutes of careful driving, Ellen makes another left turn, onto a hidden dirt path that leads even deeper into the rolling woods.

At last, she arrives—at an old cabin. An old abandoned *shack,* more accurately.

With so many dense trees and overgrown shrubs around it, it's extremely well camouflaged, practically invisible. Using her cell phone as a flashlight to help guide her way, Ellen gets out of her car and approaches.

But instead of going to the front door, she walks toward one of the trees, a leafy oak. On one of the lower branches hangs a plastic bird feeder, filled about a quarter of the way with stale seeds. Ellen unhooks it from the tree, unscrews the top, and dumps the birdseed into her open palm. She spreads her fingers and shakes, until all that remains in her hand is a rusty metal key.

Now Ellen goes to the front door. She unlocks and opens it. The hinges creak, like in a classic horror movie, but there aren't any cobwebs or cloth-draped furniture inside this cabin. The outside might look decrepit, but its interior is clean and cozy—if small and sparsely furnished.

Ellen turns on the lights, illuminating display case after display case of colorful butterflies, hung on virtually every square inch of wall. There are hundreds of specimens in total, outnumbering her home collection many times over.

And in the corner sits a small drafting desk, identical to the workstation in Ellen's attic. On it rests a glass display case that's still a work in progress, only partially filled with freshly pinned butterflies, all in perfect condition.

Ellen walks over and takes a seat, excited to get to work—when she hears something outside.

CHAPTER 34

THE CRUNCHING OF TIRES. The slamming of a car door.

Someone's here, now? Ellen thinks. *Impossible!*

She's in the middle of nowhere, a hundred miles from home, at three o'clock in the morning. She came here to be alone, to escape—and now she has a visitor?

Ellen returns to the front door and looks through the peephole.

Parked beside her Camry is a vehicle she's seen dozens of times: a white Impala. And walking toward the cabin— slowly, cautiously—is Detective McGrath.

Ellen's eyes widen in disbelief. She feels a flurry of conflicting emotions. Shock. Confusion. Anticipation. Arousal.

Flustered, Ellen hastily smooths the front of her blouse and runs some fingers through her hair, trying to make herself as presentable as possible while she waits for McGrath to knock.

But he doesn't.

Instead, McGrath suddenly kicks the door open and bursts inside, his Glock 22 service weapon aimed and ready.

"Andy!" Ellen exclaims with an almost giddy laugh. "My God, you scared me! What...what are you doing here?"

McGrath is just as surprised to see her standing there. He lowers his gun but doesn't yet put it away.

"What are *you* doing, Ellen? What the hell is this place?"

"An old hunting cabin. It's been in my family for generations."

"Who owns it?" McGrath asks. "Your house is the only property listed under your or your husband's name. We checked."

"Of course you did," Ellen says with a rueful smile. "Legally it belonged to my grandfather. After he died, it just kind of sat here. Michael and I rediscovered it a few years ago. We started coming up here sometimes to get away. It's peaceful. Quiet."

McGrath looks around at the cramped interior and floor-to-ceiling butterfly displays with apprehension. "Yeah," he says, "feels real relaxing."

"How did you find me?" Ellen asks. "I could have sworn I wasn't followed."

McGrath finally reholsters his sidearm and takes from his pocket a small electronic device about the size of a deck of playing cards.

"Last week...before our night at the motel, but after your crazy 3:00 a.m. wrong-way drag race down the 101...I came by your place and stuck a GPS tracker under the rear bumper of your car. I knew I couldn't risk losing you, Ellen."

Ellen absorbs that for a moment, trying to decide whether McGrath means it romantically as well as literally. He does.

"You were able to get a warrant to monitor the comings and goings of a suspect's spouse?"

McGrath slips the tracking device back in his pocket—and dodges the question.

"I don't regret anything I've done on this case, Ellen. Especially anything I've done with *you*. You're not like any woman I've ever met. If we'd crossed paths at a different time, different circumstances...maybe it would have been *us* spending weekends in this cabin."

Ellen nods, wistfully. It's a sweet sentiment, but painful, too.

"You're welcome to spend the night," Ellen offers. "On the couch, I mean. Unless—"

"That's all right," McGrath says, waving her off. "I wanna start heading back down the hill. Lousy cell service up here. I'm gonna ask Forensics to take a fine-tooth comb to this place, inside and out, first thing in the morning."

"You really think Michael might have brought those girls...*here*?" Ellen asks with a shiver.

"Honestly? Not a chance. He was smarter than that. But

maybe we'll find a print. A hair. A fiber. Anything we can use to find them. It's worth a shot."

With a resigned shrug, McGrath starts heading for the door.

Ellen, overwhelmed, takes a few steps backward toward her desk, bracing herself against it for support.

"Good night, Ellen," McGrath says. He holds up his cell phone. "Guess I'll see you in a few hours. I've got some calls to make."

"Sorry, Andy..."

McGrath has his hand on the doorknob when he hears the unmistakable *click* of a handgun's safety catch being flipped off.

He spins around.

He can't believe his eyes.

Ellen is aiming a compact .38-caliber handgun right at him.

"I can't let you do that."

CHAPTER

IN ALL MY YEARS with the SLOPD, I've had a gun pointed at me only once before, by a desperate coke dealer during a drug bust gone awry.

Tonight makes twice.

And it's by a woman I thought I loved.

Suddenly it all makes sense! I knew it all along—but I just couldn't see it.

Ellen is a hell of a lot more than just the killer's wife.

But there's no time for that now.

My heart is thundering. Adrenaline is coursing through my veins.

My life could be over in a few milliseconds—way too little time for me to draw my own gun, turn, and shoot first.

So I get a crazy idea.

I slap the light switch near the front door, plunging the little cabin into darkness. Then I quickly drop to the ground and roll out of the way.

Ellen yelps with shock and fires a shot—*blam!*—but it misses me by a mile.

"Damnit, Andy!" she exclaims as I frantically scramble behind the couch for cover. "Where are you?"

Ellen fires two more wild shots—*blam! blam!*—in my general direction. Again she misses me. But only by a hair.

Now it sounds like she's shuffling across the room toward the light switch herself. So I use those precious few seconds to quickly crawl around the couch and *behind* her. As soon as Ellen turns the lights back on...

I leap up and pounce.

I clasp my hands around the hot metal gun, squeezing Ellen's fingers tightly so she can't pull the trigger. Then we tumble to the floor together, our limbs intertwined.

"No, no, no!" she screams, again and again, kicking and flailing wildly as I wrestle with her for control of the weapon. Damn, she sure is feisty—and strong!

At last I manage to yank the pistol from Ellen's grip. Then I *smack* the hard steel clean across the side of her head. Ellen grunts in pain and goes limp.

I crab-walk backward a bit, then stand up, tucking her little pistol into my belt and drawing my own Glock.

"Don't move!" I shout. I keep my gun trained on Ellen as she groans and writhes. God only knows what this woman might do next, so I'm not taking any chances.

"What the hell did you do to those girls?" I demand, practically foaming at the mouth with fury.

Ellen doesn't respond.

Then she starts to laugh.

CHAPTER 36

"YOU DAMN *FOOL,* ANDY," she hisses, wiping a dollop of blood off her lip. "You know exactly what I did. What *we* did."

"You mean...?"

"That's right. Michael and I were *partners.* We picked those girls out together like we were ordering artwork from a catalog."

Ellen gestures to the hundreds of dead butterflies on the walls.

"I guess you could say we both liked collecting all *kinds* of beautiful things. This cabin is exactly where we kept them. Claire, Samantha, Maria, Patty—we did what we wanted to them, we took a few pictures, then we buried them out back, in the woods."

I'm too stunned to speak. My hands begin to tremble so much that I can barely hold my gun steady.

"Look at you," Ellen says, laughing even harder now. "You had it all wrong from the start. You thought you'd get close to me, use me, extract evidence from me, then dump me by the curb, didn't you?"

I don't answer... but what Ellen is saying, of course, is true. At least it *was*. Until I started getting to know her. Until I started *falling* for her.

"But I was the one using *you*, Detective," she snarls. "I loved my husband. We understood each other. That night he picked up Brittany, he knew you were following him. He let himself get caught to protect me." Then she adds, "He was a good man, Andy. He was ten times the one you'll ever be."

"He was a goddamn murderer!" I yell. "A monster. And a coward. And so are you!"

I feel a swell of emotions deep in my gut so powerful, I can barely describe it. Horror, disbelief, humiliation, rage. *That this bitch could have lied to me for so long...*

"I know you tried so hard, Andy," Ellen says, almost tauntingly now. "And you came so close, too. Patty was still alive just a few weeks ago. After Michael was arrested, I had to take care of her myself."

My jaw clenches like a vise. My eyes start stinging with tears. *It can't be...*

"Her body should still be pretty fresh. As for the other girls, they've probably all decomposed so much by now, not even their parents would be able to recog—"

Blam!

I'm almost as shocked by the gunshot as Ellen is.

And I'm the one who fired it.

The bullet strikes her in the throat. Her eyes bug out of

her pretty head. She starts to gag and choke on her own oozing blood.

But I just stand there, numb with shock at what I've done, watching as Ellen takes her last gasp of breath, then slumps backward against the wall.

Holy shit. I've just committed second-degree murder.

I've just killed the killer.

And yet, I feel an instant sense of tranquility come over me like a warm blanket.

I calmly reholster my handgun. I slowly push open the front door. I steadily walk back to my car. I carefully drive back down the dark, hilly road.

When I reach the main town again, I check my cell phone. Seeing I have a few bars of service, I pull over and call my partner. She answers groggily after the fifth ring.

"I solved the case, Gina," I say evenly. "I just closed it, too."

"Andy? What are you talking about? What time is it? Where are you?"

"Listen. Ellen's side of the family used to own a hunting cabin outside Santa Margarita. Dig up the address in county records, then send Hyong and his techs there right away. It's an unsecured murder scene."

"Hang on. It's a what?"

"The girls' bodies are in the backyard. Ellen's is inside, by the front door. I'll be back at my place when you're ready for me, after I pick up my parents and let them know I'll be going away for a while."

"Andy, you—you're not making any sense," Gina

stammers. "You found the girls? And . . . and Ellen's been killed, too?"

I don't blame my partner for not understanding.

Shit. I'm more confused than I've ever been in my life.

"See ya, Gina," I say.

I hang up my phone and turn it off. Then I pull back onto the road and start to head home.

As I do, I notice the sun is just starting to rise, painting the sky a vibrant orange and bloodred.

I imagine I see a swarm of butterflies, fluttering in the air.

WE.
ARE.
NOT.
ALONE.

JAMES PATTERSON

with TIM ARNOLD

PROLOGUE

THE COMMANDER SETS HER hard-shell polycarbonate suitcase down by the front door and musters up every ounce of courage she's got. These good-byes are never easy.

But this one, she fears, is going to sear a hole right through her heart.

The commander is leaving home to lead what she believes will be her last mission.

Her husband and two children are in the next room, waiting for the typical round of farewell hugs and kisses. They know their wife and mother is about to embark on yet another very important, highly classified, and quite possibly dangerous mission to outer space.

What they *don't* know is, they will probably never see her again.

The commander steps into the living room. Her family is gathered on the sofa. They've said nearly a dozen good-byes like this over the years, but right away, her kids and husband seem to sense that something's different. Their worry is palpable, written all over their faces, hanging in the air like it has all week.

At first, the commander can't look her loved ones in the eye. Her gaze falls instead on the aluminum-sheathed smart walls of their home. Then the silver, achromatic furniture. Then the concave digital holographic monitor projecting a montage of family photographs in 3-D. Like baby pictures of her two children. Snapshots from family vacations. Even wedding photos taken sixteen years ago under a spectacular celestial sky, glowing from the night's depth and intensity as if to embrace the bride and groom below—her husband's idea, a tribute to her passion for space and a symbol of their infinite love.

All of which momentarily brings the commander up short: all these images from a rich, rewarding life, each of them touching her as especially poignant, smiling down on her husband and two children sitting there on the couch, waiting.

Through the living room's giant double-paned bay window, the commander notices something outside. A sleek, black government SUV pulling up to the curb. Her ride.

The silence is deafening. She knows she doesn't have much time.

She pulls her son up off the couch and into her arms for an embrace that, for once, this teenager accepts fully, returning it in kind.

He knows something, she's thinking.

"Listen—you are so special to me, this young man of

mine, experiencing life. None of it's easy, this growing up business. I understand. But stay with it. Live life! You must know how much I love you—you need to—and I always will. Promise me that you'll keep on being yourself, no matter what else is out there."

"And remember what you promised, too, Mom. You'll start teaching me how to drive as soon as you get back. Right?"

His words catch the commander off guard. And sting her heart.

Before she has to reply, her younger daughter leaps into her arms and squeezes her around the neck in an emphatic hug.

A lump quickly forms in the commander's throat. "Sweetie, I have to. But just look at you, my special little girl. Growing up into such a smart, strong, beautiful young woman. Never forget: anything you set your mind to, you can achieve. Okay?"

Her daughter sniffles. And nods. "What I want to be is … an astronaut. Like you."

Outwardly, the commander smiles. But inside, her heart is breaking.

She had long suspected her daughter might share her love of the cosmos, especially once the girl began showing an aptitude in school for math and science. But this is the first time her daughter has voiced it herself, and the news is bittersweet. Will the girl's interest in space grow, the commander wonders, if her mission is a "success" and she never comes back? Or will her dreams be dashed forever?

Pushing those painful thoughts from her mind, the commander turns at last to her husband—her tall, handsome man with strong hands and soft eyes. Her rock for the better part of two decades.

She hasn't told him the truth about her mission, but she's afraid he's figured it out. He could always read her like a book, ever since they first met—a last-minute blind date she had almost skipped. After all, they seemed such an unlikely match. She was writing her dissertation in quantum engineering. He was a construction site foreman, who even showed up to the restaurant still sprinkled with cement dust. But he "got" her like no one else ever had. He could make her laugh, or cry, often at the same time.

They fell for each other, fast and hard. Before long, they had created a beautiful family, a beautiful life.

Her husband pulls the commander into an embrace. "Good-bye for now," he says simply.

Good-bye for now. That's been their typical send-off, their little tradition, each time she's left for a mission. At this point, it's practically a superstition. The words and tone are intentionally light. Almost glib. Deliberately far too casual to be their final farewell.

Until today.

Startled to see tears welling in his eyes, the commander kisses her husband deeply, then explains, almost pleadingly, "This mission...it's something I have to do. They picked me because they think I'm the very best one for the job. I've trained for it my whole life. I wish I could tell you more. But I can't. What I *can* say is...I love you. All of you. No matter what happens, you three will be in my heart. Forever."

And with that, the commander heads to the front door. On her way, she slides a favorite family photo (a rare printed one, not a digital holograph) out of its frame and tucks it into her pocket: her two children, infants, sitting on her husband's lap. Her daughter is hugging a favorite toy, a stuffed rocket ship.

The commander steps outside. She hands her suitcase to the uniformed driver standing next to the SUV. Then she looks up at the rich, crystal-clear night sky, flush with twinkling stars. Beautiful. Infinite. She still finds it breathtaking, every time.

Less than an hour later, the commander arrives at the highly secure Cancri 55 Interplanetary Complex, suits up, and is ushered, helmet in hand, through a maze of underground passageways to her waiting shuttle. There she joins the rest of her crew, already inside the cockpit.

Their spacecraft is moments away from departure.

CHAPTER 1

...FEEP...FEEP...FEEP...FEEP...FEEP...

Am I...*dreaming?*

...feep...feep...feep...feep...

Or is that really...the sound...*I've been waiting to hear my entire life?*

...feep...feep...feep...

"Holy shit!" I scream, and bolt upright in my desk chair, knocking a pile of empty takeout containers and coffee cups to the floor. I'm instantly awake—and already hyperventilating. I rub the sleep from my eyes, in total disbelief of what's in front of me.

The bank of giant monitors on my desk have taken on a life of their own. They're beeping wildly, flashing an endless stream of numbers and symbols.

...feep...feep...feep...feep...

"Holy shit!" I shout again, even louder.

"Holy shit, holy shit," squawks Alien, my twenty-two-year-old pet parrot, from his cage in the corner of the room.

I'm blinking rapidly, my eyes glued to my screens.

Could it really be?

After so many years of thankless, hardheaded, pain-in-the-ass persistence—could all my hard work and determination be about to pay off?

Am I really intercepting a transmission from deep space?

Could this really be a message from another world?

...feep...feep...feep...

What a glorious sound—which I was beginning to worry I'd never hear!

For years now, using my home-built supercomputer, I've been scanning the night skies. Tapping into satellite feeds. Listening to the farthest reaches of the most distant galaxies. Searching, hoping, *praying* that my long-held theory about the existence of extraterrestrial life might one day be proven true.

I've also been regularly sending *outbound* messages of my own. Digital photographs, to be exact. Communication is a two-way street, after all, even with aliens. I'd been struggling to come up with that perfect peaceful greeting when I realized: a picture is worth a thousand words, right? And what better pictures are there in the *world*— or that better illustrate what it means to be human—than ones of my kids? Claire and Ellie, my two little girls, who I love desperately, who I don't see nearly as much as I want to...

Ever since they were babies, I'd take snapshots of them all the time, then compress the files into quantum binary code and beam them out into space. It was like marking their heights on a wall, except for the entire *universe* to see.

After their mother and I divorced, she'd send me new pictures once or twice a month, and I kept on doing it. A couple years ago, my system started picking up photos of *other* people's kids being sent back. It was a nice gesture from some anonymous fellow amateur radio astronomers, no doubt—and fellow parents—who'd picked up and decoded my errant signals and wanted to participate, too. I never heard from any little green men, though...

Until... *today!*

Years ago, I set an audio alert to go off if my system ever detected data bitmaps from outer space that weren't human photos, but weren't just random "cosmic noise," either. Messages that contained some kind of pattern. Actual meaning.

...feep...feep...feep...

That's the sound I'm hearing now!

"Yes!" I howl. "Yes!!! Yesssss!!!!!"

"*Yes, yes,*" Alien squawks again. That dude always has my back.

My mind shifts into overdrive as the reality of what I'm dealing with begins to sink in. It feels like the walls of my messy LA apartment are starting to spin. I grab the edge of my computer console to steady myself.

Take it easy, Rob, I tell myself. *Get a grip. And think.*

I've dreamed about this moment for so long—but I've never actually made a game plan for when it happened.

Okay. Step one. Figure out what the hell this cascade of digital gibberish actually *means*. Is it some kind of greeting? A declaration of war? Or maybe I've just galactically eavesdropped by accident, and this message isn't directed at Earth at all.

Step two. Figure out *where* this thing is coming from, *who* it's coming from, and *why* it's coming *now*.

Step three. Tell the world! Change the course of human history—and go down in history! Redeem my reputation in the eyes of all my former colleagues. Win every scientific award and honorary degree there is! Become rich and famous! I can see the headlines now: *Aging, Washed-Up Astrophysicist Dr. Robert Barnett First to Prove Alien Life Exists. Former Colleagues Who Doubted Him Sing His Praises, Kiss His Ass!*

Wait. Hang on. Don't get ahead of yourself here, Rob. One thing at a time.

Speaking of which, what time *is* it?

I glance at the clock: four forty-three a.m. I realize it's still dark out. No wonder. Did I just wake up the entire building with my yelling? I hope not.

Now that I'm quiet, I suddenly hear something right outside—and it makes me jump out of my skin. Is somebody out there? I quickly look out the front window, up and down the street. But I can't see a soul, human or canine.

Great. After all these years of disciplined, pioneering diligence, I finally might be onto something...and I start losing my mind?

Deep breaths, Rob. Stay calm.

But how can I?

What's flickering across my computer screens is mind-boggling. It's otherworldly—literally.

Still too early to tell, but it sure looks like, yes...this could be the big one!

We.

Are.

Not.

Alone.

Like I said earlier: "Holy shit!"

But now what?

CHAPTER 2

OH, MAN. I CAN'T think straight. Gotta clear my head.

Take a walk.

Yeah, that's it. Step away for a bit. Get some air. A change of scenery. A coffee.

And I know just the spot. JP's, a grungy little coffee shop down the street that opens at five. Perfect.

I head for the door...when I realize I'm still in my underwear.

Come on, Rob, pull it together!

That's when I catch a look at myself in the full-length mirror. *Hoo, boy.* Not pretty. What happened to me? Seems like only yesterday I was a reasonably fit young man. Slim, bright-eyed. Even had a little muscle tone here and there. But now, with a growing gut hanging over two-day-old boxers, with bags under my eyes, what I see is a wrung-out, middle-aged man...and I ain't even forty!

Not only that, my apartment's a disaster—a lot like

me and my life. Dirty laundry piled on my bed, which I haven't slept in for days. Unread newspapers and magazines scattered all over. And my kitchen? It's littered with so many empty pizza boxes and old In-N-Out Burger wrappers, it's practically a biohazard zone.

The whole place looks like the lair of a mad scientist—which isn't too far from the truth. If I'm being honest, my hunt for extraterrestrial life these past way-too-many years has, well, kind of taken over my *own* life. It cost me my job, my marriage, my kids...

I tug on a pair of old jeans and a wrinkled T-shirt I pull from a mountain of clothes on the floor and stuff my wallet and keys into my pocket. I change my computer access password to a new twenty-digit random code, then I go—dead-bolting the apartment door behind me with a pair of brand-new, guaranteed-impenetrable smart locks. (One of them won't be available on the market for another six months. Don't ask...)

Once outside, I brush my thinning, unkempt hair out of my eyes and draw a long, slow breath. The early-morning Southern California air is surprisingly crisp. And thanks to the burnt-out streetlight on my grungy block, the sky looks unusually vivid.

I gaze up, and can immediately identify dozens of stars and constellations. Even Mars and Jupiter are out tonight, faintly twinkling. How amazing is it, I think, that humans have figured out how to send probes to those distant planets.

If they only knew.

But now, on to the next step. Figuring out the meaning of the alien communication I've captured, currently stored on my home computer's hard drive!

The burden is beginning to suck the breath right out of me. I start to walk but can barely stay steady. My knees are actually feeling weak. Maybe I should drive to JP's? My car is just parked at the end of the block. But no. Wobbly as my legs are, I think I'll stay on foot. At least for now.

Suddenly, I hear more barking, and I flinch as a white German shepherd rounds the corner and takes a friendly lunge at me before its owner yanks it by the leash.

"Down, girl! No! Sorry about that, sir..."

The man is younger than me, neatly dressed in khakis and a navy-blue windbreaker. I've never seen him or his dog.

"No problem," I say, offering the back of my hand to this beautiful dog. She raises her head for a scratch. "Are you...new to the area?"

"Sure am. Wife and I just moved in around the corner. I'm Joe. This is Lacy."

"I'm...uh, Hank," I say, awkwardly shaking his outstretched hand. I'm not exactly sure what compelled me to lie about my name. Just an instinct, I guess.

Joe looks like he wants to keep chatting, but I don't. "Nice to meet you," I say, and head on down the street.

Was that a little rude? Oh, well. Sorry, Joe. Your new neighbor is a little distracted right now.

CHAPTER 3

IT'S CRAZY HOW YOUR whole life can turn on a dime.

Only a few years ago I was in Pasadena, wrapping up a doctorate in astrophysics at Caltech. At least I thought I was.

My subject? Aliens. My thesis? *They're out there.*

I took a novel approach to the issue of extraterrestrial life, arguing that their mathematical likelihood was too great not to expend every resource we have to find them and make contact. And instead of trying to make contact using mathematical proofs or the table of the elements— the data we'd been transmitting into the universe for decades—we should send digital images of ourselves, and our culture. But those Caltech assholes looked at me cockeyed from day one. They said my idea "lacked empirical viability," and invited me to take it in another direction. Which I did.

I left. And never looked back.

If they didn't get it, I thought, screw 'em! It took half

a century for mainstream science to agree with Einstein's general theory of relativity. What's a couple years for Barnett's general theory of alien life?

I arrive at JP's and push open its heavy glass door, taking comfort in the familiar jingle of the old sleigh bells hung on the inside handle. The coffee shop has just opened for the day. Inside it's still empty.

"Hey, Professor!" JP yells to me as I enter. *Professor*. That's what he always calls me, and I don't correct him. "Whatcha doin' here so early, man?"

"I had to, uh, stretch my legs. Stretch my brain. Just to see if it's working right."

Juan Pablo flashes me a goofy grin. He opened this place soon after he arrived from Mexico at the ripe old age of twenty-one. Today, both it and he are cornerstones of the neighborhood. And after all the years I've been coming in, JP knows me. The real me.

I've barely sat down on the sticky red vinyl seat of my usual booth when he sets a steaming cup of coffee down in front of me.

"You okay, man?" JP asks. "Looks like you've seen a freakin' ghost."

In a way, I guess I have.

But it might also be a nice way of saying I look like shit. The last couple days in particular, I've barely slept a wink, downing about a case of Red Bull.

"I'm fine, JP, thanks," I answer, taking a sip of the thick, heavenly java he brews so well. But it's pretty obvious I'm hiding something, and he can see it right away.

"Wanna talk about it?"

"Yeah. I mean, no. I wish I could, but..."

"What's up, my friend? It's something big. I can tell. Spill it."

See? I told you this guy knows me well.

He's heard my whole life story a million times. How after I dropped out of Caltech, I joined the Air Force. How they stationed me at Edwards Air Force Base in the middle of the Mojave Desert. How within a few months, they'd accused me of "committing acts that endanger the security of the United States," all because I'd used a few military satellites and computer systems in my downtime to search for rogue extraterrestrial signals. How after my "Other Than Honorable" discharge, Marty, my brilliant, gorgeous wife, finally divorced me and moved with the kids to a nice suburban house over in Glendale. How I've been holed up ever since in my suck-ass little apartment in East Hollywood, glued to my many computer screens. No job, no friends, no women, no life. Just me and my workstation and my search for ETs.

"Well, it's hard to explain," I tell JP. "I know you think I'm a little crazy..."

"You are wrong, Professor. I think you are *really* crazy," he says with a laugh.

I nod. Maybe I am.

"Earlier this morning, I think I might have finally discovered something. Something huge. But I don't know what it means. Or what I'm supposed to do next. I just know that, for now, I have to keep my mouth shut. Which is driving me even *more* freakin' crazy!"

JP wipes his hands on his apron. He nods, almost philosophically.

"You might not *want* to talk about it. But it sounds like you have to. To someone who knows about these things. Someone you trust."

I take another deep gulp of joe, this time almost burning my tongue.

"Good point. Because if someone I *didn't* trust found out about this…"

Oh, shit! It suddenly dawns on me.

"I gotta go!" I erupt, slamming my mug down, sloshing half the coffee onto the table. "Pay you next time!" I shout as I bolt out the door.

By now, dawn has arrived, casting an eerie glow up and down the street. Already short of breath, I'm hurrying back to my apartment… because I have a growing suspicion that *someone might be following me*. How could I have been so dumb?

What's sitting on my home computer isn't just a cryptic cosmic message.

It's the biggest national security threat in American history.

And I've got to get back to it before someone else—like the military, the feds, the president himself—does first.

CHAPTER 4

IN A WINDOWLESS ROOM deep inside FBI headquarters, blocks from the White House, a veteran agent is staring at a massive wall of quantum computer monitors, each one pulsing with electromagnetic bursts.

The agent reeks of confidence, self-assurance. And with good reason. Having spent years working his way up the ranks to reach this demanding, high-level position, he's one of the most experienced people in the entire unit.

He is a member of one of the least visible but most critical divisions within the FBI: the Cyber Task Force. He and his colleagues spend countless hours scouring the deepest corners of the dark web to root out hackers, cyberterrorists. and other digital-driven threats. Their worst fear, or hope, or both, is uncovering what they call "left of boom"—a clue or tip in cyberspace preceding a threat or attack in the real world that could help save lives.

The CTF's secret weapon is known as Pleiades. Employing state-of-the-art technology, it's one of the most powerful supercomputers in the world. Its 163 racks—two-thirds of which are enhanced with NVIDIA graphics processing units—have a storage capacity of 724 *peta*bytes. There's virtually no digital system on the planet that Pleiades cannot track, monitor, or hack into.

The agent's eyes are currently scanning the trillions of bits of data flashing before him. His fingers dance across his keyboard as he runs a series of complex algorithmic programs, searching for anything unusual or suspicious. So far, so good.

Until suddenly, he gets a hit—like none he's ever encountered before.

By reflex, he's reaching for an encrypted emergency landline. Ignoring the early-morning hour, he dials his boss, still sound asleep at home.

"Chief? You need to come look at what I'm seeing here."

Within fifteen minutes, more than a dozen FBI special agents, cyber intelligence officers, and interdepartment liaisons from NASA and the armed forces have convened. Most have served in highly confidential astrophysical sciences or counterterrorism cyberespionage units. They're perched around a giant oval table covered with laptops, files, and cups of coffee in various stages of consumption. All are staring at the bank of monitors in total shock.

The previously quiet room has taken on the tense feel of a military bunker on the eve of an enemy assault.

"Barnett, Robert James," the agent explains, pulling up a dossier of the man in question on one of the screens. "Former Caltech PhD candidate. Former Air Force cyber

analyst. Current alien life theorist and amateur radio as-
tronomer."

"This guy's been on our radar for years," he continues.
"Built himself a pretty impressive home computer system,
but all it's done is send and receive some random family
photos... until tonight."

Murmurs of disbelief ripple around the table as the
agent shows them what's flowing through the suspect's
servers that the FBI recently intercepted: reams of quantum data arranged in various highly complex configura-
tions. Even the CTF commander—despite his twenty-
six-year government career on the cutting edge of science
and technology—is in absolute awe. His hand begins to
tremble... before he slams it down hard on the table.

"Get this walled off immediately!" he booms. "Highest
share level, top secret! And get a goddamn CAT team to
Barnett's apartment. Now!"

CHAPTER 5

WITHIN MINUTES, A SIXTEEN-MAN Cyber Action Team based out of the FBI's LA field office screeches up to the scene. An eight-car convoy, lights flashing, forms a crude perimeter around Rob Barnett's apartment building.

Because national security is at stake, the agents haven't yet been told the real purpose or reasons behind their mission. All they know is they are to detain one Robert James Barnett and seize all of his electronic and digital equipment—by any means necessary, including force.

The agents draw their weapons and enter the target building. With practiced haste, they head up the stairs to the suspect's third-floor apartment. To provide a perimeter, some of them stop at the second-floor landing. Others take positions inside the exit door on the floor above. The rest continue down the hall, getting closer.

Outside the apartment, an agent places an ultrasonic listening device the size of a deck of cards against the door to hear inside. He listens, but there's only silence.

Another agent has already gotten to work cracking the pair of smart locks securing the door. Opening such sophisticated wireless devices typically requires a Bluetooth-enabled smartphone with an embedded password, or an invitation from the owner. But the tech wizards of the CAT team have a workaround, and are able to gain access in twenty seconds with a password-cracking algorithm. With Barnett none the wiser, the agent now simply taps his phone's screen, and the circular LED lights on both smart locks blink from red to green and the two dead bolts recede.

The agents ready their weapons—then burst inside.

The local Los Angeles branch of the FBI's Cyber Task Force had been keeping an eye on Barnett for about six months, ever since they noticed the unusually high amount of electricity and internet bandwidth his apartment was drawing. Much like their counterparts in DC, they considered him a little intense, sure, but harmless.

As soon as they enter this mess of an apartment, however, the agents realize they have seriously underestimated this man.

It's a wreck, a sure sign of a guy without a real life. But a quick glance at the banks of high-definition monitors, rows of blinking server racks, and stacks of parallel high-powered CPUs tells them this is one of the most elaborate homemade computer setups they've ever encountered. Flanking the couch are two large vintage speakers connected to a set of amplifiers and a CD player. And over in the corner, in a cage hanging from the ceiling, perches a large parrot, bright green, eyeing them with curiosity.

While one agent heads straight to the main console, two others spread out and search the place top to bottom.

But Barnett himself is nowhere to be found.

"Looks like he bailed pretty fast," says one of them, holstering his sidearm and gesturing to the mess and filth covering practically every square inch.

Yet the agents' trained eyes are able to quickly pick out which items need special attention—that is, which need to be bagged and brought back to the lab for analysis. Like the multi-terabyte hard drives. And the reams of folders marked TOP SECRET, many of which appear to be stolen government or military files.

"Get a load of *this* little fella," another agent says. She's tapping a metal cage hanging from the ceiling. Inside, a large, multicolored parrot is watching them curiously.

"*Holy shit, holy shit,*" the bird squawks, both startling and amusing the agent.

"Forget the bird," says another agent. "Check out the *maps.*"

Tacked up on the wall next to the monitors is a giant color printout of NASA's diagram map of the Kepler-22 system, a section of the cosmos containing the first "habitable zone" planet discovered by NASA's Kepler interplanetary mission. Interestingly, one of the planets has been circled in red marker, with a series of question marks scrawled next to it.

But the agent seated at the computer console keeps his

focus squarely on the monitors in front of him. He's re-booted the system, but can't yet crack the password.

…feep…feep…feep…feep…

"It's…it's going haywire or something," he tells his colleagues.

They aren't used to hearing such nontechnical words come from his mouth, which they take as a sign their fellow agent is frustrated and frazzled.

Which must mean he's dealing with something *serious*.

So serious, the entire contents of the computer's central drive—still encrypted—will be archived, uploaded, and transmitted to Washington within minutes.

CHAPTER 6

SEALED INSIDE THE COCKPIT, the commander and her crew are beginning the meticulous final steps that will prepare their sophisticated spacecraft for takeoff, and carry them to their destination.

To her right sits the pilot. Behind him, the flight engineer. Farther back are the mission specialist and payload chief. All around, covering almost every possible centimeter of wall and console space, are decks of flickering controls.

The commander knows she's responsible for the most advanced spacecraft in existence: the *Epsilon Eridani*. It's structured from carbon nanotube composites, equipped with flexible alloy "smart wings," and outfitted with advanced EmDrives and onboard nuclear power (which would have gotten NASA's Mars rover to the red planet in seventy-five days instead of nine months). It's vastly stronger, lighter, and faster than any ship currently in operation. The most capable spacecraft the commander has ever captained, and having access to it ensures that this mission is going to be successful—a cruel oxymoron, she's thinking.

Her team's equipment is just as top-of-the-line. Each crew member wears a bright-orange custom-fit space suit and helmet made of aluminized Mylar, urethane-coated nylon, and other ultra-high-strength materials. Pressurized with oxygen, each suit is designed to protect the wearer against micrometeoroid bombardment and insulated against the extreme temperature variations the team is likely to encounter during their mission.

At T-minus twenty minutes, the commander is com-linked to the Launch Control Center to initiate the pre-flight checklist.

"*Epsilon Eridani* to Mission Control. We are standing by."

"Roger, *Epsilon*. This is Mission Control. Do you read me?"

"I read you."

"Good luck, Commander. Prepare for prelaunch protocols."

"Commence prelaunch protocols," the commander finally replies.

As Mission Control begins rattling off a long list of system tests and safety checks, the commander exchanges a knowing glance with her pilot—a look that goes well beyond this mission, way back to when they were in flight school together.

Both were recently married. Both had been away from their spouses for six intense months. And the loneliness had begun to take its toll.

It was during a final training exercise, just the two of them inside a zero-gravity chamber, blissfully adrift in little more than their underwear. Before they knew what was happening, their athletic young bodies became entangled, slowly turning, floating. Laughter at first, until their lips locked in a brief but passionate kiss. A sign of the bond forged during their training. A desperately needed release after so many hundreds of grueling hours. But a mistake nonetheless. One that neither has spoken about since, but neither has forgotten.

Once the preflight checklist is completed, Mission Control intones, "*Epsilon Eridani,* you are clear for take-off."

The Ground Launch Sequencer is turned on and the terminal countdown begins. From here, operations will be controlled automatically by the launch director inside Mission Control. The clock is ticking, on so many levels. But for now, the commander knows, things are out of her control.

In the final moments they remain on the ground, the commander removes from her space suit a tiny item of contraband she smuggled aboard. It's a major violation of security protocols, but that hardly matters now. She carefully affixes it to the corner of the side cockpit window. She smiles at it, her heart bursting with so many emotions.

It's the family photo she brought with her, of her husband and two children, her daughter tightly hugging her plush toy rocket ship.

The commander is taking them with her.

Now just seconds away from liftoff, the commander watches the rest of her crew—the pilot, the flight engineer, the mission specialist, the payload chief—all hard at work. Tapping buttons, twisting knobs, making their final flight preparations. All are so deeply dedicated to their mission, though they're prohibited by security regulations from knowing the specifics.

Even if none of them knows the truth.

The commander is briefly tempted to violate security protocols and tell them the true nature of this mission.

"Commencing final countdown" comes the voice from Mission Control. "Launch in ten…nine…eight… seven…" No, she decides. She won't. She can't.

CHAPTER 7

I'M AROUND THE CORNER and quick-stepping it back up the street to my apartment.

I gotta get back to my computer, give it a fresh look. See if I can figure out what, if anything, is *real*. If that's even possible.

Before somebody beats me to it.

Especially if that somebody works for the United States government.

I think back to that "new neighbor" I met—Joe, with his white German shepherd. He couldn't have been...*one of them,* could he? Feeling me out? Trailing me? Bullshit—right? Or is it?

No matter. Even if the feds do show up at my place, there's no way they'll get in. Bars on the windows, smart locks on the entrance—I'm in the clear.

But then again, if they do? I'm probably a dead man.

But then again, my computer and all its data are totally secure—and remotely backed up. The system is easily up to the DoD Orange Book specs, the highest level of digital encryption the government uses. (Thanks, Air Force!)

But then again...

I'm now just a few blocks from my place—when I balk. I take another lap around the neighborhood. My brain's still working overtime and I desperately gotta clear it.

Rob, will you give yourself a break? You've always been your own worst enemy!

Wanna know why your professors weren't quite taking you seriously? Because neither did you. You never even had the balls to ask out the girls you really wanted! If Marty hadn't initiated things, you probably wouldn't have ever connected with her...

And now, all of a sudden, for the first time in six years, I'm thinking about having a cold one. At five o'clock in the morning.

Insane. And of course, I know I can't.

But man, it's tempting.

After the Air Force, my drinking got way, way out of control. I started getting drunk at bars alone. Coming home after the kids were already in bed. And Marty started losing patience with me.

Soon I started drinking in the afternoons, right at my computer, trying to get a handle on the data I was seeing, thinking I could function even better with a bit of a buzz. But of course, the more I drank, the *harder* it was to focus... which made me want to drink even more... which, well, you can see where it was going.

Sure, my research started to suffer. But Marty and the

girls were paying the real price. Before long, my wife and father-in-law sat me down and had an intervention.

Which was exactly the wake-up call I needed. I went to AA, bought it—reluctantly at first, then big-time. I attended thirty meetings in thirty days, got a sponsor, the whole thing. And though my marriage didn't survive, I have not had a drink since, a genuine blessing.

But right now, *oh, man* . . . what I wouldn't give for an ice-cold—

Stop, dude!

You're onto something huge here! Something that could have a profound effect on the world we live in—the *universe* we live in! You're out there with the noble pioneers who risked everything. Who defied logic. Who alienated (no pun intended) those around them, but ultimately made the world a better place. Nobody said it was going to be easy. You gave yourself up completely to this work because you had a vision, a belief, a question. Now you're close. *Very* close.

Okay, okay!

I start to feel a little better, a little calmer, as I round the final corner to my apartment . . .

And then I see them.

I can't believe it. It's really happening.

They *are* onto me!

I spot eight black government sedans parked outside my building, lights strobing.

And I count at least a dozen federal agents in dark suits getting out and—*holy shit*—drawing their weapons!

These guys aren't just here for my computers. They're here for *me*.

I practically fling myself to the ground behind some nearby trash cans along the curb to try to hide. Of course I knock into one and it almost tips over, which would give away my position—but I grab it just in time.

Staying crouched, I watch with terror as the agents storm into my building and race up the stairs to my apartment.

Yup, I'm dead.

Obviously, they know exactly what I picked up with my computer. I don't know *how* they know, but they do. And it's clearly a matter of incredible urgency.

I gotta get the hell out of here, I realize. Get somewhere else. Fast.

But where?

Anywhere.

I just hope it's not too late.

I turn and scurry back down the street to my car, thankfully still parked where I left it a few nights ago. I pull the keys from my pocket, climb in, and turn over the engine.

It coughs. It whines. Finally, it starts.

At least something is functioning like it's supposed to in my life.

A life, it's beginning to dawn on me, that will never be the same.

CHAPTER 8

BEFORE LONG, I'M CRUISING west down Sunset Boulevard in my beat-up black 2005 Jeep Cherokee.

The car was actually a gift—a *pity* gift—from my former father-in-law, who wanted to help me get back on my feet after I got booted from the Air Force. Yeah, yeah, I know. But I was broke and jobless and needed some wheels, and I was still married to his incredible and pregnant daughter, don't forget. It's had more mechanical problems over the years than I can count, but it's generally served me pretty well.

Here's hoping that doesn't change today.

So far, so good. The engine's purring like a panther. The CD player's blaring some kick-ass Stevie Ray Vaughan. And the windows are wide open. The cool September air is streaming in and it's finally calming me some.

At least that's what I'm telling myself.

I glance in my rearview mirror, making sure I'm not being followed. I press down harder on the gas anyway. The janky old SUV grumbles and picks up a bit of speed.

I don't know where I'm going yet, but I know I'm in one hell of a hurry to get there.

I also know I'm terrified. Petrified. So scared outta my freaking brain that I'm practically numb. The full reality of my situation is just starting to become clear.

But strangely enough, I'm also feeling *good*—for the first time since I don't know when. I'm feeling excited. Energized. Alive! There's no substitute for being right, especially about something this major.

And I *am* right. Right?

Damn straight!

The friggin' US Air Force should have listened to me from the start!

Kiss my ass, Caltech!

Up yours, NASA!

But no time to start popping champagne just yet. The FBI is on my ass—along with who knows who else.

My mind is so distracted, I don't notice the traffic light turn from yellow to red. I slam on the brakes and skid to a stop just in time.

Which is when I realize what I have to do next.

I've got to get what I've seen—make that, *the alien signal I've overheard*—to the right people, so we can figure it out.

Thing is, who the hell *are* the right people?

Then it hits me.

As soon as the light turns green, I pull a screeching

U-turn, cutting off cars in both directions, getting honked at so much it sounds like an angry flock of geese.

I pray a cop doesn't see me and pull me over. That's the last thing I need right now.

Then I stomp on the gas and start heading east, then north toward Glendale.

There's only one place to start. Only one person I can share this with. I owe it to her. I owe a *lot* to her, actually. She deserves to be the first one to tell me if she thinks I've got something here . . . or if I've gone completely bonkers.

The truth is, I *need* her to be first.

And I can't get to her fast enough.

CHAPTER 9

GREAT. I'VE JUST MADE contact with freaking *aliens* and now I'm stuck smack-dab in the middle of rush-hour Los Angeles traffic.

The 2 freeway is worse than a parking lot, jammed with commuters going both ways. Impatient, I start driving like a teenager, weaving in and out of cars. I even cruise along the bumpy shoulder for a bit. Horns blast at me. I get plenty of middle-finger salutes. I couldn't care less.

When I finally reach the San Fernando Road exit, I zoom down the off-ramp, then cut through Forest Lawn Park...

And I'm suddenly flooded with memories. Like all the great concerts held here that Marty and I used to go to. Or strolling through the statuary with the kids, who would always giggle at the life-sized, highly detailed replica of Michelangelo's *David*. Those sure were the days.

And now I'm pulling up in front of our old house. My ex-wife's house.

I notice Marty has repainted it a pleasant pastel yellow instead of drab beige. God, how long has it been since I've visited? She's replaced the furniture on the front porch, too. Ditched the sagging settee on which we passed many lovely summer evenings talking about life, our kids, future *grandkids*. The rosebushes I planted and took such meticulous care of are still there, but barely. Thanks to the California drought, they look wilted. Ancient. Dead.

Like our marriage. *Oh, man...*

During my otherwise fruitless, miserable time as a grad student at Caltech, Marty Garrison was the best damn thing that happened to me. She made it all worth it.

She'd just earned a master's there in astrophysics, with high honors, and was working in the office of the dean of the graduate aerospace labs. Marty had the brains, all right, plus the beauty to match. The first time I laid eyes on her, I was done for. Tall, athletic, with rich black hair and a face that beamed self-confidence, she had me at "Hi, how can I help you?"

That was the only upside of churning through as many faculty advisors and meeting with the dean as often as I did—getting to flirt with her each time, even if I never had the balls to ask her out. One day, Marty offered to take a look at part of my dissertation, and gave me some really insightful comments. Soon thereafter, we became unofficial colleagues. Then friends. Then more. We discovered we were kindred spirits. We fell in love—deep, complex, scientifically verifiable love.

After we got married and I joined the Air Force, Marty landed a fabulous job at NASA's Jet Propulsion Lab over in Pasadena. We bought this nice little home together. Had two gorgeous girls. Things were going great. What happened?

Life happened.

No, *I* happened.

I don't see her or our kids nearly as much as I should. I know that. I also know I'm not exactly my ex-wife's favorite guy. But it was some kind of instinct that brought me here today. In the past, I've always turned to Marty for help. She's a good person, so she's always given it. And Jesus, do I need it right now.

Steeling myself, I walk up the creaky wooden stairs and knock on the door.

"Daddy!" cries Claire, my youngest, just six years old, as she flings it open. She's wearing two red bows in her blond pigtails, a *Frozen*-themed aquamarine skirt, brown pajama bottoms printed with *Star Wars* characters, and one green rubber boot. I've got to give my little girl credit: she's got style. Consistency, too. Marty sent me new pictures of Claire and her sister about a week ago—which I promptly beamed up to the heavens, as always—and she was wearing almost this exact getup.

"Hey, sweetie. Is Mommy around? I really need to see her."

Before she can reply, I hear a familiar voice call from down the hall. "Claire, get back here. What did I tell you about opening the door for..."

My stressed-out ex-wife appears in the entryway. Her hair is a frizzy mess. She's wearing a stained, oversized Caltech sweatshirt with not a stitch of makeup.

Yet to me, she looks as beautiful as the day we first met.

"Daddy's not a stranger!" Claire exclaims, overcome with a fit of giggles as if that's the funniest idea she's ever heard.

Marty frowns, not amused one bit.

"No. He's not. It just feels that way sometimes. Go back inside, baby. I'll make you breakfast in a minute."

With an adorable nod, Claire scurries off.

Then Marty levels a withering stare at me.

"Not exactly a great time, Rob."

"I know. But it's an emergency. This may sound crazy, but...I was right all along! I...I intercepted something. This morning. A message. Finally. From space!"

Marty scowls and reaches for the doorknob.

"Wait!" I plead. "Marty, please. Just listen to me."

Knowing I have about ten seconds, tops, before she slams the door in my face—maybe forever—I breathlessly explain as much as I can. The crude supercomputer I built in my apartment. The satellites I'd been tapping into. The alert signal that woke me before dawn. The streams of patterned cosmic data I glimpsed with my own eyes that finally confirmed my lifelong theory. *The freaking armed federal agents I saw breaking into my apartment!*

After I make my case—and beg for her help and expertise—I wait. Marty is silent. She's always had the best poker face I've ever seen. I forgot how much I hated it.

After what feels like an eternity, she speaks.

"Jesus *fuck*, Rob! Are you serious? Jesus fuck!"

My ex-wife is a brilliant astrophysicist and consummate professional. If *that's* her first reaction to what I've told her...I think she just might be on my side.

I can see there's still some major doubt inside her. But I can tell she understands this is too good, too big, too important not to take seriously.

Marty turns back and hollers into the house: "Girls, put your shoes on! No school today, we're taking a road trip! Hurry!"

Almost instantaneously, Claire and Ellie, my oldest, eight, scamper down the steps, hyper with excitement.

Marty and I quickly buckle them into the back seat of my Jeep and shut the doors.

"You should know, Rob," she says to me, "that I'm hoping you're wrong."

"Huh? Why?" I ask. "This is the moment I've been waiting for my entire life! It could literally be the biggest discovery in the history of humankind!"

"Exactly," she replies, lowering her voice. "If you're right...you're a dead man."

CHAPTER 10

"YOU STILL REMEMBER HOW to get there?" Marty asks.

I nod. Of course I do.

When we were married, we used to drive the forty minutes to her folks' place in Glendora almost every other weekend. And while she and her mom watched Claire and Ellie frolic in the pool, I'd crack open a beer and talk shop with her old man. In addition to being my Jeep's original owner, Dr. John Garrison is an accomplished scientist in his own right, with plenty of connections to both the public and private aerospace worlds.

If anyone can point me in the right direction, it's him.

"Get ready, girls," I say, glancing back at my happy, innocent children. "We're going to Nana and Pop-Pop's."

The girls cheer with joy as I start the engine and peel out. Soon I'm merging onto the 134, which, thankfully, is mostly clear now. So I really step on it. No time to waste.

Marty and I don't speak for the first few minutes of our ride, so the air is thick with tension. It's broken by the peal of her phone. I glance over but can't make out the name on the caller ID. With a frown, Marty answers.

"Debbie, hi, how are . . . wait . . . there's . . . there's what?"

My ex-wife's voice has grown loud and alarmed. Even the girls stop what they're doing and look up.

"Where am I?" Marty says nervously to this mysterious caller. "I, uh . . . I just stepped out to run some errands. Dry cleaning, post office, I should be back soon. My phone's about to die so if they try to call me — right. Okay. Thanks, Debbie. Bye."

Marty hangs up, shuts off her cell, and looks white as a sheet.

And I have a god-awful feeling I know why.

"That was my neighbor," she says to me. "Three black cars just pulled up outside the house. Guys in dark suits. Earpieces. Guns. What the hell, Rob?"

"Mar, I . . . I didn't . . . I . . ."

I can only stutter. At a complete loss for words.

"You just couldn't leave well enough alone, *could* you?" she snaps. "Had to keep chasing your crackpot theories. Keep ticking people off every step of the way. Caltech. The Air Force. The government. And now you've dragged *us* into it."

Of course, I understand how she's feeling. I feel sorry, and debate whether to say so. Then again, Marty could have easily shut that door on me. Could have kicked me right to the curb. But she didn't. Even knowing the dangers, she agreed to help — and brought the girls along, too. That tells me she's intrigued by what I found. And concerned. Maybe she doesn't still love me, but on some level, I know she still cares.

I'm about to respond to her—when I hear a siren. And in my rearview mirror I see the flashing red and blue lights of a California Highway Patrol car.

Shit! How did the feds find us so fast? License plate–scanning cameras? Drones? Or were they following me this whole time? What the hell do I do?

"Daddy, it's the police, you have to stop," Ellie says.

"She's right, Rob," Marty adds sternly. "Don't be stupid."

For a moment I consider flooring it. But obviously that's insane. Right?

"Okay, okay," I say nervously. I pull the Jeep over. "Everybody just be cool."

About ten seconds later, an olive-skinned, barrel-chested patrolman is sidling up to my open window. Maybe it's my nerves, but the dude looks giant. Six foot six at least. Even stranger, he's got a beard, jet-black and stringy. And in place of the typical Smokey the Bear hat, he's wearing a dark-green turban.

I've been pulled over plenty of times in my day, but never by a cop who looked like this. It must be a religious thing. The Smith & Wesson sidearm on his hip sure looks department-issued.

"Good morning, Officer...Singh," I say, squinting in the sunlight to read the name tag above his glistening badge, an attempt to be friendly. "What seems to be—"

"License and registration," he says gruffly.

Damnit. As soon as he runs my info through his system,

an alert is going to chime in every FBI and DHS field office from here to Chicago! I'll be detained. Arrested in front of my family. Carted off to some CIA black site. But what choice do I have?

"Not a problem, sir," I answer.

I open the cluttered glove box and start rummaging through it. A small avalanche of candy wrappers and unpaid parking tickets tumbles out.

"Do you know how fast you were going back there?" he asks. "I clocked you at ninety in a sixty-five. You in some kind of hurry?"

"Uh...no, sir. I mean, I am. In a hurry. We're taking the kids to, um, spend a day with their grandparents."

The patrolman grunts. What I told him was the truth—at least part of it. He can see my two girls whispering and giggling in the back seat. But will he buy it?

I find the Jeep's registration. *Think of something, Rob!* But I can't. And I'm all out of time. Knowing I'm sealing my fate, I hand it over, along with my license.

The officer turns to head back to his car, when little Claire points to him and blurts out, "Hey, mister, did anyone ever tell you you look like Chewbacca?"

The patrolman stops in his tracks. And looks deeply offended.

Just when this couldn't get any worse!

Claire and Ellie buckle over in hysterics, but Marty and I are mortified.

"Girls!" Marty snaps. "Don't be rude. Tell the officer you don't mean that."

"But he does, Mommy, look!" Ellie says, pointing to the image of the character printed on her little sister's *Star Wars* coloring book. "He's so tall, and big, and his beard!"

"Officer, I'm sorry," I stammer, trying to smooth things over, "they're just being silly."

"Oh, *are* they?" the officer asks, his face still tight.

But then, a huge smile spreads across his face. "Do I *sound* like him, too?"

Incredibly, the cop lets loose a deep, nasally roar—a darn good Chewbacca impression, if I do say so myself.

Ellie and Claire go nuts. The officer beams. He does it again, even louder.

A highway patrolman doing voices during a traffic stop? Seriously? And here I thought discovering alien life would be the strangest thing that happened to me today.

"I've got two of my own about the same age," he says to me, leaning into my window, dad to dad. "Look, I know you can't wait to hand 'em off to Grandma and Grandpa and have some alone time. But slow down and drive safe. Okay?"

I can barely hide my absolute shock as the patrolman hands my license and registration back to me.

"Yes, sir!" I say, a little too enthusiastically. "Absolutely. Thank you!"

"You all have a good day."

I watch the officer get back into his squad car and drive away. No arrest, no ticket, no feds swooping in, nothing. Marty and I share a look of shock. And relief.

Maybe the universe is even crazier than I thought.

CHAPTER 11

"INITIATING GRAVITATIONAL BOOSTER SE-QUENCE."

"Roger," Mission Control responds. *"Epsilon Eridani,* you are clear to proceed."

The commander turns to the flight engineer—who is rapidly executing a string of mind-numbingly complex calculations on her holographic touchscreen control panel—and asks: "Current orbital positioning?"

"We're looking good, ma'am," the flight engineer responds. "I'm finishing the final telemetry projections now. Then we'll be ready to separate."

"Very well."

Next, the commander's attention turns to the pilot.

"Heading and flight vector?"

"Modifying to two-six-niner-five, Commander. Fly-by-wire coming offline."

"Aye," the commander responds, as the gloved fingers

of the pilot's left hand dance across his translucent panel, while his right hand gently tilts the control stick.

On both the outer port and starboard sides of the spacecraft, rows of tiny thrusters make a series of minute adjustments to the ship's flight path. Currently, the *Epsilon Eridani* is in low orbit. But that's about to change in a very big way.

By firing, then jettisoning, their booster rockets at the right moment, the crew intends to harness the power of Earth's gravity to slingshot their craft more efficiently and thus deeper into space than they could otherwise travel. It's a tried-and-true technique, but one that requires extraordinary planning and the utmost precision.

It's also the crew's point of no return.

Once they leave orbit, there will be no second chances.

No room for error.

No turning back.

If the commander is going to be fully honest with her team, if she is going to reveal what she and she alone knows about their mission, if she is going to offer her crew members the opportunity to back out…now is her absolute final opportunity.

To abort the mission at this junction would be incredibly costly. It would also be career-ending, perhaps for everyone on board. Yet it would be doable.

After booster separation, it becomes all but impossible.

Only now does the weight of this dilemma fully sink in for the commander—when she and her crew are literally weightless. Her face remains calm and professional, but inside, her mind is on fire.

Then she gets an idea.

A cowardly one, but still.

Perhaps she can find a minuscule mechanical problem, a technical excuse to abort the mission, without anyone being the wiser. Unlikely, but worth a shot.

"Full life support and eco-stasis check?" the commander asks. "Is there anything—anything at all—out of the ordinary?"

The mission specialist swivels his seat around to face her. He is immediately concerned. This request is not part of the standard pre-separation protocol. At all.

"Can you please repeat that, Commander?"

"Before we're flung into deep space, is it so wrong to want to review the systems that will be keeping us alive?" she asks, rhetorically.

"Of course not, ma'am," the mission specialist replies, still a bit rattled. But he obeys, and runs a complete ship-wide diagnosis.

"Life support and eco-stasis fully operational," he says. "O-2 filters, rehydrators, nitrate converters, primary and redundant plutonium generators. All running optimally."

Normally this would be comforting news. But to the commander, it's the opposite. If this mission is going to be halted, it is now completely in her hands.

"Commander," the flight engineer interjects, "we're entering our optimal launch window. We're ready for your command."

Glancing down at the photo wedged into her console of her children and husband, the commander suddenly feels an overwhelming pang of self-doubt. She begins to question every major life decision that's brought her to this point. Where did her belief in this mission come from? Will her family ever fully understand why she accepted it? Is it truly the right thing to do? How will history judge them? *Whose* history, anyway?

"We are awaiting your order for booster combustion and separation," the pilot repeats. "We're nearing our window's termination, Commander."

When the commander remains silent, the pilot adds sternly: *"Ma'am?"*

The mood on the bridge is growing tense. *What's going on?* the crew wonders.

The commander has mere seconds left to make up her mind.

At last, just as the sun is beginning to rise above the planetary horizon, she does.

Her mouth dry and scratchy, the commander whispers: "Boosters . . . engage."

The pilot and flight engineer snap into action, executing the command.

The ship's rear rockets instantly erupt with thousands of tons of propulsion.

The *Epsilon Eridani* groans and shudders as it leaves orbit, hurtling higher, higher, higher into space.

Once the boosters' fuel is fully expended, the flames snuff out. Next, the empty rockets separate from the craft

CHAPTER 12

I MAKE THE FINAL turn onto my former in-laws' winding, private road and their quaint, Spanish-style cottage comes into view. It's been years since I've visited, but it feels like I was here only yesterday.

Claire and Ellie clap and cheer in anticipation. And it's no wonder. Marty's parents are both so warm and loving toward their granddaughters, always spoiling them rotten. What kids *don't* like getting to skip school to frolic in a swimming pool, play with a cute dog, and eat ice cream sandwiches?

I drive through the property's wide-open iron gate. (I'd told Marty's father a thousand times to keep it locked, but he always ignored my advice, chalking up my concerns to paranoia.) I pull the Jeep up in front of the house and toot the horn.

As Marty and I get out and start unloading the girls, Karen and John, trailed by Newton, their yappy schnauzer, emerge from the front door to greet us—with a mixture of joy and confusion. They're delighted to see their daughter and grandkids, but are clearly *not* so thrilled to see their former son-in-law, the guy who basically abandoned the family years ago to drink and chase a cosmic fantasy.

"What a wonderful surprise!" Karen exclaims, wrapping Claire and Ellie in a tight embrace. She seems to sense my and Marty's unease immediately. "How about we get you girls inside and into your swimsuits," she says. "Come."

When the three of us are alone, John moves to Marty and gives her a long hug. "It's wonderful to see you," he says, "but don't the girls have school? What are you doing here?"

"It's a long story, Dad," my ex says. Then she gestures to yours truly.

I start to go in for a man-hug, but John extends a chilly hand instead. I don't exactly blame him. It's actually more than I deserve. Humbly, I shake it.

"Hello, Rob," he says. "It's been…quite a while."

"I know," I reply. "It's good to see you, John. Considering the circumstances."

"And what would those circumstances *be,* exactly?"

"Why don't we, um…head inside," I suggest. "I need to talk to you. I need your help. With something important. Something that could change our entire understanding of the universe as we know it."

John shakes his head in disgust. "Son, you listen to me. If this is another of your ramblings about sending aliens photos, about intergalactic radio transmissions, you—"

"*Please,* Dad," Marty interjects. "Just hear him out. For me?"

God, what a woman! How did I ever let her slip away?

John is clearly still unhappy about the situation, but he can't say no to his little girl. With a huff, he turns and heads back into the house.

I give Marty's shoulder a grateful squeeze and the two of us follow him inside.

But before I shut the door, I hear a faint whirring noise high overhead. It's distant, but getting closer. It starts growing louder and louder. Before long, it's nearly deafening.

I look up...and gasp.

A helicopter—police? government? military?—is soaring high in the sky above.

It flies directly over the house, then keeps going, finally disappearing behind the crest of a nearby hill.

It takes me a solid few seconds to catch my breath.

Was it just an LA Sheriff's Department chopper on a routine patrol of this neck of the San Gabriel Mountains?

Or was it someone else—tracking me, watching me?

I tell myself I'm just being paranoid.

But am I?

CHAPTER 13

MARTY AND I FOLLOW her father down the hall and into his private study, which is lined with mahogany bookshelves. On the walls hang a collection of framed, antique sketches of early airplanes. An original blueprint of NASA's 1961 *Saturn I* module. And John's many impressive degrees and awards, including his PhD in astrophysics from Stanford and the National Medal of Science bestowed on him by President Clinton.

I should probably mention that brilliance runs deep in Marty's family.

About a decade ago, my father-in-law retired from a long and distinguished career as head of Boeing's Advanced Space Access Team in nearby Torrance. He and Karen purchased this cozy cottage in the hills, where they've lived ever since. But John still does some consulting here and there on various top-secret aerospace projects for the government and private sector, which has kept him up to date on all the latest technological developments in the field, both domestic and foreign.

Sure, the guy might hate my guts. But there's nothing I can tell him about my research or discovery that John won't at least know *something* about.

"Now what the hell is going on?" he demands, slamming his office door.

"Let me show you," I say. "I just need remote access to my home system."

John flips open the MacBook on his desk and spins it to face me. "Go ahead."

I smile awkwardly. "Actually, that's not going to work."

Whether the FBI confiscated my supercomputer's hard drives this morning or not, I thankfully had the foresight a few months ago to set up a real-time, thrice-encrypted multivalent phantom server, encoded across a randomized network of dark-web server farms all around the world.

In layman's terms? I backed up all my files to a very top-secret cloud.

Problem is, I'll need an equally robust computer system to open them.

Luckily, I know I've come to the right place.

John understands exactly what I'm asking for. Grumbling under his breath, he heaves a moveable bookshelf to the side to reveal a hidden titanium-reinforced wall. He taps a code into a digital keypad and the wall slides open . . . exposing a small inner chamber lined with slim monitors, blinking server towers, and quantum processors.

This is one of the few things my father-in-law and I have in common. His might be a little fancier than mine, but we've both built makeshift homemade supercomputers.

I hurry over to a console and get to work, logging in to my remote portal with a series of thirty-six-digit alphanumeric passcodes I've committed to memory. Before long, I've pulled up the streams of data qubits I first saw early this morning.

The repeating pattern is right there, clear as day.

But the "meaning" is still an absolute mystery.

"Have a look," I say to my ex-wife's father. "See for yourself."

John squints at his computer monitors, at first with extreme skepticism. But the anger creasing his face slowly turns to confusion...then astonishment.

"Oh, my God," he utters, eyes growing wide with amazement. "This...this is...I..."

He's so flabbergasted, he can't even string together a complete sentence!

Marty leans over his shoulder to see the pulsing data herself. She sits down, her eyes never moving from the screen; she's even more incredulous than her father.

"Where are you getting this from?" she asks. "What's the source?"

"It's actually a synthesis of two different feeds," I explain, typing rapidly and pulling up a spinning map of the globe on-screen showing a pair of blinking dots—one in central Russia, the other in South America. "A classified former Soviet listening station and a radio telescope within the Atacama Large Millimeter Array in northern Chile. That's what makes this so unique."

John is still reeling. "Do you...do you understand... what this *means*?"

"Not a damn clue," I say. "That's what I was hoping you could help tell me. But I do know... *it means something*. No way in hell this is just random cosmic noise. It's a string of repeating signals aimed directly at us from deep space—from a part of the infinite night sky we haven't fully probed. And *that* means..."

I can barely contain myself as I finish the sentence.

"...my theory was correct all along! Some*one* or some*thing* is out there! Sending us a message, trying to make contact!"

I look to John, who has turned white as a ghost. He puts a shaky hand to his head and sits down, struggling to process it all.

"Okay, let's just think this through," says Marty. "Obviously the government is going to want to keep a lid on this. And that means, they're going to want to keep a lid on *you*, Rob—if you catch my drift. The only way to protect yourself that I can think of...is to *translate* the message. Figure out what it's actually *saying*, to give yourself some leverage. Which, of course, is easier said than done."

I nod gravely. I'm fully aware of the incredible danger I'm in—we're *all* in—and the many challenges that lie ahead.

"The question is, *how*?" I say. "We barely have the

computing power to *visualize* these data qubits, let alone interpret them. If only there was some way—"

"There is."

John slowly stands again and looks me square in the eye.

"Northrop Grumman. They have a facility. Up in Antelope Valley. They call it Tejon Ranch."

"Sure, I know it," I say. "Not far from Edwards Air Force Base, where I used to be stationed. I've seen sat-feeds of the place. Looks like nothing but an abandoned airstrip and a couple empty hangars... right?"

John frowns and shakes his head.

"Wrong. That's just what they *want* you to think."

CHAPTER 14

"IF YOU REALLY PUSH the folks at Northrop," John continues, "they'll admit the place is an old research facility. But they'll tell you it's basically abandoned. In reality..."

I lean forward, anxious to learn whatever tidbit he's about to spill.

"...it is. At least on the surface. But underground? It's a massive system of buried tunnels, some a mile deep. They contain twenty-two levels of intergalactic communication and data analysis capabilities like you wouldn't believe."

For a moment, I'm too startled to say anything. Truth be told, I *don't* believe it. And apparently, my former father-in-law can read that skepticism all over my face.

"I know it sounds improbable," he says. "But it's true."

"Dad," Marty says, "how do you know? It must be just a rumor."

John shakes his head.

"About a year ago, I consulted on an aerospace project for Northrop. I've been to Tejon Ranch. I've seen what it really is. The technology that place has is on the cutting edge of interstellar communication capabilities." He gestures to the computer screens, still blinking with the patterned data message. "If anybody outside the government stands a chance of translating this, it's them."

I consider what John is saying. It all sounds amazing.

Except for one tiny little problem.

"Okay, even if Northrop *was* willing to touch this thing with a thirty-foot pole," I say, "how exactly do you expect me to get inside that place? Knock on the door and say, 'Hi, I'm a disgraced scientist who just made contact with aliens. Mind if I borrow your nonexistent supercomputer system for the afternoon?'"

"He's right," Marty says sullenly. "There's just no way—"

"There's *always* a way," John replies. "You just get to that ranch. Let me handle the rest. I still know a few researchers there. They'll be waiting for you at the main gate. Once they recognize what you've discovered, they'll help you—just like I did."

I'm overwhelmed with conflicting emotions. This man I admire so much, who was once family, whose daughter I used to love—and on some level still do—is not only showing me the professional respect I've always craved. He's willing to go to bat for me. Risk everything. Because he believes in me. Because he believes in my discovery.

"I...I don't know what to say," I stammer.

"Say *good-bye*—to Marty and the girls. They'll stay here with us, where it's hopefully safer."

I nod. With federal agencies looking for me, of course that's the wisest option. Still, the idea of being away from them again makes me feel awful—because being *with* them this morning has made me feel so wonderful.

I'm overwhelmed with conflicting emotions from all sides. Marty and the kids. Being with them again reminds me of how much I love them, how important they are to me. What the hell was I thinking? I wasn't. I buried myself in this crazy project that looks like it's about to pay big dividends, good, bad, or otherwise.

And the only way to justify my selfish isolation, my addiction to it, is to honor Marty and the kids, and my work, by seeing it through. Whatever it takes. It's also about my professional integrity—if there's any left to be had.

While John remains in his office to start making some calls, Marty and I head to the backyard. There we find Claire, Ellie, and Newton all splashing happily together in the pool. Karen is sitting on a chaise longue, watching her granddaughters and their dog.

"Girls," Marty calls to them, "come say good-bye to your father. Quickly."

Claire and Ellie hop out of the water and scurry over to me.

I kneel down and wrap their little wet bodies in a giant hug.

"So, listen," I say, fighting the giant lump growing in my throat. "I just found out I've got to take care of some very important work stuff. I'm sorry I have to go, but—"

"Will you visit us again?" Claire asks, her face bright with hope.

"Of course!" I insist. "Before you even know it. It's been so much fun being with you guys today. Listen to Mommy and Nana and Pop-Pop, okay? And always remember how much I think about you two. And how much I love you."

"We love you, too, Daddy," Ellie says, and both she and her sister tighten their embrace around my neck.

God...I would give *anything* to freeze this moment in time forever. The photos Marty sends me—and I send into space—are nice, but *nothing* beats the real thing. It takes everything I've got to tear myself away from them. I promise myself I'll see my girls again soon. That I'll be a bigger presence in their lives. A better father.

And this time, I really mean it.

After I hug Karen good-bye, Marty and I step out alone onto the front porch.

"You're sure you can handle this, Rob?" she asks, gazing up at me with those beautiful green eyes.

How the hell did you let this incredible woman go?

"Honestly? I'm not," I admit. "Mar, I'm *terrified*. I've got a message from outer space and it's up to *me* to decode it! But I *have* to handle this. For you and the girls. For myself. For...for the future of the human race."

Then I add with a little smile: "No pressure, right?"

Marty chuckles, happy for this shred of comic relief. Then very tentatively, she leans in and gives me a quick kiss on the lips. I feel my whole body tingle like it was our first kiss all over again. Then we both pull away—just as John steps out onto the porch as well.

"Ready to hit the road?" he asks.

"Ready as I'll ever be," I answer, holding up my key to his old Jeep.

"I don't think so," John says, snatching it right out of my hand. "Follow me."

CHAPTER 15

JOHN MARCHES DOWN THE porch stairs and heads for the garage around the side. I hustle along after him, confused as ever.

"You're going to be racing across the desert," he tells me, "then up some rocky foothills. Winding roads. Treacherous switchbacks."

"Right," I reply as he yanks open the garage door. "All the more reason for me to take the four-by-four, no?"

The inside of the garage looks like a tornado swept through. Tools, car parts, wires, old furniture, and boxes and boxes of computer equipment, floor to ceiling.

Except in the back left corner.

There, something is covered with a wrinkled gray tarp.

"The Jeep is what they *think* you'll be driving," John says, heading for this covered object that stands about three feet tall. "They've got your plates. I'm sure they've put out an APB. You need speed and agility. But most of all, *anonymity.*"

With a bit of a flourish, he pulls off the tarp to reveal a motorcycle so sleek and aerodynamic, it might as well be a mini spaceship.

It's a Ducati 899, a bike that was clearly designed to go *fast*.

"Wow!" I can't help but exclaim. I feel like a little kid on Christmas morning. The motorcycle is absolutely stunning. "How long have you had this thing?"

"I bought it two years ago," John answers. "Wasn't easy convincing Karen to let me. It's perfect for cruising through the countryside, or along the coast. Or in *your* case...outrunning the feds. Here. Try these on."

John hands me a black protective leather jacket and a pair of padded riding gloves. They all fit, well, like a glove.

"Now climb on. Give it a try."

I do, instinctively squeezing the brake handle to stabilize the Ducati while I straddle its contoured leather seat. I rode a clunky old Honda Rebel in college, so I'm familiar with how to handle a bike. But this one is like nothing I've ever been on before. Even in park it feels nimble. And futuristic. Almost ethereal.

I turn the ignition key and a small rectangular screen lights up, displaying the bike's data. It looks less like a motorcycle dashboard than the cockpit of a plane. I shift into neutral, press the starter button, and roll the throttle just a touch. The Ducati responds instantly with a low, throaty roar.

"Tank's about half full," John says, reaching for one of

two helmets hanging on a nearby hook. "You may need to top it off at some point before you get there."

He hands me the helmet. It's neon-green DayGlo, full-face with a clear visor, so it offers not just excellent protection but a bit of a disguise, too. I slip it on, and adjust it so it's snug and secure. Then I flip up the visor and give John a deeply grateful look. I realize in that moment that he's the closest thing to a father I've ever really had.

"John, I...I don't know how to thank you."

"Not now," he says, waving off my sentimentality with one hand while rummaging through a plastic bin with another. "You've got an opportunity here—no, a *responsibility*—to shine a light on something earth-shattering. Something history-making! That's a major accomplishment you should be proud of."

I swallow hard, overcome with pride. Everything I've worked so hard for...all that I've sacrificed...all the mistakes I've made...the toll it's taken on my family, my health, my life...

"But you won't be alive to enjoy it," John continues, snapping me out of my trance, "unless you get your overeducated ass to Tejon Ranch in one piece. Do you hear me?"

I nod, and see he's been tinkering with what looks like a small GPS device, which he affixes to my handlebars next to the throttle.

"This is a Garmin Zumo 350LM. Just follow the directions I programmed. It's a pretty roundabout route, so it should help you avoid too much traffic *and* throw off anybody trying to follow you. You're looking at a two-hour ride at least."

"Got it," I say. "Good thinking."

"Oh, one more thing. Leave your phone here."

"That's okay," I say. "I turned it off hours ago."

"Do you really think that's going to prevent the suits from tracking it? Gimme a break, Rob. You're smarter than that. Take these instead."

He thrusts into my hands a few cheap, disposable cell phones.

"When I'm working on a top-secret consulting gig," John explains, "I like to keep some lying around, just in case. They'll do in a pinch. Then just toss 'em."

Nodding, I stuff the phones into my jacket pocket. "Anything else?"

John gives my shoulder a firm pat. "Godspeed. Now get going."

I snap my visor shut, shift into first gear, give the bike some gas, let out the clutch, and roar—more like *fly*— out of the garage, down the driveway, and past the open gate.

I'm about halfway down Glendora Mountain Road, just starting to get comfortable with this zippy little bike, en- joying the sense of freedom and the cool breeze whipping around my body, when I spot something that makes my stomach drop.

Tearing across Foothill Road about a half mile down the hill is a convoy of three black SUVs. Their sirens are off but their blue lights are flashing.

And they're headed right for me!

No way it's just a coincidence. It's gotta be the FBI. Maybe they really did manage to track my powered-down iPhone like John said. Or maybe they just checked my file and wagered that I'd turn to my former in-laws for help. Maybe that helicopter that flew overhead twenty minutes ago spotted me. Or maybe...maybe...

Snap out of it! I scold myself. It doesn't matter. I can't let them catch me.

Thinking fast, I apply the brake, then steer my bike off the road and down a slight embankment. I spot a dense grove of trees, and maneuver my motorcycle and myself behind them. As soon as I'm in position, I kill the engine—

Seconds before the SUVs whiz past my hiding spot. They continue flying up the road, toward the family I left behind—once again.

Have I lost my mind? No.

I know I'm right, and that I'm doing the right thing.

I also know I just dodged a bullet.

I pray my luck lasts just a little bit longer.

CHAPTER 16

DR. JOHN GARRISON IS standing on his front porch. He's been watching his former son-in-law—a decent man, a flawed man, a man obsessed, a man who might be mere hours away from changing the course of human history—speeding away on a high-performance motorcycle toward a top-secret corporate research facility deep underground.

John is hopeful that Rob will be safe and successful. But he also has grave concerns. He waits for the sound of Rob's bike to completely fade away into the distance. Then he waits for the cloud of dirt it kicked up to dissipate as well. The trillions of dust particles swirling through the air under the California sun have created a kind of mysterious haze, which feels like an eerie metaphor for what's happening.

"Iced tea, honey?"

Karen, John's loving wife of more than forty years,

is standing in the open doorway, beckoning her rattled husband inside. He can see, already seated at the kitchen table, his daughter and two beautiful granddaughters waiting for him. How could he resist?

After locking the front door behind him, John takes a seat on the cushioned wicker settee next to Marty. He gives her hand a tight squeeze, and they exchange a look that speaks volumes. Despite Rob's many imperfections, they both still care about him deeply. They're both extremely proud of him.

And they're both scared to death for him.

Karen sets out some glasses and begins to pour the cold, amber liquid from a giant pitcher—when a sudden pounding at the front door startles her, causing her to spill it everywhere.

"FBI! Open up!"

"Oh, my God," says Marty, clapping her hand over her mouth. Her girls whimper with fright, and cling to her desperately.

"It's all right," John says to his family, his voice low and reassuring. "I'll handle it."

As the knocking and yelling outside grow even louder, John calmly opens the front door. More than a dozen government agents in dark suits and sunglasses—looking straight out of *Men in Black*—are standing before him. Three black SUVs are parked in his driveway, boxing in Rob's empty Jeep.

"John Garrison? We're here to search the premises," one of them announces.

"I'd like to see your search warrant first, if you don't mind," John replies calmly.

But just as the doctor expected, the agents ignore his request and blow right past him—shoving him out of their way, nearly knocking the older fellow to the ground. They have also drawn their sidearms, keeping them aimed low but ready.

John struggles to hide his fear. Whoever these guys work for, apparently the rule of law doesn't apply to them. At least not at the moment. Maybe never.

The agents quickly spread out all across the house and property, checking every floor, every room, every closet, every nook and cranny. Marty, Karen, and the girls stay huddled in scared silence at the kitchen table, where John rejoins them.

"Now listen here," he says to the agent who seems to be in command. "Charging into my home, guns blazing, terrifying my family. What the hell is this about?"

Of course, John already knows the answer. But playing dumb is part of his act.

The lead agent steps right up to John and glares at him in a show of intimidation.

"An issue of national security," is the gruff reply. "We're looking for a dangerous fugitive. Currently the most wanted man in America. So do *not* give me any shit."

"I see," John says. "Well, if it's Barnett you're looking for, he's long gone."

This *really* gets the lead agent's attention. "So you admit he was recently here?"

"Of course. His phone is sitting right there on the counter. And his car is parked outside. Feel free to look around all you want. But you won't find him."

"Where did he go? When?"

"My wife, see, was going to make some brownies for my granddaughters," John answers, "but we were out of flour. So Rob took a walk to the market at the bottom of the hill. You probably passed it driving up. He should be back within the hour. At least I hope so. You're welcome to wait here for him. Care for some iced tea?"

The agent eyes John with deep suspicion. The old man appears to be telling the truth, but the agent is smart and seasoned. He's about to order a team to head back down the hill and verify John's story, when he hears some critical news via his earpiece.

"Copy that," the agent says into his wrist mic. Then to John: "Don't move."

He leaves the house and jogs over to the detached garage. Two agents are already inside. One is on his knees, inspecting what appears to be a few drops of shiny motor oil on the concrete.

"Check this out, boss," the junior agent says. "Looks fresh. But the space is too tiny for a car. Maybe it's a lawn mower or something, but I thought you'd want to see."

The lead agent nods, already snapping on a latex glove to inspect it. He gently touches the oil spot. Sure enough, it's still wet—and warm.

"That lying SOB!" he says under his breath. "Run

Garrison's DMV records. He owns a *motorcycle*. Find out its make and plates."

The agent stands. His expression grim with determination.

"Barnett didn't go to the damn supermarket. He went on the run. I want to know where. And goddamnit, I want to find him!"

CHAPTER 17

THE COMMANDER IS ON the flight deck floating gently, peacefully. She has been staring out through a porthole at the trillions of stars all around her for the better part of an hour. Racked with growing guilt and misery, she has been trying, desperately, to find some shred of solace in the infinity of outer space. But she has failed.

Her incredible burden continues to weigh upon her. It feels heavier than the force of 10 G's. With the *Epsilon Eridani*'s final destination fast approaching, she knows she cannot keep the true nature of their mission a secret for much longer.

So the commander has decided, at long last, to tell her team the truth.

She keys the com-link on her control panel. "Attention, all crew," she intones. "Please assemble on the flight deck immediately for an urgent briefing."

Not surprisingly, confusion and concern ripple throughout the ship.

The pilot, just waking from a scheduled sleep break, is still groggy, but perks up right away. He is soon propelling himself through the ship's corridors toward the cockpit.

The flight engineer is in the reactor room, monitoring the ship's engine core. She is also apprehensive, but is quickly on her way as well.

The payload chief is in his quarters composing a video message to his wife and two young children back home. Alarmed by the interruption, he pauses the recording and moves to join the others.

Lastly is the mission specialist, who is in the midst of eating a rehydrated meal: lumpy spaghetti and mushy meatballs. Dumping the unfinished contents in the ship's computerized compost bin, he heads up to the flight deck, too.

Once her crew is assembled, the commander takes a brief moment to compose herself, which only further unsettles them. They can sense something is amiss.

Finally, the commander speaks, slowly and with deep seriousness.

"Each of you has known since the day you accepted this mission that it brings with it enormous responsibility. As well as enormous risk. Like the great distance we're traveling through uncharted space. And the giant payload we're carrying."

"You mean the most advanced exploratory probe ever designed?" the payload chief interjects with a forced smile. "I wouldn't really call that a 'risk,' ma'am."

"Copy that," says the pilot. "And I think I speak for all

of us when I say we have the utmost faith in you, ma'am, to guide us to our destination and back."

And back. The commander swallows hard. Her crew isn't making this easy.

"I appreciate that," she replies, "more than any of you could know. Which is why what I'm about to share is incredibly difficult for me."

The commander takes a deep breath.

"The fact is, we...we are not going back."

The crew members exchange confused looks.

"What are you talking about?" asks the flight engineer. I've charted a course to the probe launch point, Commander, as well as our return journey, which will last—"

"You've been misled," the commander says. "All of you. We won't be making that return journey. Because we are not launching a probe. We're not even carrying one. Our payload is, in fact...a five-million-megaton nuclear warhead."

"That's ridiculous," says the pilot. "I don't understand."

"The purpose of our mission is not exploration. It is *annihilation*. For decades, our top astrophysicists and interplanetary astronomers have been observing intergalactic evolution. Their focus has been on one planet in particular—a world that has given them great cause for concern. We have been chosen...to *end* that world."

Stunned silence—followed quickly by confusion. And bubbling anger.

"My God," whispers the payload chief. "I get it now. This is a suicide mission!"

WE. ARE. NOT. ALONE.

The commander averts her eyes. "I suppose that is one way of describing it."

Each of the crew struggles to process this unthinkable bombshell, each in their own way. The pilot with stoic resignation. The flight engineer with fearful whimpering. The payload chief with shocked horror.

But the mission specialist explodes with white-hot rage.

"You lied to us, you bitch!" he exclaims. "You knew all along, and you—"

"I had no choice," the commander responds, contrite. "My orders came from the very top. If I'd revealed our true purpose earlier—"

"None of us," the mission specialist screams, "would have agreed!" The veins at his temples are throbbing. "We have families. We have our whole lives ahead of us—*had* our whole lives. You signed our death warrants without our consent!"

The commander tries to stay calm, hoping to keep the volatile situation under control. "I can't imagine how you all must be feeling. But what you must *understand* is, our sacrifice is for the good of the entire species. The entire universe. Our lives may—"

"No!" cries the pilot, who glimpses out of the corner of his eye—a split second too late—the mission specialist lunge at the commander, brandishing a screwdriver.

The pilot instinctively hurls himself through the air in between the commander and her assailant, right as the mission specialist thrusts the tool—stabbing not the commander but the pilot, deep in his shoulder.

The pilot cries out in agony as the other two crew members join the melee.

After a frenzied, weightless scramble, the others manage to subdue the mission specialist. The flight engineer hurriedly opens the cockpit's first-aid kit and readies a digital syringe filled with 20 cc's of ketamine, a powerful synthetic sedative.

"No, don't!" shouts the mission specialist, still flailing wildly. "She lied to us! She's sending all of us to our deaths! Don't you fools understand that?"

But the other crew members remain loyal. The flight engineer jams the needle into the mission specialist's thigh and within seconds he goes limp.

Everyone else begins catching their breath. Only now does the pilot stop to examine his stab wound. His injury isn't life-threatening, but it's painful and deep. Globules of his blood are floating throughout the cockpit like red rain.

"Thank you," the commander says to her crew. "You... you all saved my life."

But no one responds. The irony is clear as day.

The commander reassumes control. She signals the flight engineer to cue the shape-memory wings to fully withdraw into the fuselage, and the spaceship sails on.

CHAPTER 18

I'VE BEEN CROUCHING IN this prickly thicket of trees, my motorcycle hidden next to me, for a good fifteen minutes now.

I've been trying to steady my nerves and plan my next move—and also make sure there aren't any more FBI vehicles bringing up the rear.

Figuring the feds have probably reached my former in-laws' place by now and have started questioning my family and conducting a search for me, I decide to hit the road again. I stand and start to inch my bike out of the brush—

When I hear the SUVs speeding back down the road.

Shit, that was fast!

I push my motorcycle back on its side and dive back behind the trees, just in the nick of time. The convoy rumbles past me, making the ground tremble.

I guess the good news is the feds aren't terribly interested in John or Karen or Marty or my girls. That's a relief, for sure.

But the fact that they spent barely *any* time on the property fills me with dread.

It means they know I'm on the run. They probably know I borrowed John's Ducati. And they may even know where I'm going.

Okay, okay. Think, Rob. What now?

I still have to get to Northrop and Tejon Ranch. That much I know for sure.

But how?

The route John programmed into the Garmin for me was deliberately indirect. But it will still take me there via a few major freeways—roads teeming with California Highway Patrol and probably fitted with license plate–scanning cameras at every bend.

Great.

Now that I've completely lost the element of surprise, I guess I'd better stick to back roads from here on in. It may take me a hell of a lot longer, but it's worth it, even if it's just for my peace of mind.

I pick the bike back up out of the bushes, then power up the Garmin and begin plotting an alternate route as quickly as I can—aware that the longer the device stays on, the higher the risk they'll be able to track it.

But even if the feds don't, I'm still just one lone man on an unusual motorcycle, who's being hunted by a small army of government agents in broad daylight...

Daylight. Of course!

With the sun so high in the sky, it's gotta be a hundred times easier for the FBI or Highway Patrol or whoever to spot me. Right?

Maybe I should hide my ass until nightfall, or at least sunset. Even if it improves my chances of getting to Northrop undetected by one percent, isn't it worth it?

I rack my brain. Then I remember: there's a quaint bed-and-breakfast-type place just a mile or so up the mountain, with a cozy coffee shop and café on the ground floor. Back when Marty and I were still married and would spend the holidays with her parents, their out-of-town relatives would often stay there. And since I'm a train wreck in the kitchen, I was usually assigned to "taxi duty," shuttling them back and forth.

Point is, I can hang out at the B and B, have a few cups of joe, maybe even a shot or two of something—*No*, stay sober, Rob!—until sundown, then scram.

Best of all, I now know how to get there with my eyes closed.

I quickly shut off the Garmin, drop my helmet visor back into place, and roll the Ducati back up the embankment onto the road.

I restart its engine, say a little prayer, and off I go.

CHAPTER 19

"CHECK, PLEASE," I SAY to the kindly middle-aged woman who has been patiently topping up my coffee mug and bringing me meals for the past ten hours.

"Sure you don't want one more, hon?" she asks. Then she adds with a smile: "Unless you're in some kind of big ol' rush."

I chuckle, trying to be as friendly as I can—and also to seem as normal as I can. To try and cover my tracks, I told her that I was taking a "staycation"—spending a rare day off work being served delicious food and relaxing and catching up on some reading.

All day, I've been sitting in this little café, sipping about a gallon's worth of coffee and pretending to read a stack of newspapers. But really, my mind has been racing a mile a minute as I waited anxiously for nightfall and tried to plan my next move.

I've also been thinking about *why* I'm even trying to

make that next move to begin with: *the message I intercepted from space!*

That's the key to all of this, and it's still the biggest question mark of all.

Even if it's "just" a friendly, intergalactic greeting, it would be an earth-shattering, history-altering event.

But what if it's something more? A warning. A demand. A threat.

This could be the start of the end of the world! Why now? Why me?

"Here ya go, hon," the waitress says, setting down my check.

I nod thanks, then pay the bill in cash, leaving a ridiculously large tip. I hope it's enough to erase any suspicions she might have about me and for her not to call the local police, which is the absolute last thing I need right now, especially after that last run-in.

Soon I'm back on the open mountain roads again, speeding toward Tejon Ranch. The sun has just set and I'm very happy to have the extra cover of darkness.

I also had the brains to buy an old-fashioned folding map—remember those?—back at the bed-and-breakfast, so now I can keep my Garmin off for good. I'm relieved to be off the grid...unless the feds have figured out a way to track paper, too! (I'm only joking...but then again, I wouldn't put it past them.)

After about ninety minutes of driving, I flip my visor up and let the cool, pine-scented evening air hit my face. It feels like I'm flying—cruising along this high-altitude road and with the lights of Santa Clarita twinkling below, both calming and exhilarating.

But then a different kind of light catches my eye.

The "low fuel" indicator on the Ducati's dashboard is on.

Seriously?

John did tell me to top up, but it completely slipped my mind. I've only got another fifty miles or so to Northrop. I wonder: can I make it? No, not a chance. And it's definitely not worth the risk of getting stranded in the middle of nowhere.

Cursing under my breath, I pull over on the gravelly shoulder and whip out the paper map.

There's a gas station just half a mile away, off a route labeled Spunky Canyon Road. Who comes up with these names? Whatever. I'll take it.

A few minutes later, I'm sputtering into Hal's, a tiny, run-down convenience store with two old-school gas pumps out front—as well as two rough-looking mountain men sitting in rocking chairs and smoking cigarettes. They eye me as I park my motorcycle by one of the pumps...which I see has a handwritten sign duct-taped to it: PAY INSIDE. Fair enough. I yank off my helmet, nod a silent hello at the men, and enter the store.

A third grizzled fellow is behind the counter. He's got a long beard and is wearing an old trucker hat stained all different colors from dirt, sweat, and motor oil.

"Help you?" he huffs, absorbed in what I can see is a nudie magazine. I place a crumpled twenty on the counter.

"I need about fifteen dollars on pump two, please. I'll come back for my change."

The man gives me an unnervingly long look. Is he suspicious? Did I say or do something wrong? Did the cops put out a description of me already?

Finally, the man grunts, snatches up my money, and punches some keys on the antique cash register, the kind that actually dings with a real bell when it opens.

Back outside I go. I unscrew the gas cap, insert the nozzle, squeeze the handle...but nothing happens. I guess the cashier hasn't turned on the flow yet. I glance back inside. Sure enough, he's on his cell phone. He looks back at me and holds up a finger as if to say "one second." I see him flip a switch under the counter. I try the gas pump again and thankfully, the fuel starts to flow.

Under the uncomfortable watch of all three men, I fill up the tank. It comes to just over thirteen dollars. I debate whether I should forget my seven measly bucks and just hop on my bike and burn rubber. Because something about this whole situation just isn't sitting right. But then I worry that that might look even *more* suspicious. So I casually saunter back into the store.

"Sure is a nice bike you got there," the cashier says. I can see he's holding my change, but he doesn't give it to me. "Mind if I ask where you got it?"

"Thanks," I reply. "I'll be honest. It's not mine. It's on loan from, uh...a friend."

The man nods but still doesn't hand me my money. "You lost or something?"

"Lost? Not at all. It's a beautiful night. I'm just out for a ride."

"Thing is, we don't usually get too many folks of your type around here."

I don't like where this is going. Not one bit.

"What do you mean, my type?" I ask, as innocently as possible.

"You don't live in the mountains, do you? No, you look to me like some kinda brainiac. Lemme guess. Accountant maybe. Computer whiz."

I shrug. "You got me. I live in LA. And, um, yeah...I guess you could say I stare at computer screens all day. Could I have my change now, please?"

But still the man doesn't give it to me.

Now I'm *really* getting nervous. Even though I'm sure this guy is probably just a lonely dude making conversation, my mind runs through a dozen grim scenarios.

"Why don't you hang around a minute," he says. "I've got somebody on his way over wants to talk to you."

Well, shit. Now I *know* this is bad news. He's been trying to stall me! Whoever wants to chat, I can guarantee the feeling won't be mutual.

"Sorry," I say, turning and heading for the exit. "I'm kind of in a hurry. Keep the change."

"A hurry?" the man repeats. "I thought you said you were just out for a ride."

Just keep going, I think. *Get out of here, Rob. Get on your bike and go!*

So I try to do just that. Without responding, I push

open the store's door, stride over to my Ducati, mount it, and start the engine—

When I see the ominous strobing of a red and blue bubble light.

A Santa Clarita Sheriff's Department cruiser is pulling in, blocking my escape.

CHAPTER 20

NOT GOOD! THIS IS NOT GOOD!

I know I haven't done anything wrong here, but of course I'm not about to speed away with a cop five feet in front of me. But now what?

Just be cool, Rob, I tell myself. *And think.*

A forty-something officer climbs out of the Chevy Charger, beer belly first. His lip is fat with a wad of chewing tobacco. He strolls over to me, tugging his duty belt higher on his hips, then resting a hand on his sidearm.

"Evening, sir," he says. "Can I see some ID, please?"

ID? Shit!

If Officer Friendly here runs my license through his system, you better believe it will send up a giant red flag in the FBI's system, too. Those suits will be on me faster than the speed of light in a vacuum. (Even under stress, I can't help the nerdy science joke.)

"Of course, sir," I say, slowly reaching into my back

pocket and fishing out my wallet. "Mind if I ask what this is all about?"

"I just like keeping tabs on folks coming and going in this neck of the woods. Make sure the unsavory ones stay out. You understand, don't you?"

"Well, sure," I reply. "Except, last I checked, 'keeping tabs' doesn't give you sufficient probable cause to stop someone and ask for identification, does it?"

The deputy's face hardens. I'm not trying to be a smart-ass here, honest. The last thing I want is to piss this guy off. But I do want him to know that I know my rights, which might just be enough for him to think twice and let me go. Not likely, but . . .

"Save it for a judge," the deputy says, spitting a gob of brown tobacco juice on the concrete just inches from my feet. "Am I gonna have to ask you again?"

Hey, it was worth a shot.

"No, sir," I say as I hold out my license. The officer angrily snatches it away, then waddles back toward his car. If I'm going to make a break for it, it's now or never.

"Don't you move a muscle," he snaps.

And reluctantly, I obey. Instead of running, I just stand there, frozen, watching him through the windshield typing my info into his mobile laptop. I'm trying desperately to maintain my best poker face, even though I can feel my forehead, neck, and underarms all growing damp with sweat.

Meanwhile, watching *me* are those two guys out front in rocking chairs, along with the third man inside the store. I can tell they're getting a kind of sick pleasure from this whole scene, which only makes my blood boil hotter.

The cop seems to be taking a terribly long time. His screen is probably flashing a message like NATIONAL SECURITY THREAT! DETAIN! DETAIN! My heart is beating right out of my chest as I imagine the sheer hell that is about to rain down on me. A throng of federal agents swooping in, all armed to the teeth. A black helicopter roaring across the sky. A burlap sack being thrown over my head. Getting hurled into the back of a van and whisked off to a black site for the rest of my life—all because I devoted it to following my dream.

The suspense is killing me! Just get it over with already!

Finally, after what feels like forever, the deputy heaves himself out of his vehicle.

"My apologies for wasting your time, Mr. Barnett," he says, politely holding out my license.

Wait, what?

"Hal behind the register over there," he continues, "he's a buddy of mine. Had two separate holdups in the last four months, so he can be a little jumpy. Thought you looked like one of the suspects, so he called me on my cell. I told him the chances of a bad guy coming back to a place he robbed and actually *paying* were pretty slim. But that's what friends are for."

I take my ID with trembling hands and slide it back in my wallet.

"So...you're saying...I'm free to go?"

The deputy flashes me a big, dumb grin.

"Unless you've got a warrant out for your arrest my computer doesn't know about. Or you've committed some *other* crime you'd like to confess to."

I laugh, maybe a little too hard. "No, sir! Thank you, sir. Have a good night, sir."

The cop gives me a quick wave, then gets back in his car, reverses, and drives off.

Holy shit! I don't believe it. I just dodged *another* bullet!

But . . . how? How is it even possible?

Doesn't matter. I'll worry about it later. Like when I'm accepting my Nobel Prize.

I'm not going to push my luck any more. I'm a man on a mission: to decode an alien message! As I tug my helmet back on and gaze up briefly at the beautiful canopy of stars up above, so rich and dazzling this far away from the bright lights of LA, I'm reminded of its importance.

I've got in my possession the world's first message from *another* world.

But what the hell are they trying to tell us?

It's up to me and me alone to get it to Northrop and find out.

Now.

CHAPTER 21

ACCORDING TO MY TRUSTY paper map, I'm only a few miles away from Tejon Ranch.

So close!

If I were driving on normal city streets, it might only take me a couple minutes to cover that distance. But on this narrow, increasingly winding mountain pass, I'm probably looking at closer to half an hour. Which is fine. I've made it this far; I'm definitely not stopping now. I am *going* to translate that message.

So I keep moving, easing my bike around every sharp curve and blind switchback. The route is feeling increasingly remote and deserted, but I take that as a good sign. After all, if *you* were building a multibillion-dollar top-secret research facility, wouldn't you want to place it as far away from civilization as possible?

My lights catch a raccoon scurrying across the road ahead of me, followed by three furry offspring. It's pitch black out here, and the sky is richer, more beautiful for what it could be hiding.

And then, at last, up ahead... I see it.

Not the ranch itself. I'm still about a quarter of a mile from the perimeter. At least I think I am. Instead, I see some kind of *preliminary* security checkpoint: a tiny shed with a light on inside and a retractable arm blocking access to the road beyond.

Instinctively I slow down my bike—and start to panic.

This isn't how it was supposed to happen.

John told me to go in through the main gate, that he'd have people there waiting for me, people to escort me inside. He didn't say anything about an *outer* gate. True, I took a different route to get here than he suggested, but this is still the only road that leads to the front entrance.

Maybe Northrop added this extra layer of security since John was last at the ranch. That's the only explanation I can think of. And indeed, as I get closer, I notice that the gatehouse looks prefabricated, almost like a metal tool-shed you could buy at Home Depot, and the arm seems rather thin and flimsy, like it was made out of balsa wood. It's quite possible—I'd even say it's *likely*—that this entire checkpoint was put up in the recent past.

Not like that does *me* any good tonight. So what do I do?

Well, like I said... I didn't make it this far to stop now.

I consider using one of the burner phones John gave me to call him and ask his advice—and to make sure he really did get in touch with his pals inside the ranch—

before I try to get in. But I'm positive the feds have tapped his cell and landline. I'd be giving them my exact location, wrapped up in a bow. That would be a death sentence.

So I guess I'm on my own. Here goes nothing.

I slowly pull my bike up to the gate. A baby-faced rent-a-cop, a kid who looks barely a few years older than my daughters, hastily steps out to intercept me.

"Can I help you, sir?" he asks, affecting as tough a persona as he can muster.

"I sure hope so," I answer. I flip up my visor and hold out my license. "My name is Robert Barnett. I believe I . . . have an appointment."

The security guard levels a suspicious gaze at me.

"An appointment. Here. At nine o'clock at night?"

"Look," I say, gritting my teeth, "can you just check the visitors log? It's very, very, *very* important. Trust me. Please."

Warily, the guard does so. He scans my ID with the slim digital device he's holding. I can't see the screen, but I do see it flash green. I also see the guard's eyebrows lift in total surprise.

"My mistake, Mr. Barnett. You're all set. Let me raise the gate for you."

Ha! John came through for me.

I can barely contain my elation as the guard ducks back into the shed. I lower my visor and rev the throttle, ready to drive onward.

But the gate stays down. And I see the guard latch the door shut behind him.

Then I notice that beneath the door...the grass and weeds growing along the shoulder don't stop when they reach the shed wall. They keep going underneath it—as if the shed was simply plopped down on the ground *very* recently.

Oh, shit...

This isn't an outer-perimeter checkpoint at all.

It's a fake. A decoy.

This is an ambush.

"FBI! Hands in the air!"

A dozen heavily armed federal agents suddenly spring up from their hiding spots on both sides of the roadway, barking orders and training their rifles right at me.

No, no, no!

I stay frozen, too stunned to speak, too horrified to move. I feel numb. All around me, time seems to slow down.

The next thing I know, I'm tackled and thrown face-first off my bike and onto the rock-hard concrete. Thank God I'm wearing John's helmet, or my brains would probably be spattered everywhere. I feel it get pulled off and the burner phones ripped from my pockets while my hands are yanked behind my back and cuffed.

"Robert James Barnett, you are being detained under direct order from the secretary of homeland security, for violation of civil code section—"

"Goddamn you guys!" I yell, struggling in vain but as best as I can against my unlawful arrest. "Listen to me! I'm not a security threat..."

I thrust my chin up toward the heavens.

"...but maybe *they* are! I'm in possession of critical information that the world needs to see. But first, what *we* need is to *understand* it. You have to believe me!"

Yet my pleas fall on deaf ears. I'm gruffly hauled to my feet and practically dragged away toward a black tinted-window SUV that is speeding toward us from the direction of the ranch, kicking up a giant dust cloud behind it.

"No, please, please!" I scream as one of the vehicle's rear doors opens—and I'm tossed inside.

CHAPTER 22

"CALM DOWN, MR. BARNETT. We're on the same team."

The voice—tranquil and soothing—is coming from the front passenger seat.

I look over to see an older man, African American, salt-and-pepper hair, thick horn-rimmed glasses. He's wearing a bland dark suit like the other government agents on either side of me, but he has a refined, almost professorial air about him.

"Same team? Yeah, right. Forgive me for thinking you're full of shit."

"Think whatever you want," the man says. "All we'd like to do is ask you some questions. The more you're willing to cooperate, the better it will be for everyone."

I've finally caught my breath a bit and have started to calm down like the man commanded. Of course, I'm still absolutely petrified—about who exactly these folks are, where they're taking me, and what in God's name is going to happen next.

"You think *you've* got questions?" I exclaim. "I picked up some kind of alien FaceTime message in my freaking living room! And look what happened!"

The man nods. "Yes. That's one very impressive computer setup you've got in there. Seems you're quite the expert on extraterrestrial communication. Which is why we're especially glad you're here now. We're looking forward to having your help."

My help? What is this dude talking about?

"Where are we going?" I ask. "At least tell me that."

Gesturing through the windshield, the agent says: "Look for yourself."

To my astonishment, we're not headed for a secret military plane to take me to Guantanamo Bay. Nothing like that at all.

We're arriving at the Tejon Ranch main gate...which is being *opened* for us!

We ride along in silence for a few moments through what does indeed look like an old, abandoned military facility. We finally reach a giant rusty hangar. The SUV stops, all the agents exit, then my door opens and they escort me out as well.

"This way, please," the man in the glasses says, as if I really had a choice.

Strangely, inside the hangar is an elevator—a modern one. We step in and the metal doors close. Then we begin to descend, lower and lower...

Until finally we exit into what can only be described as a *laboratory of the future.*

I'm in total disbelief as I'm escorted down an endless corridor, brightly lit, lined with massive blinking, humming quantum computer terminals that seem to go on in every direction, floor to ceiling, forever.

"My name is Special Agent Stephen McKinley," the man says as we walk. "I'm assigned to a little-known division of the FBI that handles... *unconventional* threats."

"Well, I'm not exactly the most conventional guy myself," I reply with a smirk. McKinley actually cracks a smile. Trying to piggyback on his goodwill, I say: "Hey, think we could take these cuffs off? I mean, if we're 'on the same team' and all?"

I watch as McKinley gives a subtle okay to one of the other agents escorting us, who unlocks the restraints. Grateful, I rub my wrists as we keep moving.

"My department only became aware of your little research project early this morning," McKinley explains. "But a number of other federal agents—not to mention some of your fellow scientists at this Northrop research facility—have apparently been monitoring your work for some time."

Hang on... my "fellow scientists" have been monitoring my work?

I actually have to suppress a little smile of my own. If what McKinley is saying is true, maybe the scientific world doesn't actually see me as the crackpot they insist I am.

McKinley places his face up to some kind of small

lens mounted beside a steel-reinforced door. It bathes his features with a flash of white light—a high-tech facial-recognition scanner. Then it blinks and the door slides open with a hiss.

We enter a massive control room, with giant flat-screen computer monitors covering every inch of wall. The space is buzzing with scientists and agents who barely register our entrance.

"Rob, meet your new colleagues," McKinley says as three painfully geeky techies approach us. My kind of people! "Dr. Leo Conrad, Dr. Seth Chan, and Dr. Rafael Axen."

Dr. Conrad speaks first, offering a limp but excited handshake. "Wonderful to make your acquaintance, Mr. Barnett. Let me be the first to say, the cosmic data you managed to capture and recognize on your home system was highly impressive."

"Thanks, Doc," I reply. Slowly but surely, my fear is morphing into pride.

"You're obviously no criminal," McKinley interjects. "But you did obtain what we believe is an extraordinarily sensitive message from an intelligent being from outer space—which we quickly accessed and copied for ourselves. Because the Bureau believed you planned to go public with that discovery, hopefully you can understand why we felt the urgent need to track and detain you."

"I do."

"Take a look around," Dr. Conrad says. "What you're seeing is every single drop of quantum-computing power we have being used to try to *decipher* your data. Due to the uniqueness of your home setup, there are a few elements of its algorithmic expression we were hoping you could help clarify."

"And then," says Dr. Chan, barely able to contain his enthusiasm, "we can hopefully finish our *translation*! Because right now? We are very, very close."

CHAPTER 23

THE MISSION SPECIALIST IS starting to wake up.

He's groggy, disoriented, and his reflexes and reaction time will be impaired for quite a while. Still, having proven himself to be an unpredictable threat to the crew's safety, none of them is taking any chances. He's tied down to a chair in the cockpit with some spare electrical cords while the others take over his tasks.

The pilot is floating nearby with another syringe of sedative, just in case.

After checking her console, the commander slowly turns to face her colleagues.

"Everyone," she says solemnly, "we will soon be locked in on our final destination. I am going to connect with my family and...attempt to say...some kind of farewell. I invite all of you to do the same, if you so choose."

The commander watches her team begin to disperse. She is still conflicted about having lied to them, but is beginning to forgive herself.

Yet she is aching to her very core knowing she will never see her family again.

Keeping her eyes glued to that wonderful old photo she snuck aboard of her husband and two children as infants, she considers making a video message for them—but she doubts she could get through it without bursting into tears. So instead, the commander swings a keyboard out from under her control panel and begins typing.

My sweet children, my dear husband—

If you felt I was hiding something from you all when we said good-bye...I was.

I don't know how to tell you this except directly: I am not returning home from this mission.

I won't pretend to be able to explain the full nature of our purpose, except to say that I believe we are playing a key role in saving the entire universe. I am weeping with sorrow, but I am also honored and humbled to be making such a sacrifice.

I know that one day, you all will join me, wherever it is we go next. Until then, please carry my deep love for all of you in your hearts, and know that I will be watching over you, always.

—Your loving wife and mother

It is all the commander can do to hold herself together. She has never felt so out of control.

The pilot sees this and reaches over to her, placing his hand on her forearm. Their eyes meet, and their kindred souls connect, once again. He tries, silently, to offer her a kind of reassurance, born from their years of training and similar experiences—and from the grim fate they now share. It helps. But only so much.

And so the commander recommits herself to the mission's latest tasks at hand, trusting that her family, history, and the entire universe will ultimately understand why she made the decision that she did.

The *Epsilon Eridani* continues cruising within the L-1 point, orbiting the sun, stabilized by the gravitational pulls between that star and the ship's target planet, a mere 1.5 million kilometers away.

The commander's current priority is to review their latest communications, both sent and received.

The contents of these communications will determine what happens next.

CHAPTER 24

DOCTORS CONRAD, CHAN, AND Axen are huddled around an enormous tower of computer monitors and quantum processors. Agent McKinley is observing from nearby.

I'm watching in awe as a torrent of numbers and symbols flutter across the screens.

"As you can see, Dr. Barnett," Dr. Conrad says, "we're using a fault-tolerant quantum computation model to minimize de-coherence. But this is where we keep getting stuck."

"Any ideas?" asks Dr. Chan. "You know this data better than anybody."

At first I say nothing—not because I don't have any ideas, but because my lips are frozen in a big, dopey grin.

I may not technically hold a PhD, but I'm certainly not going to correct them. I just can't express how amazing it feels, after all these agonizing years, to finally be taken seriously by some fellow scientists.

But I force myself to snap out of it. No time for pride. This is deadly serious stuff.

"Let me take a look," I reply, nudging my way between the trio to a free keyboard.

I hit a few keys and quickly skim the data readouts. I see the problem immediately—and I realize that this remarkable computer system can probably handle my complex solution.

"Okay," I say, "I think you're on the right track. But the noise threshold is still too high. I'd also double your density matrices to match my qubit input rate. Like this."

I execute the commands, and within seconds, the streaming data begins to ebb and pulse, like a river changing course.

Soon, the data flow changes again. It actually looks like numbers and symbols are starting to rearrange themselves into some kind of order. I think it's working!

"Barnett, you did it!" Dr. Chan says.

But Doctors Conrad and Axen are too stunned to make a sound.

And so am I.

Because before our eyes, it appears as if the data is turning into...

"Letters!" I blurt out. "Look!"

"Yes, yes, it's deciphering," exclaims Dr. Chan. "We're getting our first word!"

We're all watching something we simply can't believe. Something that defies all earthly logic as we know it, every bit of scientific research ever done.

WE. ARE. NOT. ALONE.

A message—or at least the start of one, sent from outer space, emerging painstakingly slowly, one letter at a time:

3α677δ58ø58ϖ485ε25χ5θ46Δ9ηφ853π2737τ2θ5...

M

"Oh, my God," says Dr. Axen. "That's an *M*!"

It is! Clear as day. And it leaves me absolutely dumbstruck.

7ç6å9β32α7μ82π6ε43δ5θ96Δχ28η8φ49μ73τ83δ9ϖ3...

E

"An *E*, holy shit!" exclaims Dr. Axen.

3α6θ3χ65β3ψ25θ23ε7α86π3χ20μ06Δ4ψ88β3τ89ε2...

R

"An *R*?" asks Dr. Chan. "Are they spelling *Mercury?*"

"Hang on," Dr. Conrad says, typing furiously. "It's not complete yet."

8ϖ39β60α7δ34Δ382ϖ86ε5χ19Δ9θ65η3ψ5π373τ5ç6...

C

"A *C*!" shouts Dr. Chan. "It *is* spelling *Mercury*. Is that where this has been coming from?"

But then...

4å4β3θ2α37μ88π3ψ25θ23ε7θ96Δχ2β32α7μ06Δ4δ7...

Y

"*Mercy?*" I ask as that final letter becomes clear and the first chilling word of the message is complete. "I...I don't understand. Mercy for *what*? Why would aliens start by saying *that* to us?"

It's Agent McKinley who answers me. He looks strangely...*calm?*

"A fair question, Barnett," he says. "But it has to be understood... in context."

"Context?" I ask. "I'd say a message from extraterrestrials is pretty damn unique!"

I look around at the other scientists for confirmation, but oddly, all are silent.

"Actually," McKinley says, "it's not. We've been receiving... *other* messages. For quite some time now."

And just like that, my head starts to spin. I can barely stand straight. It feels like the floor below me has instantly turned to Jell-O.

Did this guy just say "other messages"? Is he freaking serious?

McKinley reads my mind. He nods, gravely.

"That's right," he says. *"Dozens."*

CHAPTER 25

"THIS FORMAT," MCKINLEY CONTINUES, "is more or less how all the others came in. Streams of patterned cosmic data that we would slowly decipher, letter by letter."

"But this latest one," Dr. Chan interrupts, "the encoding was different."

"It was more algorithmically complex for some reason," Dr. Axen adds. "Probably so the signal would cut through all the cosmic chatter more clearly—because it's an important one. Which is why we needed your help."

"Wait, wait, wait," I stammer, trying to steady my dizziness and absorb what I'm hearing. "Go back to the part about those *other* messages. What did *they* say?"

Dr. Conrad starts to answer, but McKinley quiets him by raising his hand.

"Let's let these three get back to work deciphering *this* one," he says. "Barnett, you come with me. I'll tell you everything."

Agent McKinley has to practically drag me into an empty adjoining conference room separated from the bustling main lab area by thick glass walls. As soon as he shuts the door, the room becomes pin-drop silent.

"You may want to have a seat for this," the agent suggests.

But I'm way too jittery for that. So while McKinley sits down calmly at the large mahogany table, I pace back and forth.

"What I'm about to tell you," he says, "is—in the interest of national and global security—of the utmost secrecy. Do you understand?"

"Yes!" I shout, at the end of my rope. "Out with it already!" The suspense is killing me.

"We've been tracking these signals, these messages, for a while now," McKinley says. "Nine years, seven months, two weeks to be precise."

My head starts spinning. If this agent is telling me the truth...

Earth has been secretly receiving alien communications for nearly a decade?

"It took us almost half that time just to figure out how the hell to decipher them. But once we landed on the unique combination of quantum digital physics, it was like we'd stumbled on the Rosetta stone. Suddenly, all the messages we'd intercepted up to that point could be translated. It's still not clear who or where they're coming from. But whatever life form is sending them...they know an awful lot about our planet and species."

"Jesus Christ," I mutter. "What did they say?"

"The messages express increasingly grave concerns about our behavior. Our judgment. How we live our lives. How we live *with* one another."

"Who's . . . we?" I ask.

"The undeniable implication is *all* of us," McKinley explains. "Every last human being on the planet, all seven billion. According to these messages, the human race— by both our actions and inactions—is guilty of engaging in 'perilous endeavors.' These aliens have been sending observations, suggestions, and recently . . . warnings."

I have to grip the edge of the conference table now to brace myself.

"Warnings? Like what?"

"Like we've been tempting fate by allowing our global nuclear capabilities to grow unchecked. Like we've been destroying our own environment. Like our worsening disagreements over culture, religion, and resources have not just halted humanity's development, but have actively put our species' future in jeopardy—and thus, by extension, *other* species' futures as well."

I'm left absolutely aghast. And utterly terrified.

Because I'm slowly starting to understand.

"*Dysgenics,*" I say. That's the opposite of evolution: the passing down of *harmful* traits and other disadvantages to future generations.

"Correct," McKinley says. "But these life forms don't just see human beings as harming *ourselves.* They view us as a threat . . . *to the rest of the universe.* Their messages have been warning us that unless we change our ways…we may be facing…*human extinction.*"

My legs start to give out. Finally I take that empty seat at the conference table.

"Fine, okay, so you guys have been getting all these messages," I say. "What the hell have you been doing about them?"

"Since they first started coming in nine years ago, we've been sharing the data streams directly with the White House, our closest allies, and a secret select committee at the United Nations. We've hoped they'd be willing to abide by the aliens' recommendations and take on some of our species' challenges. We've tried, certainly. But look at our messed-up planet, Barnett. We haven't exactly made much progress."

Now my gut is in an absolute knot. I try to speak, but my throat is too dry to make a sound. I try to think, but my mind is too frenzied.

Just then, the glass conference room door opens and Dr. Axen pokes his head in. I notice right away his face is as white as a sheet.

"Agent McKinley?" he says, his voice quivering with fright. "We've finished deciphering the complete message. You really need to see this."

CHAPTER 26

IT'S TWO A.M. ON the East Coast. Most of the country is fast asleep.

But on the "Watch Floor" of the White House Situation Room underground complex—the epicenter of the federal government's 24/7 vigilance over national security threats—one man is wide awake.

Byron Stannis, a stout, compact fellow with decades of military and intelligence experience, is in charge of the Watch Team's overnight shift. He has also been a key member of Operation Obsidian Sky, the government's top-secret monitoring of the ominous extraterrestrial messages that have been incoming for nearly ten years.

Stannis is currently seated in front of two tiers of curved computer monitors, participating in a secure video conference with representatives from the Pentagon, the National Security Council, NORAD, the Cyber Ops team stationed at Northrop's classified quantum computer lab at Tejon Ranch in Southern California, including crackpot amateur scientist Robert Barnett, whom Stannis has been monitoring for months, and various allied leaders from around the globe.

And joining, from aboard Air Force One, is the President of the United States.

"What you are seeing, ladies and gentlemen," says Dr. Chan at Tejon Ranch, "is our complete rough translation of what appears to be . . . their *final* message."

Stannis was given this intel just minutes earlier, and reading it left him gut-struck.

He can't imagine what will happen when the content is actually spoken aloud.

"And needless to say," Agent McKinley chimes in, "given the escalating tone of *recent* similar messages, we believe this warning should be taken extremely seriously."

"Yes, I think we can all agree on that," the president says. "Let's hear it."

Dr. Conrad clears his throat and, from his tablet, reads the most difficult, most momentous few sentences of his entire life.

"*'Mercy . . . is no longer an option,'*" he says—as every person on the video conference lets out a horrified gasp. "*'We have sent you innumerable messages about your planet. About your species. About your future. We have made our concerns clear to your leaders. We have implied them to select individuals. We have tried to help you. But you have not listened. You have not changed. You have only . . . gotten worse. Therefore, you leave us no choice. Good-bye.'*"

And with that, the video conference turns deafeningly silent.

The national security advisor slumps in her seat, shaking her head in shock.

The admiral representing the Joint Chiefs of Staff crosses his arms and sets his jaw in a furious grimace, not used to feeling so helpless.

Stannis leans back and covers his face, as if that might somehow remove him from this utter nightmare that is all too real.

Finally, the secretary of defense looks directly into the president's eyes.

"Sir, what could that mean?"

The president's expression is grim but stoic, resigned but brave.

"It means...only an act of God can save us now."

CHAPTER 27

YOU LEAVE US NO CHOICE.

The commander has just read—for practically the hundredth time—the complete text of the final message that her home planet's leaders recently beamed down to Earth.

A copy was relayed to her vessel when the *Epsilon Eridani* first entered the Milky Way galaxy a few hours earlier. But the commander did not know what the contents of that message would be before she opened it.

It has confirmed her worst fears.

The commander was never involved in the top-level discussions that brought about this decision. She holds a high rank in her home world's starship fleet, but such matters are way above her pay grade.

She was certainly aware of the High Council's ongoing deliberations regarding the "Earth problem," as it was called, along with the various methods they employed to try to fix it. *Homo sapiens* are a relatively young alien race, similar in many ways to her own. They possess incredible potential—for both good and bad—but their capacity to do harm was projected to be much more likely.

Their civilization's ruling classes were given years of warnings to improve their behavior, ample time to change course. Hundreds of "ordinary" human beings were selected, too, and were sent cryptic *individualized* messages. These were never as explicit, nor did they reveal their alien origin. But they were laden with great personal meaning: familiar songs, inspiring aphorisms, touching images. They were intended to encourage the receivers to reexamine their lives and make *small* changes to their behavior. But by and large, this failed as well.

The commander, for years, had secretly rooted for the human race to heed her leaders' calls—or show even the slightest signs of improvement. Yet when she was tapped to lead the mission that would vaporize the blue planet, she knew that their window of opportunity had closed.

Humans' days were numbered.

And so were her own.

YOU LEAVE US NO CHOICE.

Is she doing the right thing? Is their annihilation justified? She believes so. But how can she be completely sure?

The High Council might have decreed Earth's destruction, but it will be up to *her* to order the launch of the nuclear warhead that actually does it, her finger on the button. Until the very last possible moment before she presses it, the commander will be hoping for a miracle.

And not just for the human race.

For her ship, which will be engulfed in the warhead's cosmic inferno.

For her loyal crew, whom she misled about this mission from the start.

And for herself. For her loving husband. For her dear, precious children.

You leave us no choice.

Closing the message window, the commander takes another look at the photograph of her family wedged into her console: so much love, so much longing, so much joy, so much regret—all triggered by one simple image.

She swore an oath to carry out her orders to the best of her ability.

And she will.

It just kills her that this is how it has to be.

With tears brimming in her eyes, the commander keys her com-link. She speaks slowly and steadily, trying with all her might to keep her voice from wavering.

"Attention, all crew," she says, "we are nearing our flight's final stages. Our primary mission objective appears to be a *go*. Commence launch initiation sequence."

A chorus of "aye-ayes" comes back at her through her headset.

WE. ARE. NOT. ALONE.

Her crew—even the formerly livid mission specialist—is now courageously embracing their fate. She couldn't be prouder of them, or more moved.

As the blue planet comes into view now through the *Epsilon Eridani*'s windshield, the commander steels herself for what's ahead.

She has made her peace with the grim calculus that requires her to kill so many humans, for the good of billions of *other* species throughout the universe.

But she is still torn up inside at having to kill her innocent team and herself.

If only there was another way...

CHAPTER 28

WHAT'S HAPPENING DOESN'T SEEM real. It *can't* be real. But it is.

I just watched, via encrypted video-link, the leader of the free world receive the news that our planet—after years of warnings—is about to come under some kind of attack from alien beings.

The president declared he'd be initiating Continuity of Operations protocols. He also ordered all American military forces and nuclear silos around the world to be put on red alert, and urged every other country—friend and foe alike—to do the same.

But then, he pinched the bridge of his nose in despair, and acknowledged what everybody else on the video conference was thinking. Or at least what *I* was thinking.

"Not that any of it," he said, "is likely to make a damn bit of difference."

The call ended only a few minutes ago, but news has already spread throughout the underground labs. It's a madhouse, with scientists and agents scurrying everywhere.

"Agent McKinley!" I call, trying to grab his arm as he hurries past. "What happens now? What do we do?"

But he angrily brushes me off.

"What do we *do?* We build a time machine. Go back ten years. Tell the world about these goddamn alien warnings and convince people to take them seriously!"

His stern face finally shows the momentous fear he must be feeling. The fear that *all* of us are feeling. I understand what he's saying perfectly.

We're royally, epically screwed.

How could we humans have been so stupid?

I get that the government wanted to keep a lid on the whole receiving-coded-emails-from-little-green-men thing. Hell, just think how much *I* freaked out this morning when I intercepted one—and I'd been expecting it for years.

"At least let me call my family!" I plead. I explain to McKinley how, when I was ambushed at the front gate a few hours ago, security guards snatched away the burner cell phones John had given me. I need a phone.

"Word is *going* to leak about an impending attack," I say. "Chaos is about to descend not just on Southern California, but all across the world. Roads are going to be jammed. Phone lines, internet access—it's all going to be overwhelmed! If the world is really ending, Agent, I have to say good-bye to the people I love. Please?"

McKinley frowns. I can tell he's feeling the same way

about *his* family. He's not thinking like a federal agent any-more, but like a husband and father. Same as me.

"My office," he says, yanking a white plastic fob off his keychain. "Make a left at the end of the hallway. Third door on your right. There's an unclassified priority land-line on my desk. Use it—before it's too late."

McKinley thrusts the fob into my clammy hands. Be-fore I can thank him for this act of kindness, he spins and disappears into the frenzied crowd.

I don't have a second to waste.

I sprint down the hall, elbowing my way through the chaos. I turn left, and soon find a door with McKinley's name on it—locked. I hold the key fob up to the plastic panel located where the doorknob should be, and it buzzes open.

Relieved, I burst inside. It's blandly corporate and sparsely decorated. His desk is practically clear—except for two telephones: a high-tech encrypted one...and a "normal" one beside it. I jam the receiver against my ear, then frantically dial Marty's cell number, which, thank-fully, I still have memorized all these years later.

It rings. And rings. And rings.

As I wait, I start to imagine what might be happening up on the surface. As soon as word gets out, it will be chaos. Looting, rioting, hell. A total breakdown of law and order. All human progress and civilization—gone in seconds.

The line keeps ringing. My heart keeps racing. Finally, my ex-wife picks up.

"Marty!" I blurt. "Thank God, it's me!"

"Oh, my—Rob, are you okay? Where are you?"

The sound of her voice, of her genuine care and concern for me, fills me with joy and relief—but also with searing pain. This woman I once loved so much, the incredible mother of our two wonderful girls...she has no idea this will probably be the last time we ever speak.

"I'm fine, Mar. I made it to the ranch, we translated the—look, it doesn't matter. Where are Claire and Ellie?"

"They're asleep. It's midnight. Are you sure you're all right, Rob? You sound—"

"Wake them up!" I exclaim. "I have to talk to them, too. I have to...*we* have to..."

I force myself to take a deep breath before I say these next unthinkable words.

"We *all* have to...say good-bye."

CHAPTER 29

"GOOD-BYE?" MARTY ASKS. "What are you talking about? You're scaring me, Rob. What's going on?"

My breathing is sharp and ragged. I'm brimming with so much emotion, I can barely form complete sentences.

And even if I could, what the hell am I supposed to say? Where do I even begin?

"I'll tell you what's going on. I promise. But in case time runs out...there's a lot more I want to tell you all first. Now wake the girls, Marty. Do it, please!"

I don't mean to alarm her, but our situation—our *planet's* situation—is dire.

"Okay, okay. Hang on."

I hear rustling on the other end as she heads to the second-floor guest room with the red wooden bunk beds where Claire and Ellie are fast asleep. I spent so much time in her parents' house when we were together, I can picture exactly what she's doing—including stepping on that creaky third stair on her way up. For years, it drove me nuts that my father-in-law had the time and brain-power to consult on top-secret government computer engineering projects, but could never spare a few minutes to fix a step.

Now I'd give *anything* to be back in that house, bounding up that old, rickety staircase, able to hug all three of my girls one final time.

Funny how the end of the world makes you realize what really matters.

How it makes you regret almost every decision you've ever made—and all those you didn't.

How could I have been such a lousy husband?

How could I have taken Marty for granted?

What the hell was I thinking, searching for alien life instead of focusing on the incredible life *we* created? Why did it take a goddamn message from outer space to make me realize how much I miss and adore my precious family?

And how could the *human* family have screwed this up so much?

A tiny part of me thinks maybe we do deserve what's coming.

"Girls, wake up," I hear Marty saying. "It's your father. He needs to talk to us."

Claire and Ellie utter groggy hellos. Hearing Marty's voice when I called got me choked up...but hearing my little girls makes my eyes wet almost instantly.

"Hey, you guys," I say, trying to sound upbeat and disguise the overwhelming fear and dread I'm struggling with. "I just wanted to tell you...how much *I love you.*

And how I always will. No matter what happens. Now and forever. I couldn't be prouder of you guys, and I always will be. Do you understand?"

"Daddy, are you crying?" asks Claire. I can hear in her voice that her little lip is quivering. She was always so smart and empathetic. I know I can't lie to her.

"I am," I say, smearing a tear across my cheek. "But I'm crying because... I'm happy. Very, very happy. To talk to my little angels."

Which is the truth. There's no one in the world I'd rather be speaking to right now.

Especially since the world is ending.

"We love you, too, Daddy," says Claire.

"Yeah, and we're proud of you, too!" squeals Ellie. "We miss you!"

Tears are streaming down my face now. It's all I can do to whisper: "Okay, you two. Back to bed."

"Will you be home soon, Daddy?" asks Ellie, the one I can't lie to. What do I say?

"I... I hope so, sweetie. But I promise I'll see you soon. Somewhere, somehow."

Marty takes back the phone. As she walks into the hall and closes the bedroom door, I can hear her sniffling. I haven't told her anything about the other messages, the aliens, the impending attack.

But I know immediately my brilliant ex-wife has figured out *everything*.

"How much time do we have left, Rob?" she asks quietly.

I tell her the truth. I don't know. But not much.

Then I tell her how much she means to me. How she and our girls are the very best thing that's ever happened in my otherwise pathetic life.

Marty, sobbing hard now, tells me she loves me, too. That my life *isn't* pathetic, because it's rich and full of meaning. Because my family loves me and my work paid off and I've helped make a difference in so many people's lives.

I'm moved beyond words. There's so much more I want to say—

When I notice a growing commotion in the hallway outside.

Scientists and agents are rushing all around, shoving one another to get through, barking frantic orders, terror in their eyes. It's sheer pandemonium.

Which can only mean one thing.

"Mar, I...I gotta go. I love you!"

I force myself to hang up, one of the hardest things I've ever done. But there's no time to think about that now.

I rush out into the hall and join the stream of people. It seems an even mix of some folks hurrying back toward the main lab, others running for their lives.

"Hey!" I scream, trying to get someone's—anyone's—attention. "What the hell is happening? Where's everybody going?"

A young lab assistant finally takes pity on me. She slows down just for a moment, and breathlessly shouts back, "They're here!"

CHAPTER 30

I'M STANDING IN THE underground lab's bull pen again, with dozens of employees crammed in like sardines. But other than some muffled sobs, the room is eerily silent.

Because we're all too goddamn stunned to make a sound.

Displayed on the giant wall of monitors is a grainy image—coming from a US military spy satellite—of an unidentified flying object hovering approximately 100,000 miles above Earth, roughly half the distance between us and the moon, and well out of range of even our most advanced fighters and nuclear warheads.

The object is triangular in shape, but has a bulbous nose cone, like a submarine.

It's a dazzling metallic color, covered in shimmering mirrored panels.

It's an alien spacecraft, orbiting our planet!

I've seen some pretty incredible things in my life. My

wife on our wedding day. The birth of our children. The transmission of an encrypted extraterrestrial message right in my living room, just this morning. But sweet mother of God...

This is a whole other level beyond my wildest dreams.

I'm witnessing humanity's first contact with an alien species—one that's made very clear its desire to completely annihilate us!

My body feels paralyzed. My mouth is dry. The floor suddenly seems wobbly, like a trampoline. But my gaze stays fixed on that floating metal vessel.

"It's doing something!" cries Dr. Chan. "Look!"

Sure enough, the underside of the ship seems to be... *opening.*

It's hard to make out in the darkness of space, but a gigantic hatch appears to be slowly retracting to reveal a massive object, long and cylindrical, with thrusters and fins.

The technology may be alien, but it's clear as day what we're looking at.

A terrifyingly powerful weapon.

Panic sweeps through the lab. Screams of terror echo from every corner.

Those sons of bitches, they're really going to do it!

Our species, our entire planet, is about to end in... Hours? Minutes? Seconds?

My head actually hurts as I try to process it. Billions of people, all around the world, are about to be turned to dust! Our species has some problems, sure, but we don't deserve to end like this!

Especially not all those *children,* so innocent.

It's the thought of *them* losing their lives that pains me the most. They had nothing to do with our civilization's mistakes, or our leaders' failures. Nothing at all.

Of course I think of my own kids first, Claire and Ellie. But then I think about all those digital pictures my home supercomputer received over the years, from parents all across the world. They always made me smile, wherever they came from. Such happy, beautiful families. Such inspirations. Such beacons of hope. Such…

Wait.

Hang on.

No. No way. It's impossible…

"Dr. Axen!" I shout, noticing the scientist racing past me, his eyes red from crying. "I need to ask you something about—"

"Ah, forget it, Barnett, there's no point. It's all over!"

"No, no, just listen to me, please! When Dr. Conrad read that message on the video conference, there was that one line, something like: *We implied our concerns to certain individuals.* Do you remember? What did that mean?"

"Oh. *That.*" Axen rubs his eyes and sniffles. Then strangely, he smirks.

"In one of the messages we intercepted…they said they'd grown tired of dealing just with our planet's 'elite.' So they'd decided to reach out to some *ordinary* people, too. Never said who, or how they were going to do it. And we never picked up any stray signals, or got reports of any civilians claiming to be communicating with aliens. I always thought they were bluffing, but—"

"*When* did that message come in?"

Dr. Axen shrugs. "A couple years ago. Does it really matter?"

Yes, yes! I'm thinking. *Maybe more than you could ever imagine!*

"This may sound nuts," I say, "but I think maybe *I* was one of those people!"

Dr. Axen just rolls his eyes and starts to head off again—so I grab his arm.

"I'm serious! My two little girls... for as long as they've been alive, I've beamed digitized pictures of them out into the cosmos. A sort of peaceful greeting. To anybody who might have been listening. A few years back, my super-computer started getting encrypted pictures of children and families *back*."

Dr. Axen's expression slowly begins to morph from dubious to disturbed.

"I just assumed they were from other radio astronomers," I continue, "but I never figured out who. No way it was just a coincidence!"

"Okay," Dr. Axen says, "maybe you *were* one of the chosen. Maybe those creatures in that ship up there *were* sending you random kids' pictures, *were* trying to communicate. So what? Now they're pointing a goddamn warhead at us!"

"I know," I say. "*I know.* But... I think I have an idea how to stop them."

CHAPTER 31

THE LAB IS QUICKLY descending into chaos. Scientists and agents are abandoning their posts in droves. Not like I blame them. If you just found out the world was about to end, would you really hang around the office?

By a stroke of luck, I spot McKinley amid the madness. I fight my way over and corner him, with Dr. Axen by my side.

Frantically, breathlessly, I try to explain my insane idea.

In a nutshell, I want to bombard the alien vessel.

With pictures.

"For years they were trying to reach out to me," I say, "but I never reached back. At least not in any meaningful way. If those aliens are so damn worried about the future of other species, let's make them realize whose futures they're snuffing out—*our children's*. Put a face on all the *kids* they're about to murder!"

McKinley is furrowing his brow so much, his bushy black eyebrows are actually touching. Not a good sign.

"Are you out of your mind, Barnett? You really think we're going to save the human race with a couple Sears family portraits?"

"Not a couple," I answer, growing indignant now. "Thousands. *Millions.*"

He's clearly still skeptical. "And how exactly are you going to—"

"That facial-recognition scanner by the lab entrance? We use its software to comb the internet, find every image of every child's smiling face we can. I can write that program in thirty seconds, and this place has more than enough computing power. Then we reverse-encrypt the pictures with the same quantum-encoding sequence from the aliens' messages to *us*... Then we use the lab's video conference satellite to beam the photo stream directly at the ship. Easy!"

I hold my breath as McKinley digests my outlandish, decidedly *not* easy scheme.

"I know it sounds far-fetched," I add. "Even insane. Desperate. But think about it, Agent. What in God's name do we have to lose? Let me try it. *You owe me that!*"

Exasperated, McKinley throws his hands into the air.

"If you two really want to spend your final moments on this earth emailing baby pictures to aliens, be my guest. Here." He yanks off the key card strung around his neck and tosses it at me. "This will give you top-level access to every computer server on the ranch."

McKinley starts to rush off, but turns back and adds reluctantly: "Good luck."

"The primary terminal—this way!" Dr. Axen exclaims, dragging me through the disorderly bull pen to a monstrous cluster of computer monitors and server towers. I slide McKinley's key card into the slot and the system lights up like a Christmas tree.

"You start writing that re-encryption script," I say to Axen. "I'll find the pictures."

I quickly get to work, harnessing that facial-recognition software and adding just a few extra lines of code. The lab's system is soon scouring the World Wide Web at a mind-numbing pace, downloading around sixty thousand children's photos per second.

As they flicker past me, I glimpse birth announcements. Holiday cards. Class pictures. Graduations. Vacation snapshots. First steps. It's all incredibly moving.

But my delight is cut short when I glance back at those giant monitors showing the hovering alien vessel.

I see the weapon underneath it is slowly being aimed—*directly at our planet!*

"I'd love to get that re-encryption code any day now!" I call sharply to Dr. Axen, whose fingers are dancing across three different keyboards like a concert pianist's.

"Got it!" he shouts back. "Start transferring the photos!"

I do, and dozens of zettabytes of pictures start to be encoded into the same system of numbers and symbols I helped translate just a few hours earlier.

Immediately I begin uploading them into the video conference satellite system, then beam them out into space. I use the same wavelength frequency I did for

Claire's and Ellie's pictures all those years—a few of which were certainly included among the millions of others that are uploading right now.

And then?

I sit back and exhale, and let the quantum computer do its thing.

All around me is pandemonium. Screaming, crying, a total breakdown of order—and that's inside a secure underground facility filled with seasoned professionals.

I don't even want to *think* about the hell that must be breaking out on the surface.

I just hope that Marty and the girls are staying calm and safe.

Picturing my beautiful kids is the only thing keeping me going right now.

And maybe, just maybe, the images of *millions* of kids will spare our species from annihilation.

"That's the last of 'em!" Dr. Axen shouts over the chaos, lifting his hands from his keyboard as if it were a hot stove. "They're all encoded. Now what?"

I look back at the dark image of the spacecraft.

The weapon underneath is still poised for firing.

"Now . . ." I say wistfully, wiping a tear from my eye, "we wait. And hope."

CHAPTER 32

"MISSILE IS ARMED FOR launch," says the payload chief. "Trigger coming online."

The commander nods solemnly as a small, red plastic box emerges from her console.

Inside is a single black knob.

A quick twist of her wrist and the weapon strapped to the underside of their vessel—a five-million-megaton nuclear warhead—will fire.

Obliterating an entire world.

Obliterating *themselves,* as well. The horrific nuclear vortex that will be created when Earth is vaporized will be inescapable for hundreds of light-years. Highly advanced as it is, the *Epsilon Eridani* will not be able to outrun it. Nor can the missile be fired from a practical "safe" range.

The crew's one and only choice is suicide.

Closing her eyes to think of her husband and kids once more, the commander touches her hand a final time to the photograph of her family. This will be the last time she sees their image with mortal eyes. So this is how she wants to remember them. At their very happiest. Their very purest. With the rest of their beautiful lives still ahead of them.

With her other hand, the commander opens the trigger box and grips the black knob. It must be done.

"Brace for launch in five...four...three..."

"Wait!" cries the flight engineer. "Don't fire, don't fire!"

The commander's blood pressure skyrockets. "What is it?" she demands.

The flight engineer is working the touch controls on her panel in a frenzy.

"We're being hailed. An incoming visual distress message, overloading our comms frequency. Multiple zettabytes of data. Are the rest of you seeing this?"

Their own control panels buzzing and flashing, the crew confirms that they are.

"Is it from the High Council?" the commander asks with cautious hope. "Maybe they've changed their mind. Maybe they're calling off the—"

"No," explains the flight engineer. "It's coming...from Earth."

The commander is completely befuddled. Nowhere in the mission briefing did her superiors say to expect any communication attempt from the blue planet. Nor is there any set protocol for handling it.

"Very well," the commander says. "I suppose...put it on-screen?"

"Stand by," replies the flight engineer, who transfers the message to the colossal display panel at the front of the cockpit.

And then the distress call plays. It's unlike any the commander has ever seen: a stunning cascade of images.

A heart-wrenching stream of photographs of human children of every age, background, and creed.

Millions of them—smiling, laughing, crying, crawling, playing, learning, *living*.

An avalanche of youth and hope. Innocence and potential. Love and pure joy.

Which leaves the commander dumbfounded. She feels like she's being buried under an emotional avalanche. It's staggering. Overwhelming.

The commander's lip begins to tremble. Soon her whole body follows.

The enormity of what she's about to do—all the young lives she's about to end—suddenly hits her in a new and deeper way than ever before.

But so does a sense of hope. Of *promise*.

Perhaps humans have reexamined their species, after all. Perhaps their eyes have been opened to the value of future generations and their place in the greater universe. Perhaps they really have learned something from her species.

Perhaps they deserve a second chance!

The commander knows, of course, that this decision is not hers to make. All her training is telling her to twist that black knob as she was originally ordered—or at the very least, communicate this development to the High Council to ask for their input.

But the commander has had enough.

She can no longer in good conscience carry out her mission.

It may cost her her career, but it will save her life—and those of billions of others.

It will keep these human children united with their parents, just as she will soon be reunited with her own.

"Attention, crew," she says, as the pilot, flight engineer, payload chief, and mission specialist all listen, rapt. "Our primary mission objective...has changed. We *will* be firing our payload, but *not* at Earth. Instead, we will use it as thrust—to slingshot us back home. Plot a return course and flight-nav. Launch on my command."

It takes her flabbergasted but overjoyed crew a few solid seconds to fully register what's happening—but they quickly oblige, snapping into action. A new flight path is charted and the warhead is re-aimed.

"Missile is *again* armed for launch," says the payload chief. "Trigger online."

With ineffable admiration for her team, unshakable belief in the power of hope, and unimaginable excitement to return home...the commander grips the black knob.

"Brace for launch in five...four...three...two..."

CHAPTER 33

I HAVE TO REMIND myself to breathe—and blink. My eyes haven't moved from the monitors showing the spacecraft in almost five long minutes. My hands are clammy. My brow is dripping with sweat. My heart is thudding right out of my chest.

There's no way of knowing whether the vessel received our image transmission, let alone if it worked. And as the seconds tick by, I'm starting to lose hope.

"Dr. Axen," I say grimly, "at least we can say we tried. It's been an honor—"

"Fucking shit!" he suddenly exclaims. "Missile hot, missile hot!"

It can't be. It can't!

I glance back at the monitor and see, with horror, *that the weapon has been fired*!

"No, no, no!" I wail. My knees buckle and my entire body tumbles to the ground.

The unthinkable has just become reality.

The entire planet is about to be destroyed!

But then, a strange sense of tranquility washes over me. Maybe it's the cosmic inevitability of our situation. Or the fact that eight billion people are now united by a common fate for the first time in human history.

Whatever the reason, my heart rate slows and my breathing returns to normal.

And then I realize: if the world is about to end, *I want a front-row seat.*

Quickly but not frantically, I bound through the lab and back toward the entrance. I push open the door and call the elevator. I ride it up to ground level, then exit the giant hangar and step outside. I see a few people running for cover, but I stand perfectly still.

I look up at the night sky, a blanket of darkness stretching on to infinity. There's a bit of cloud cover, but I can still make out dozens of twinkling constellations.

Then I gaze in the direction where I know the alien spacecraft is hovering—and from which the weapon is hurtling toward us—even though both are way too tiny and far away to see with the naked eye.

But no matter. Simply being aware of their presence is enough for me.

Ditto Claire, Ellie, and Marty.

You don't always need to *see* something to be profoundly affected by it. It could be an alien race from a distant galaxy. A nuclear missile speeding toward you. Or the unshakable love you feel for the people you care about most.

I wonder what it will look like when the weapon strikes. How quickly the planet will be vaporized. Whether I'll feel excruciating pain, or won't feel a thing.

I take one long, final deep breath of the crisp California air.

And then I see it. *Brilliant lights in the sky!*

The most enormous, powerful, jaw-dropping explosion I've ever witnessed...

Huh?

The ground trembles a bit below me, and strong gusts of wind batter my body. But clearly the weapon was detonated high in the atmosphere, a few miles at least.

Oh, my God...

I see the heavens light up in spectacular fashion. A firestorm emanating in every direction—there for all the world to see, and celebrate. *Oh, my God.*

They spared us!

We're alive! My family is alive! Humanity is alive!

My plan worked!

I tumble backward onto a patch of grass in a giddy fit of laughing and crying, total shock and excruciating relief.

I watch in silent awe as the epic explosion in the sky starts to die down. The billowing smoke begins to dissipate and once again a few stars become visible.

I've never seen anything so beautiful in my life.

And I hope I never do again.

ABOUT THE AUTHORS

JAMES PATTERSON has written more bestsellers and created more enduring fictional characters than any other novelist writing today. He lives in Florida with his family.

SUSAN DiLALLO is a lyricist, librettist, and humor columnist. A former advertising creative director, she lives in New York City.

MAX DiLALLO is a novelist, playwright, and screenwriter. He lives in Los Angeles.

TIM ARNOLD had a regular column in *Adweek* during his thirty-five years in the advertising business. Currently a blog columnist for the *Huffington Post,* he continues to actively consult for a wide range of clients.

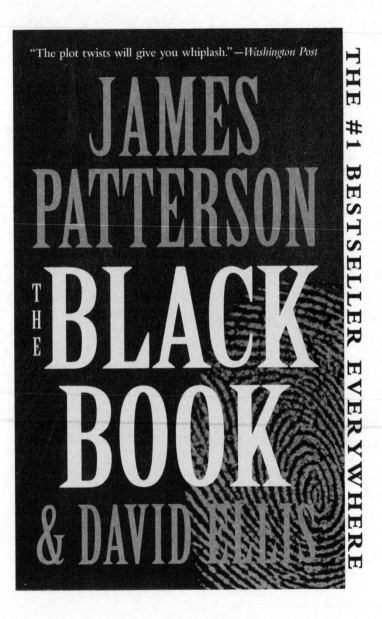

"The plot twists will give you whiplash." —*Washington Post*

JAMES PATTERSON

THE BLACK BOOK

& DAVID ELLIS

THE #1 BESTSELLER EVERYWHERE

THE BLACK BOOK

I have favorites among the novels I've written. *Kiss the Girls, Invisible, 1st to Die,* and *Honeymoon* are top of the list. With each, I had a good feeling when the writing was finished. I believe this book — *The Black Book* — is the best work I've done in twenty-five years.

Meet Billy Harney. The son of Chicago's chief of detectives, he was born to be a cop. There's nothing he wouldn't sacrifice for his job. Enter Amy Lentini, an assistant state's attorney hell-bent on making a name for herself — by proving Billy isn't the cop he claims to be.

A horrifying murder leads investigators to a brothel that caters to Chicago's most powerful citizens. There's plenty of evidence on the scene, but what matters most is what's missing: the madam's black book.

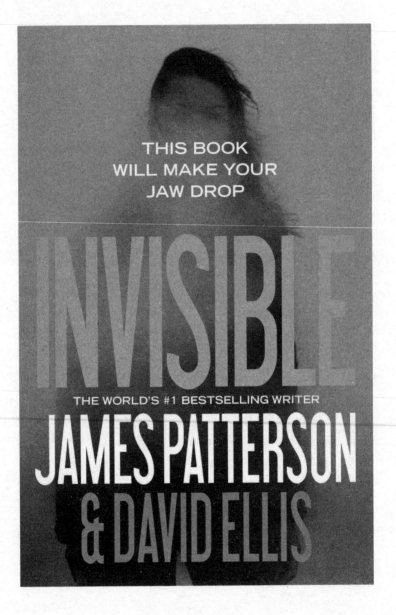

INVISIBLE

When I started writing *Invisible,* it seemed like every other TV network was telling the same kind of police stories, robberies, and crime twists. So I wanted to tell a different kind of suspense story, one that would really make your jaw drop. In the novel, Emmy Dockery is a researcher for the FBI who believes she has stumbled on one of the deadliest serial killers in history. There's only one problem—he's invisible. The mysterious killer leaves no trace. There are no weapons, no evidence, no motive. But when the killer strikes close to home, she must crack an impossible case before anyone else dies. Prepare to be blindsided, because the most terrifying threat is the one you don't see coming—the one that's invisible.

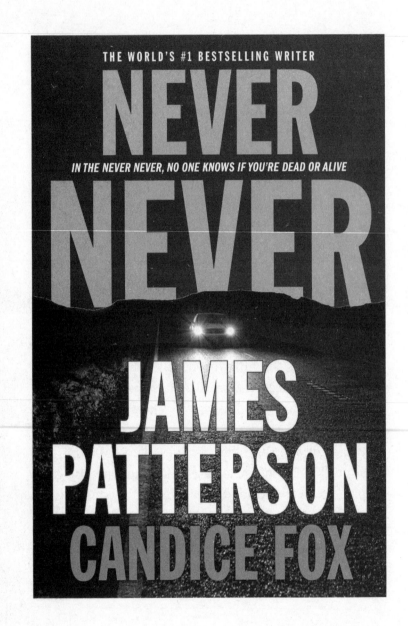

THE WORLD'S #1 BESTSELLING WRITER

NEVER NEVER

IN THE NEVER NEVER, NO ONE KNOWS IF YOU'RE DEAD OR ALIVE

JAMES PATTERSON

CANDICE FOX

NEVER NEVER

Alex Cross. Michael Bennett. Jack Morgan. They are among my greatest characters. Now I'm proud to present my newest detective—a tough woman who can hunt down any man in a hardscrabble continent half a world away. Meet Detective Harriet Blue of the Sydney Police Department.

Harry is her department's top Sex Crimes investigator. But she never thought she'd see her own brother arrested for the grisly murders of three beautiful young women. Shocked and in denial, Harry transfers to a makeshift town in a desolate area to avoid the media circus. Looking into a seemingly simple missing persons case, Harry is assigned a new "partner." But is he actually meant to be a watchdog?

Far from the world she knows and desperate to clear her brother's name, Harry has to mine the dark secrets of her strange new home for answers to a deepening mystery—before she vanishes in a place where no one would ever think to look for her.